T0103882

ALEXANDER ALEXANDROV

A MAN ALONE

iUniverse books may be ordered through booksellers or by contacting:

iUniverse LLC
1663 Liberty Drive
Bloomington, IN 47403
www.iuniverse.com
1-800-Authors (1-800-288-4677)

ISBN: 978-1-4917-3615-9 (sc)
ISBN: 978-1-4917-3614-2 (e)

Library of Congress Control Number: 2014910328

Printed in the United States of America.

iUniverse rev. date: 07/01/2014

ROMANIA
Danube
Pleven
Varna
YUGO SLAVIA
SOFIA
Black Sea
Burgas
Plovdiv
Haskovo
Svilengrad
Edirne
Kurdzhali
TURKEY
GREECE
Sea of Marmara

BULGARIA

Prologue

Bulgaria, 1980s

Zhivko Mladenov's breathing was raspy, coming in deep gulps as sweat poured from his forehead and down his flushed cheeks. The man in front of him nodded, and the fight was on.

Zhivko launched a hopeful roundhouse kick, but Andrei Mitov casually brushed the blow aside. This was too easy. Undaunted, he again raised his right leg into position and attempted a second blow. The instructor instinctively brought his left arm down in a defensive position. The movement was swift and precise, perfected after more than twenty years of service in the special forces. Zhivko's shinbone collided painfully with the outstretched arm of the instructor, causing him to lose his balance and hop on his support leg to remain standing.

The veteran watched silently. He could have gone for the kill and ended the training match, but instead, he stepped back. Mitov wanted to test the young recruit by letting him come to him … assuming he had what it took.

Zhivko narrowed his eyes and contemplated his next move. He regained his footing and stepped forward. The numbness that had temporarily incapacitated his leg dissipated. Mustering all his strength, he launched a front kick directly at the instructor's abdomen. It was a powerful blow, and he was hopeful.

This time, the instructor caught his leg with both hands and forcefully pushed it down. The impact, delivered with two blunt and hard lower palms, temporarily immobilized him. Zhivko's shinbone was throbbing and beginning to swell. A kind of tingling pain spread through his leg.

He was standing on just his left leg now, the other leg barely touching the cold mat below. A quick glance at the clock on the wall revealed that the training session was into its third hour, well past the designated ninety minutes. His red shirt had long ago turned burgundy. Sweat was pooling around his eyes and beginning to blur his vision. Fatigue had set in, and he unknowingly lowered his hands.

Mitov immediately got angry. He had told him many times never to let his guard down.

The punishment was swift and unforgiving. It was the best way to reinforce the basics and the only way to separate the committed recruits from the wannabes. A trained boxer, the instructor unleashed his fury on his human punching bag.

Bam! Mitov's fist slammed into the boy's head, just above the left ear. The blow was as unexpected as it was powerful. The dull thud reverberated throughout the empty gym as Zhivko fell, barely catching himself with his arms. He began to see stars and nearly lost consciousness. Colorful images danced against a black backdrop as his skull felt ready to explode.

Dazed, Zhivko crawled on all fours and raised his hand to his head, which was pulsating. The pain was astounding, but he also felt overwhelming embarrassment and shame. He gritted his teeth in anger.

"Get up!" screamed the instructor.

Zhivko scrambled to his feet. The world was spinning, but at least he was beginning to see clearly. Survival instincts merged with a desire for revenge. He stepped back to assess the situation.

"You're pathetic!" the instructor said loudly, taunting him. Plenty of other recruits had been quickly dismissed from the program. Psychological strength was crucial. If you were not willing to push yourself beyond your limits, you didn't belong. It was easier to improve a weak body than a weak spirit.

Zhivko regained his mobility and began shuffling side to side, boxing style. The injured right leg hurt with every movement, but he did not let that bother him as adrenaline surged through his veins. He focused his eyes and let fierce determination distract him from the pain.

Long ago, Zhivko had promised himself never to let anyone beat him, even if it was just a training session. The instructor was waiting, calm and in control. He was old enough to be his father.

The throbbing in Zhivko's head was clouding his thinking. Still, he studied his opponent, planning his attack. He raised his left leg and aimed for the side of the knee.

The instructor moved aside.

Zhivko caught up with him and tried again.

The instructor stepped away, and the kick swung through the air.

The third attempt was similarly unsuccessful, but the instructor made a mistake. He had stepped too far to the left and lost his center of gravity. Zhivko saw this and reacted.

His right leg came down hard on his opponent's knee. Finally, a blow had connected! He was exhilarated, yet his leg was begging him to stop.

The instructor was surprised. He was sure the recruit would have given up by now. Others would have.

Instead, Mitov watched as Zhivko cocked his leg back without putting it down, delivering another blow to the same knee. This time, the man's leg folded, and the knee buckled and hit the ground. He looked up just in time to see a clenched fist over his head.

"Stop!" he yelled and raised his hand. Zhivko pulled back his arm and looked at the instructor. For the first time that day, his features relaxed and a shy smile appeared on his tortured face. His eyes were wide with accomplishment.

"Well done," the man said, getting up and wiping sweat from his brow. "You trained well today."

"Thank you," said Zhivko, his chest heaving as he tried to control his heavy breathing. His bruised and battered body collapsed on the mat, finally succumbing to exhaustion.

Chapter One

Summer 1997

The military truck traveled quickly along the paved road, and the driver focused as he observed the conditions ahead from his perch. About thirty minutes earlier, the sun had sunk below the skyline, and a late summer chill descended over the Bulgarian border town of Svilengrad. The road led away from the city and southwest toward the Turkish metropolis of Edirne. Traffic was light and consisted mostly of freight trucks carrying goods between Europe and Asia. The border was approximately fifteen kilometers away when the driver veered onto a narrow, potholed auxiliary road.

A gust of wind rippled through the truck's camouflage net.

The men sitting in the back could not see outside but immediately tensed. The heavy vehicle's large wheels left a trail of dust in their wake. Zhivko tightened his grip on the AK-47. Tonight's task was to bust a drug depot, confiscate the goods, and arrest the smugglers. He had been on many missions before, yet small beads of sweat still gathered between his fingers.

He looked around at the faces of his comrades—a total of twelve men, all supremely trained and ready to serve their country. They were serious now, staring ahead quietly. Their camaraderie had been forged through years of earning their living by facing danger. The specifics of the mission were given to them last minute as a safety precaution.

In his mind, he went over the commander's instructions once more.

Two stay behind to guard the entrance and protect the truck. Another three are to position themselves along the perimeter of the rectangular compound, one on each side. The remaining seven charge the warehouse. The commander is going to follow the men and coordinate.

The windowless industrial warehouse was less than a kilometer off the international road and surrounded by a tall fence. The paint was peeling off, and the facility looked dilapidated. The entire compound was approximately three hundred by five hundred meters, with a security booth placed at the entrance. The building was completely unlit, nothing but shadows and silhouettes in the twilight.

"Doesn't look like there is anyone here!" the driver shouted. "The barrier is raised."

"Go through and stop," said Veselin Iliev, the commander. Zhivko knew that Iliev had been on many missions and earned praise for guiding his team safely and successfully. He had never lost a man during his fifteen years as unit commander, though rumor had it the pressures of the job did cost him his first marriage. Apparently, he knew better than to try a second time.

"Got it," the driver replied. His foot remained firm on the accelerator.

"I want Pavel to enter the warehouse first," Iliev said. As the most senior of the twelve commandos, Pavel Rachev was the squad leader and the person closest to Iliev. The commander had also been a squad leader years ago, before promotions within the Ministry of Internal Affairs gave him political and bureaucratic responsibilities unrelated to the daily management of the commando unit.

Zhivko looked at Vassil Velev, a communications specialist sitting next to him. The two were good friends, having served in the military together. He expected him to cut the tension with a funny remark or a playful grin, but Vassil instead looked sullen and lowered his eyes.

"Get ready," the commander said with a grunt. The men grabbed their ski masks and put them on, twelve identical soldiers moving stealthily in the night. The truck slowed down sharply and came to an abrupt stop. Heart rates accelerated in anticipation.

"Go!" Iliev yelled.

The men poured out of the back of the truck, their feet hitting the pavement with a thud. Weapons raised and ready, they fanned out. Zhivko was among those assigned to charge the building. Heavy rubber shoes beat against the pavement as he ran along with the group, scanning the right flank. The truck's powerful headlights provided illumination.

Suddenly, a dog appeared, running wildly from the opposite end toward the commandos. It barked ferociously—teeth bared menacingly.

Pavel fired two shots, and the canine fell, blood coloring the fur on its belly. The men continued. They were now no more than fifty meters from the entrance to the warehouse. The group advanced cautiously.

"Perimeter secure!" someone shouted over the radio. "There is no one here."

They must be inside. They don't know what's going to hit them.

Zhivko remained focused. He knew well that the most difficult part was just ahead.

The group leader got to the entrance, rifle aimed at the sliding metal door. He raised his hand and pointed with two fingers. Vassil and another man rushed to the side of the door and gripped the handle, leaning back as they readied to thrust. The leader nodded. The door flew open with surprising ease.

The men looked inside, trigger fingers ready. The light didn't penetrate far into the dark warehouse, and visibility was poor. The driver received an order to maneuver the large vehicle near the entrance and point the headlights directly inside. The commandos maintained their positions and waited. The night was silent and the sky starry.

The truck revved up its engine and moved in behind them while the leader gestured with his hand, careful never to take his eyes off the target. The men shuffled inside, their eyes scanning the new surroundings. A number of tables were arranged next to each other along one wall in the far corner. A few chairs were haphazardly scattered around the tables, while small tubes and pipes littered the floor.

The air was dense and smelled foul. There were numerous overturned plastic containers. The layer of dust on the floor showed traces of chaotic activity. Pillars running along the middle divided the warehouse into two halves.

"Stay alert," Pavel warned. "They could be hiding."

Zhivko looked up at the ceiling. The roof was made of thin sheets of metal, spartan except for a large idle fan. There were no connecting beams, no places for someone to avoid detection. His eyes scanned the warehouse again, but there was no one. The group moved to the center, and the leader gave the order to spread out. A quick and thorough inspection ensued.

"What's going on?" Iliev asked over the radio. "Report!"

Pavel sounded a little incredulous. "We don't see anyone."

"Maintain position."

The men remained steady, rifles aimed, eyes searching for a target. *They must be here.* Their anxiety was rising.

Iliev walked in with a quick military step, head moving from left to right. He stopped near one of the support pillars and looked around. Empty. The men were visibly starting to get nervous. Zhivko could sense the sweat sliding down his temple. The ski mask was becoming heavy and uncomfortable.

"Is there anyone on the roof?" the commander asked, bringing the radio to his mouth.

One of the newest squad members, assigned to guard the compound entrance, replied, "We have not seen anyone. One of us would have noticed movement."

Zhivko saw Iliev frown. "What about along the perimeter? Did you double-check?"

The radio crackled again.

"Nothing here," the man along the east side replied.

"Or here," the man on the west side added. "We checked all three sides thoroughly."

The initial confusion gave way to despair and anger. One of the men gave a nearby chair a powerful kick, sending it flying through the air. It hit the ground with a sharp sound that bounced off the walls and echoed throughout the empty building.

"Fuck!" the commando yelled and tore off his mask.

"Relax!" ordered Pavel.

"This is bullshit!" the commando continued, running both hands down his face. Standing just over 190 centimeters and with a body built for power, Simeon was the most imposing figure in the group and had a reputation for speaking his mind. "They obviously left in a hurry."

The men looked at each other, stunned and scared. The unthinkable realization was beginning to settle in.

The unit had been compromised. Someone had tipped off the smugglers.

Chapter Two

Tuesday, September 2, 1997

Mira Lyubenova held on tight to the straps of the large duffel bag and briskly walked down a crowded sidewalk in Sofia, Bulgaria's capital. She twisted her arm uncomfortably to check her watch and frowned. The press conference was about to start without her. Something sharp was poking her in the back with every step, but there was no time to stop and readjust the contents of the bag.

The Ministry of Internal Affairs was located on the corner of Gurko and September Sixth Streets, or at least she thought so. With the collapse of communism, the street names had been changed. Either way, the building was readily recognizable by the large statue of a lion situated in front of the main entrance. Mira looked both ways and crossed the street in a hurry, her flat athletic shoes ideally suited for her quick feet—comfort over elegance.

She plopped her bag on the scanner and handed her press ID to the guard. The policeman put his cigarette down and raised the document to his eyes. The young woman in the picture was conservatively dressed in a dark suit and wore a touch of lipstick, her hair pulled tightly into a ponytail. Today, Mira's dark-brown hair was messy and flowed loosely over her shoulders. She was wearing a plain dark shirt that had in some places untucked itself from her casual jeans. No makeup. Her nails were manicured but not polished.

"You're just in time," the officer said. "Down the hall and to your right. There are plenty of people there; you can't miss it."

"Thanks," Mira said and retrieved her bag. The officer nodded and gave her a warm smile. She was probably one of the better-looking reporters he'd seen that day.

The doors to the conference room were open, and the chatter of journalists was echoing down the poorly lit hallway. Mira walked through the entrance, careful not to trip over the wires snaking across the floor. The cameraman adjusting his view of the podium paid her no attention.

Most of the seats were taken, with the exception of those located in the back. Mira moved along the side, next to the wall, and approached the front. She spotted an open seat in the first row and confidently walked toward it. There was a small camera and a battery pack placed on the seat, but Mira picked them up and gently placed them on the floor next to the chair.

"Those are mine," protested a photographer crouching on the ground. "I have to take pictures."

"The chair is not for your equipment," Mira said plainly, taking a seat and setting the bag down between her legs. Her tone was calm yet firm, with a conviction the photographer took as a sign there was no point in arguing. The man frowned and returned to his camera.

Mira opened her bag and pulled out a pen and notebook. She then grabbed her tape recorder and checked the battery. All was in order. She leaned back and blew the loose strands of hair away from her angular face.

Mira looked ahead and saw Yordan Stoyanov standing just a few meters away, quietly conferring with one of his aides.

"Let's keep this short, shall we?" he said, leaning into the woman to make sure no one could overhear. "There really isn't much that I want to discuss anyway."

The aide, a thin woman in her fifties, wearing a long gray dress, nodded in agreement.

"I understand, sir. I will do what I can."

The room was nearly full, casual chitchat and random sounds filling the air. The aide scanned the crowd and got up on the platform.

"Thank you for coming. The minister wants to say some words, and then we'll open the floor for questions. Please keep in mind that time is limited."

Mira wanted to sneer. *Limited by you.*

The aide stepped aside, and Stoyanov walked behind the podium. The TV cameras immediately turned on, and the photoflashes started going off. The minister adjusted his glasses and looked down at his notes. His new suit was neatly pressed. He was no doubt hoping he would look good and impress the viewers, but his efforts did not move Mira.

"Good afternoon," he began. "I want to take this opportunity to inform the public that the Interior Ministry has taken into account their concerns and will respond accordingly. My belief is that our measures will bring the desired result."

Stoyanov explained that in response to calls from citizens, more police officers would be put on night duty, particularly in the bigger cities. All disturbances against the public order, even when seemingly insignificant, would be looked into, he assured them. Finally, the police would take additional measures to ensure the security of fans at professional soccer games. The beautiful sport would not be tarnished by hooligans looking to get into a fight.

The minister concluded his speech and looked confidently at the journalists assembled before him. Mira rolled her eyes but nevertheless wrote everything down. Like most of her colleagues, she could jot notes with lightning speed.

"I will now take your questions."

Mira immediately raised her hand but was not picked. Stoyanov fielded a question from the back and explained that because of budget cutbacks, the police would not be able to buy any new equipment this year. The second question also went to someone else, but Mira was prepared for the third round.

"Minister," she said loudly as soon as there was a moment of quiet, "I would like to ask you something."

"Go ahead," the forty-five-year-old man pointed to her with a practiced gesture and quickly pushed up his glasses. Poise and appearance were important, particularly when he was probably going to be on the evening news.

"Is it true the economic sanctions imposed on warring Yugoslavia five years ago have led to a sharp rise in organized crime?"

Mira pressed the "on" button on the tape recorder and raised it in the air.

Stoyanov cleared his throat and searched his mind. The room felt a little hotter. He made a point of giving his aide an icy look.

He began cautiously. "Obviously, the sanctions were a challenge for us. But we have to support the international community's efforts to bring peace to the countries of the former Yugoslavia. We have been taking all the measures necessary to make sure that domestic criminal groups are not emboldened by the chaos across the border."

The minister saw another raised hand and wanted to call on someone else.

"What about smuggling?" Mira asked. She was standing up now, making sure she had everyone's attention. "We all know that smuggling activities increased in the wake of the sanctions."

She saw Stoyanov shift uncomfortably and try to hide his annoyance. He didn't like it when reporters did not play by his rules.

"The government is constantly monitoring the situation," he assured her, making certain his voice conveyed authority. "The border police are coordinating their efforts with the local police stations, and we will crack down on smuggling. We have time for just one more—"

"What about police officers assisting the criminal groups?" Mira interrupted. She had no intention of leaving without asking that question. A renewed excitement gripped the hushed crowd.

"I beg your pardon?" Stoyanov said, digging his fingers into the podium and staring at the young reporter.

"There are suspicions that some current and former police officers are helping the smugglers." Mira tried with little success to control her breathing. Her pale cheeks flushed red. "Are you aware of this?"

The minister grunted his frustration.

"Missus ..." he began slowly.

"Miss," Mira corrected. The audacity impressed some of her more demure colleagues, whose smiles insulted the minister.

"I understand," Stoyanov said, visibly annoyed. "I was appointed to this position last year and have not yet received proof of a police officer engaging in such activities. That's just media speculation." He liked that accusation and raised a finger in the air for dramatic effect. "But I can assure you that if we learn of ministry personnel violating their professional commitments, they will be dealt with severely. Thank you all for your time."

A second wave of flashes followed Stoyanov as he picked up his notes and walked off the platform, disappearing from view by going into a room with restricted access.

Mira turned off her recorder and sat down. She took the small tape out and hid it in her front pocket, where she could feel it press against her thigh. She cursed herself for forgetting her scrunchie and once more brushed back her messy hair. The cameramen unplugged their equipment and folded tripods. Mira threw the duffel bag over her shoulder and followed the crowd out of the conference room.

It was warm outside, and at the nearby park, parents lazily observed their children playing. The narrow street was nearly jammed with cars, and no one noticed a black Mercedes pull out and follow the young woman as she walked.

Chapter Three

Wednesday, September 3, 1997
10:05 a.m.

Zhivko picked up a loaf of bread and tucked it under his shoulder. The neighborhood supermarket was poorly ventilated and depressingly half empty. He walked down the sparse aisles and grabbed a package of ham and a few bottles of mineral water. A middle-aged woman in a white robe handed him a four-hundred-gram square of feta cheese she quickly cut out from a larger block dunked in a tank of water. She also gave him six eggs and cautioned against buying more.

"They aren't fresh," the woman warned and smiled at him. "Better come back tomorrow; they say we'll have some delivered in the morning."

"Thank you," Zhivko replied and nodded.

The woman held his eyes for longer than necessary before looking away.

The line at the counter consisted of a pregnant woman and a frail old retiree, slowly counting his change coin by coin. Zhivko waited patiently for his turn, eventually tossing his groceries in the plain white bag handed to him by the cashier.

The narrow street cut through a quiet neighborhood in northwestern Sofia. Zhivko walked slowly, admiring the still-green trees planted along the sidewalk and glancing at the occasional cat scurrying out of the way. Behind him, a yellow tram came to a stop and its doors flung open with an unmistakable thump. Seconds later, it circled around a small garden and headed in the opposite direction, the wheels making a loud screeching sound. The morning weather was too cold for a short-sleeved shirt but too warm for his thin leather jacket, even when unzipped.

Zhivko neared his building, a new eight-story structure that was among the tallest in the area, and was puzzled to see a police car parked in front. It was a plain Russian-made Lada sedan, white with dark-blue insignia on the sides and the trunk. He approached the building and started walking along the side, toward the main entrance located in the back.

Something was obviously going on. It must be one of the neighbors' kids again. The family on the second floor had three rowdy teenage sons, and at least one of them was always misbehaving.

Zhivko was approaching the flight of stairs leading up to the entrance of the building when he saw two police officers push through the door.

"Hold it!" one of them said loudly, looking down at him with steely eyes. "Who are you?"

"I live here," Zhivko replied with a baffled look. "Why?"

"Are you Zhivko Mladenov?"

"Yes," he answered with a pause. "And you are?"

"Officer Pashev," replied the middle-aged cop with graying hair. "Are you a member of the special forces?" The tone was harsh and accusing.

"Yes."

The two cops exchanged looks and then charged down the stairs, the large and heavyset one taking two steps at a time while Pashev trailed behind him.

"Don't move!" the heavyset police officer instructed. "We have orders to bring you in."

Zhivko stood still. Confusion swept over his mind and body like a cold chill. He could sense his heart begin to beat faster as he assessed the situation.

The two cops were now standing in front of him, one on each side.

"Don't try anything," Pashev said, reaching for his handcuffs.

"What's going on?" Zhivko asked bewildered. "Are you *arresting* me?"

The entrance opened, and a tall, thin man in civilian clothing emerged. He briskly walked down the stairs and approached the three men with purpose.

"I'm Inspector Ivanov, Fourth District Precinct," he said tersely, looking directly at Zhivko. "I was called in to do a search of your apartment." He leveled an accusatory stare.

"What?"

"Sixth floor, apartment eighteen?" Ivanov spoke quickly, his eyes still locked on Zhivko. A cocky smirk was spreading over his face.

"Yes …"

Ivanov smiled. "We found drugs and money up there." He delivered the line plainly and with the gravity of a seasoned professional. Zhivko could tell the inspector was looking for a criminal, not a suspect.

His mind blanked. "That can't be," he replied, glancing at the faces of the men in front of him. "It's not possible."

"Would you like to explain how a stash of over ten thousand dollars found its way into your bedroom?" Ivanov smiled again, revealing a row of yellowing teeth. His raspy voice testified to years of tobacco abuse. "I know how little you boys make."

"This is crazy!" Zhivko erupted. "Someone must have placed that there; it's not mine."

"Come with us to the precinct, and we'll talk about it," the heavyset officer said. "I don't want this to be difficult."

Pashev waved him forward. "Come on; give me your hands."

"Let's not make a scene," Ivanov implored. A woman on the second floor was watching them from her balcony, a pan of wet laundry in her hands. The youngest of the three brothers was also observing closely and with trepidation.

"Give me your hands," the chubby cop ordered.

Zhivko's mind raced. *What the hell is going on?*

"Give me your hands." This time, the voice was sterner and more unforgiving.

"No." He sensed his training was taking over as adrenaline shot through his veins. Zhivko dropped the groceries, breaking some of the eggs. The yoke splattered against the transparent bag. Heavy beer bottles clinked against each other as they fell to the ground.

"I'm not going anywhere." His eyes became cold and calculating, his muscles tense.

Ivanov shook his head in disappointment while the two cops looked at each other.

"This is your last chance; I'm not going to ask again."

Zhivko stepped back. *No way.*

The two cops charged at him from both sides, each aiming to grab one of his arms. Zhivko lunged to his right, toward Pashev. He raised his arm just in time to avoid it being immobilized and landed a powerful side punch across the man's face. The blow to the nose temporarily incapacitated him.

The overweight cop tried to tackle Zhivko from behind, but he didn't have the time.

Zhivko moved forward swiftly and pushed Pashev in the chest. He then used his sweeping leg to create a tripping point behind the injured man's knee. The loss of stability occurred instantly, sending Pashev to the ground. Arms flailed helplessly.

Zhivko turned around immediately and threw a blind, straight punch. The top two knuckles of his right fist connected with the chin of the overweight officer, loosening a lower tooth and forcing the man to backpedal.

He spun around in a split second and grabbed Pashev's gun from its holster. The cop was bleeding profusely from the nose, and the double impact to the head had taken away his ability to react.

A standard-issue nine-millimeter automatic. Judging by its weight, Zhivko figured the Glock 17 was fully loaded. He tightened his grip on the gun and pointed it at the overweight officer.

"Don't move."

The cop was holding his hand to his mouth, trying to stop the bleeding. Zhivko stepped to the side and glanced at Ivanov. The inspector was standing still, an expression of shock on his face.

Zhivko took a few steps back so he could see all three men without turning his head.

"Take your weapon out, and put it down."

The man wiped his bloody hand on his shirt and reached for the gun. His fingers left thick, wine-colored lines across the blue shirt.

"Slowly."

The police officer put the gun down at his feet. Meanwhile, Pashev regained his awareness but lay completely motionless with fearful eyes looking up at Zhivko.

"Kick it away."

The cop's kick sent the gun bouncing across the platform, banging loudly against the concrete.

"What are you doing?" the policeman asked with a muffled voice, bringing his hand to his mouth again and wincing in pain, revealing his bloodied teeth.

What am I doing? Zhivko searched his mind for an answer but came up blank. He looked at Ivanov and then back at the two cops. Pashev pushed himself up from the concrete and was now in a crouching stance.

"Go in the building, close the door, and handcuff yourselves to the radiator pipes," he ordered. "Do it now. I will be watching."

The three men convened at the stairs and started walking up, acutely aware the gun was pointed at them. The woman from the balcony briskly pushed her son inside and closed the door. The boy glued his nose to the window.

The overweight cop coughed violently, his body twitching. His nose was no longer bleeding, but it still hurt like hell. It was swollen and probably broken.

Satisfied his instructions had been completed, Zhivko turned to the street. It was empty. He ran toward it and looked in both directions.

A teenage girl on the opposite sidewalk was casually walking her dog. Zhivko hid the gun behind his leg. The girl glanced at him and continued walking.

I need time to think. What were the police talking about? There was nothing out of the ordinary in my apartment. And if there was, surely it was placed there by someone else. Have I been framed?

He scratched his head. *I get along well with everyone.*

Zhivko looked up and down the street again, uncertain what to do but keenly aware backup would be arriving soon. The girl with the dog was rounding the distant corner and about to disappear. At the other end, a woman was carrying two heavy bags in both hands.

Zhivko placed the gun under his belt and covered it with his jacket. He began walking toward the supermarket, his pace quick but not fast enough to catch anyone's attention. A glance behind revealed that no one was coming from the driveway next to his building. He continued walking briskly.

In the circular garden, old men were throwing crumbs to the pigeons. A taxi was parked in front of the supermarket, the driver lazily reading a newspaper. No wailing police sirens could be heard. Instead, a chestnut fell from one of the branches above, bounced against the pavement, and rolled away. Zhivko stopped to think.

It was risky to take the tram. Too many people would see him, and the wide windows would leave him exposed. Being confined in a tram car would make it all but impossible to get away should something happen. A short walk north was a park with thick vegetation and few trails.

That would do. He desperately needed to escape and collect his thoughts.

Chapter Four

Kiril Dimitrov watched as Ivanka slid her toned legs forward, her toes ironing over the small folds of the soft silk sheets. The twenty-three-year-old woman propped herself on her elbows and arched her back, raising her breasts. She smiled seductively as the wind from the open terrace door made her body stiffen and the perky nipples harden.

Kiril looked at her approvingly, a tight-lipped smile forming. As always, he was freshly shaved, skin almost boyish in texture. His full hair was expertly groomed and styled. He was serious, powerful, and wealthy. Appearance was everything in his line of work and among the people who constituted his social circle. The image would be incomplete without the appropriate clothes, car, or female companion.

And she was no ordinary woman. Ivanka could inspire erotic fantasy in the most saintly of men.

He kept his eyes on the sultry blonde, her naked curves capturing his lascivious imagination.

The phone on the table near the window rang jarringly. Kiril had been sitting in his armchair with one leg over the other and did not appreciate the interruption. He got up and walked toward the phone, letting it ring once more while he stopped to run his hand through the blonde's long platinum hair. She leaned in and seductively ran her fingers up and down his ribs.

"Hello?" he said with a clear voice.

The man on the other side was equally unemotional. "Hi, colleague, it's your old friend calling."

The words were deliberate. The participants never used their real names, intentionally preferring more generic terms. Secrecy and confidentiality were of utmost importance, a necessary precaution in case someone else was listening.

"It's good to hear from you," Kiril replied. A few meters away, Ivanka swung her feet over the bed and onto the floor. "How was work?"

"It was a busy day."

The man put one hand in his pocket and pushed the phone closer to his face.

"Give me a status report," he commanded, looking over the large balcony at the lawn below. The grass around his two-story house was freshly cut and the bushes along the perimeter shaped into perfect rectangles.

"Everything is done," the voice on the other end reported. "The operation was successful."

"What about the commando?"

There was a heavy sigh and a moment of hesitation. "He got away."

Kiril's expression changed abruptly, anger creeping into his voice. His grip on the phone tightened.

"What happened?"

"He escaped arrest," the man on the other side clarified. "But don't worry; the police are on him. It's just a matter of time. Everything has been taken care of."

"Are you sure?"

"Of course, colleague."

The words didn't soothe Kiril. He had built his entire life around discipline, order, planning, and execution and objected to things not going his way.

"Are you sure?" he repeated heavily.

"*Da.*"

"That's good, my friend," he said. "Follow the plan without mistakes, and I will make sure you get your money soon."

"Thank you."

Kiril closed the balcony door and pulled the nearly transparent white curtains across. Ivanka was looking directly at him and batting her eyelashes.

"And one more thing," he said, sensing his concentration slipping. Ivanka tiptoed in his direction and slowly wrapped her hands around his torso. "Make sure you keep the car clean and running."

"Of course."

The line went dead, and Kiril returned the receiver to its cradle. Ivanka pressed herself against him and kissed his neck. She had heard most of the conversation but did not understand the subject matter. Nor did she care. She was thinking of how abruptly her life had changed.

Her first photo shoot for a select men's magazine was about a year ago. Her parents disapproved, but with unemployment rising and wages in the small town dropping to just barely above subsistence levels, their moral objections were brushed aside. She was suddenly the highlight of glamorous parties attended by wealthy men. The opulence she was enjoying now was addictive, and Ivanka had no intention of going back to her previous life.

Her fingers traced a circle around one areola and softly squeezed it.

The man eyed her lustfully. Already beautiful, to him, she looked even sexier with the cosmetic improvements he had paid for. His crotch was beginning to heat up.

Chapter Five

The jogger breathed rhythmically, his trained lungs expanding and contracting without difficulty. His breathing was deep but not hard, for he was athletic and could easily sustain this pace for at least an hour. The worn-out sneakers were beginning to rip, and the ends of the shoelaces unraveled more and more with every day, but he did not have money for a new pair.

It had been dark for over an hour, and the park was quiet, except for the odd romantic couple and the occasional dog walker. There was a deserted children's playground at one end, a slide shaped like a large white elephant easily distinguishable in the darkness. At the other end, about four hundred meters away, was a shallow artificial pond, lilies floating on top of dirty water. His feet pounded against the pavement as his eyes nervously scanned the surroundings. He had been jogging for approximately twenty minutes, but thus far, no one had given him the sign. It was probably too dark for anyone to make out his face, but he was wearing a hoodie as a precaution. The cool air occasionally got inside and chilled his neck.

He briefly considered jogging away and calling it off. Doubts surfaced once more and called on him to leave the situation and pretend nothing had happened.

He looped around the lake and began another lap.

Meanwhile, a dark Mercedes quietly approached. The vehicle drove away from the narrow, lit street and merged into the semidarkness. The large trees with their abundant, heavy leaves provided ideal cover as the driver, a former wrestler named Nikolai, intentionally picked a secluded place and turned off the engine. He and Stefan, the man in the backseat, got out.

"Stay put," Nikolai ordered the third man, sitting in the passenger's seat. "Don't get out of the car, and don't make any noise. We shouldn't be too long."

The man nodded, and the doors closed softly.

Nikolai was short, but his muscular frame packed incredible power. He had had Olympic aspirations until a devastating knee injury ended his dream. His current employment wasn't exactly what he had expected growing up, but it did come with certain benefits.

Unlike the other two members of the group, who came from distant regions of the country, this was his home turf. Born and raised in the big city, he did not think much of its allures or vices. For him, the capital was a given; it could not change or corrupt him in any way. He was not so sure about his two subordinates.

Nikolai and Stefan made their way through the park with purposeful, direct steps. They intentionally kept their heads down as they approached a specific point midway between the playground and the pond. There was a white bench there, nestled between the trees and next to a large, rectangular meadow. They sat down. Nikolai raised one leg to his knee while the other man lit a cigarette. They waited.

The jogger's silhouette appeared in the distance, still too far to be heard. There was no one else nearby. The tip of the cigarette blazed orange in the dark.

The jogger looked to his left, now just a tad more nervous.

Two men, one smoking and playing with his lighter.

"Excuse me, do you know the time?" asked one of the men.

"Sorry," the jogger said in between deep breaths. "I don't carry a watch."

That was the password. Nikolai got up and stood in front of the hooded man, trying to look him in the eyes. The facial features were not clearly recognizable even at point-blank range, but he had no doubt.

"How have you been?" he asked, the tone slightly friendly.

The jogger was deliberately dismissive. "Don't get cute with me," he replied, the summer night air caressing the sweat from his flushed cheeks. The man smoking the cigarette threw it on the ground.

"Do you have the money?" the jogger asked. He could only see the basic outlines of the men's faces, making a positive identification impossible.

Nikolai reached into his unzipped leather jacket and produced a dark plastic envelope. The bills inside were new, not a scratch, tear, or fold. He was curious how the boss always had money like that, but he didn't have the courage to ask.

"It is all here," he said, handing over the envelope. "Just like we promised."

The jogger took the envelope and opened it. His fingers rapidly flipped through the bills, but he could not tell their denominations.

"It's all there," Nikolai said with a half smile. "Trust me."

"Looks like I'll have to." The jogger placed the envelope in his sweatpants. "Now what?"

"Now nothing," Nikolai said calmly. "We will contact you if we need to."

"How about you leave me alone?" The jogger phrased it as a question, but his voice was firm and sharp. "I am finished helping you."

Nikolai said nothing.

"Go home," Stefan said. "Take care of your pregnant wife."

The jogger's eyebrows immediately narrowed as the words struck him personally. How much did these men know about him? And how did they know it? He lowered his head and ran away, the darkness of the park enveloping him within seconds.

Chapter Six

The office of *Trud* was located on a narrow street near the center of Sofia. It was an old building, erected in the earlier part of the twentieth century, its facade and interior consisting of faded, scratched stone. Pigeons assembled outside on the ledges and sometimes took refuge in the nooks. The lobby was perpetually poorly lit and dusty.

Mira pulled open the heavy door and walked in. She hurried across the black marble, taking off her duffel bag as she made her way toward the old elevator.

It was busy on one of the upper floors. Impatient, Mira walked to the stairwell and started ascending the stairs, taking them two at a time.

"Here comes our star reporter now!" shouted Martina, a young woman in her early twenties, when she saw Mira walking in. "How was the press conference?"

"Not much different from the many other ministry press conferences," Mira replied, taking out the recorder and notepad from the duffel bag and placing them on her crowded wooden desk. The large newsroom occupied most of the fourth floor, the desks of the journalists placed in sequential pairs, one opposite the other. News clippings and colorful postcards from across the world were pinned to the walls. Someone frequently left one of the windows open, allowing a cacophony of street noises to enter.

"Anything suspicious?" Martina asked, pushing her chair across the parquet around the desk and toward her colleague. She arched her eyebrows. "Are there any secret connections to the shadowy criminal underworld that you are about to uncover and write about?"

Mira smiled. Her younger colleague, who had been a bit of a protégé before striking out on her own, was a source of positive energy and had a quirky way of lightening the mood.

"I don't know," she responded. "Maybe."

"Ha," Martina chewed her pencil and reclined in the chair. "Well, I am sure you'll figure it out."

"Let's hope so," Mira responded, turning on the computer. "And what are you working on?"

"Just following the travails of the so-called celebrities." Martina used her legs to push off and wheel herself back behind her desk. She was wearing a plain, short-sleeved shirt, her thick brown hair falling down over one shoulder. She was shorter than Mira and with more delicate features but a slightly wider nose.

Mira laughed.

"You won't believe some of these people," Martina said, shaking her head. "It's so shallow and tasteless it's almost surreal!" She laughed loudly and started typing. "It's what makes this job interesting."

"Give me an example," Mira asked as she plugged her headphones into the recorder and prepared to listen.

"Well, let's see," Martina began. "There's this babe out of …" She scratched the side of her head. "I forget the name of the town, but anyway, she is quite hot and recently appeared naked for a men's magazine. The tabloids are jumping over each other trying to cover her every move."

Mira turned up the volume on the recorder and nodded to indicate she wanted to listen. Martina closed her mouth but continued when she saw Mira could not locate the start of the recording.

"She has catapulted herself into elite circles, so to speak. She is now dating this mobster—or at least it's rumored he's a mobster. Her clothes alone cost tens of thousands."

Mira paused the recorder and raised her head, catching Martina's brown eyes. "What's the charm in writing about stuff like that?" she asked.

"It's exciting," Martina answered joyfully. "Which model has fake tits, who is banging whom … for example, this girl …" She stopped for a second to think. "Ivanka, her name is Ivanka; hers are this big." Martina mockingly raised both hands ridiculously far in front of her size-A breasts as an illustration. "Must be painful," she concluded.

Mira smiled and turned the recorder back on. "I'm sorry," she said. "But I have a lot of work to do."

"No problem."

The phones in the newsroom were ringing regularly, other reporters were coming and going, and one of the interns was frequently turning on the television in the corner and flipping the channels to check the news. Mira was glad she had learned long ago to block out all disruptions and focus.

In the distance, the sun moved down toward the horizon, and a shadow descended over the office. The traffic on the street below calmed and became infrequent. The phones were not ringing as often.

Mira put down her pen just as Martina yawned and stretched her arms. At that moment, she looked over and saw the editor in chief, Anton Hubchev, emerge from the main entrance. The man walked quickly, and, as always, appeared to be short of breath and about to break a sweat.

One of the financial reporters raised his hand, but Hubchev waved him away. "Not now," he said with authority. "I'll get to you in a minute."

A large, unfit man with a progressively widening waist and a workaholic's penchant for cigarettes, Hubchev believed in a hands-on approach to managing his staff. He walked over to Mira's desk and knocked his fingers on the surface.

Mira pushed her chair back and looked up.

"Have you heard the news?" Hubchev asked, running his hand over his neatly trimmed beard.

"What news?"

"The police just announced that they have identified someone from the special forces as a possible mole for the drug traffickers. They tried to arrest him earlier today."

Mira put her elbows on the desk and placed both hands on her face. *They arrested someone? Does this mean they are acknowledging the corruption within their own ranks? Is there definitive proof someone is secretly working for the smugglers? This certainly changes the article …* She took a few seconds to think and then looked up at her boss.

"This news was just released?"

"Yes."

"Is there a name, a photograph?"

"They will be releasing a name shortly," Hubchev said. "I am going to be in my office. I've sent someone junior to cover things from the ministry. I'm sure we will be informed in due time. As for you,"

Hubchev began, scratching his face again and pointing with a shaking index finger, "I want you to stay here. This is a big story, and we gotta be on top of it."

Mira nodded and processed the information. It was going to be another long night.

Hubchev breathed in heavily. "I know you have been doing a lot of research on your own. Talking to your anonymous sources, poking around where you should not be, asking questions of people who don't like to be in the spotlight."

Mira did nothing except avert her eyes.

"I don't know exactly what you do or how you do it." Hubchev scratched his chin and sighed. "I only ask that you stay safe."

The man put his heavy hand on Mira's shoulder.

"You are safe, right?" His eyes expressed genuine and almost parental concern.

"Yes," Mira nodded. There was a trace of uncertainty in her voice.

"You sure?"

"I think so." She could smell the nicotine on his breath but pretended it did not bother her.

Hubchev seemed reassured. "That's good," he said, removing his hand. "Glad to hear it. But if you need me to assign you protection, get you a bodyguard or something, tell me immediately."

"Of course."

Mira saw that Martina had stopped typing long ago and was listening intently to the conversation.

Hubchev grabbed his belt with both hands and pulled it up for reassurance. He wore loose jeans and an oversized black shirt just underneath an oversized dark vest with a number of pockets. A pen protruded from one, a napkin from another. The contours of a zipped-in wallet were also clearly visible.

He cleared his throat and looked at Martina.

"What are your plans?"

"I'm just about finished," the young woman responded with barely disguised joy. "I'm going home and hope to sleep well because tomorrow night I am going to hit the clubs to see if our filthy-rich compatriots will provide me with something juicy. You know, the usual."

"Okay," Hubchev nodded. "Don't do anything stupid."

"No, sir." She smiled.

The editor gave her a content look and left. He moved a few desks away and leaned in to talk to one of the other reporters. Martina waited until the man was out of earshot before speaking to her friend.

"So, you're not going home?" she asked. "You are going to stay here late into the night?"

Mira shrugged. "Looks like it." She felt most alive and inspired during these moments. The hunt for the truth and the story behind it animated her with a strong sense of purpose.

Martina lowered her eyes and reached for the drawers, grabbing her purse and popping a stick of gum in her mouth. "Listen," she began, looking across the desk at her colleague. "I don't mean to intrude on your personal life or anything, but I think you have been working too hard."

Mira breathed in with annoyance. She hated when the subject was raised. She knew Martina was right.

"Your devotion is admirable, but you are hurting yourself," Martina continued, apparently taking Mira's silence as an opportunity to press her point more forcefully. "You should pay more attention to yourself. When was the last time you went to a beauty salon or went out for a girls' night out with the rest of us?"

Mira laughed uneasily. "Not recently."

"My point exactly," Martina said. "This job is killing you. You've already lost one fiancé, and if you keep this up, how are you going to find a second?" She stabbed the question straight into Mira's heart.

Mira was wounded. She preferred to keep her sadness hidden deep inside, away from any outsiders.

"Sorry if that was too blunt."

"No worries," Mira replied, feigning indifference.

"I'm heading out." Martina slung the purse over her shoulder.

"Okay. I'm going to stay here. I have to get my head around this. I will see you in the morning."

"I am sure you will." She waved good-bye. "You will probably be the first one in."

Martina walked out and headed for the elevator. She pulled open the metallic cage door and closed it behind her. Once in the lobby, she skipped down the final steps and breezed through the entrance, making sure her sweatshirt was firmly tied around her waist. She liked to carry it with her in the event that it got unexpectedly cold.

As she walked down the street and around the corner, a man sitting silently by himself in a nearby café looked up. He took notice of her leaving, but as she was not the target, he continued to sip his drink quietly.

Chapter Seven

Zhivko told the hotel receptionist he was a traveler, visiting the city for one day just to see a friend. A shy smile followed, part of his attempt to blend in and not raise suspicion. It was a plausible explanation, and he had delivered it convincingly to the bored woman behind the counter. It probably did not matter much, because he intentionally chose a cheap and obscure little hotel on the outskirts of Sofia, the kind of run-down dump that gave shelter to penniless travelers, long-haul truck drivers, cheap prostitutes, and sleazy adulterers.

The receptionist did not ask for his ID before directing him to the second floor with a dismissive wave. She returned to her crossword puzzle before he had a chance to thank her.

The room measured just four by three meters. The bed cover had holes from cigarette burns while the raggedy pillow featured two colorful stains, one darker than the other. He preferred not to know their origin.

Zhivko threw his jacket on the bed and looked outside the window. There was a neon sign on the outer wall, the bright light shining through the double-pane window, which was cracked on one corner. There were dead flies at the base. The place was awful, but it would have to do for one night. He doubted his name had been released to the public, but it was still too risky to be seen in the center of the city.

Just a few hours ago, he had been leading a normal life, looking forward to relaxing on the couch.

Trying to make sense of the events had made his head hurt. He sat on the edge of the bed and rubbed his hands over his face, pressing on his eyes to force concentration. The mattress screeched. There was a loud noise from outside as someone's heavy footsteps echoed across the corridor. Deep-bellied male laughter was followed by a soft and distinctly feminine voice, the words indistinguishable. A door slammed shut, and there was silence.

Zhivko looked around the barren room. In one corner was a wooden stand holding a yellow rotary phone with a circular dial on top.

Tomorrow morning, he would have to go and empty his bank account, for if formal charges were levied against him, the authorities would probably freeze it—not that there was much money anyway.

Also, there was an open-air market nearby, and he needed to buy some personal items.

But first, he needed to find out what had happened. Zhivko reached for the phone and spun the dial.

"You're late," his wife said curtly, looking over her shoulder as she washed the dishes. The open kitchen door allowed a view into the foyer. "I ate dinner by myself."

"I'm sorry," Vassil said, taking his sweatshirt off and sitting down to untie his shoes. He got up and used his T-shirt to brush the drops of sweat from his forehead. The sweatshirt he hung on a hook in the foyer, next to his wife's purse. It was a gift for their anniversary.

Vassil walked over to Yulia and hugged her gently from behind, placing a kiss on her cheek.

"It is good to see you," he said romantically into her ear. She was delicate and petite, her gentle features always soft and capable of instantly awakening his masculine impulses.

"Aha," she replied, turning up the water flow and continuing to scrub a pan. The skin on her fingers was wrinkled, and the detergent was wearing away her nail polish.

"Let me help," Vassil said. "In your condition, you should not be cleaning the dishes."

He attempted to push Yulia away from the sink, but she refused to move.

"You know what? I agree," his wife replied with a quick turn of her head. Her striking red hair was disheveled and the brown eyes alive with anger. "I should be lying down on the bed, getting ready for sleep."

Vassil stepped back, surprised by the unexpected outburst.

"Then please do that," he pleaded. "Let me finish the dishes."

"No," Yulia said with more than a trace of bitterness, throwing the sponge into the sink and turning around to face him. She was visibly tired. "It will take you too long. Take care of the baby while I finish."

Vassil looked at his son. The ten-month-old child was crawling along the kitchen table, pushing a little fire truck across the smooth surface. The boy glanced up at him with wide eyes and lifted an outstretched hand.

Vassil walked over and kissed the child's head.

"He needs to blow his nose," his wife instructed, rinsing the pan one last time before putting it aside to dry and picking up a dirty dish. "And he was crying like you wouldn't believe until just now, which means you need to change his diaper."

Vassil leaned forward and took a sniff.

"Ewww," he said in disgust and smiled. "Let's wash you, shall we?" he asked and picked up his son with one hand, grabbing the fire truck with the other.

"I am taking him to the bathroom, honey."

"Don't use more water than necessary!"

He was already walking down the corridor.

Vassil flipped the light switch and stepped inside the small, damp room. There was a shower with a bathtub to the left, a toilet to the right, and a sink against the wall in the middle. He placed the baby in the bathtub and pulled off his shirt. The child smiled happily and waved both hands in the air.

"Hold on, son. Hold on," Vassil said with laughter. He pulled off the wool socks and placed them near the door, where they were least likely to get wet.

The baby lay down on his knees and attempted to crawl along the bathtub, hands awkwardly placed in front of him. He pawed at the slick surface, the little fingers looking for traction. Vassil freed the diaper from the child's pudgy legs and placed it aside. Next, he reached for the removable showerhead and adjusted the water temperature to lukewarm.

The kid squealed with delight, the playful brown eyes looking up at his father lovingly. The child's mouth opened wide, tongue protruding in an attempt to articulate words. The kid laughed noisily and started splashing around, hitting at the water with his palms.

Vassil knelt near the bathtub and watched his son. *Soon you will have a sister to keep you company.*

"Okay, now turn around." Vassil aimed the water at the child's butt and made sure the drain was free. The child's voice filled the small room.

Vassil spent another five minutes bathing his son before shutting off the water and wrapping the child in a large towel. The baby reached for his dad's nose and tugged on it.

Vassil exited the bathroom and flipped the switch off.

"Is everything taken care of?" his wife asked, her frustrated eyes focusing on the child. She had removed her plain white apron and used it to wipe water off her shirt. A spot near her left collarbone was nevertheless visibly wet, and one bra strap was falling down her arm.

"Yeah," Vassil said, tapping his baby's little nose with his index finger. "Our boy is ready to go to bed." He cradled the child and walked into the bedroom, gently placing the youngster in a wooden crib and removing the towel.

The boy giggled and started sucking his thumb.

Vassil reached for a pile of clothes nearby and retrieved two pieces that would serve as pajamas. He dressed his son quickly and gave him a kiss on the cheek.

The baby giggled again and waved an improvised good-bye. Vassil stepped back, turned off the light, and closed the door. He was hoping the kid would fall asleep quickly, allowing him to spend a few precious minutes of intimacy with his wife.

Yulia stood in the hallway, occasionally glancing at the mirror near the front entrance. The accumulated effects of fatigue and stress were beginning to adversely affect her beauty. The pretty oval face with narrow lips was frowning.

"We can't go on like this," she said sternly as soon as the bedroom door was closed.

"What do you mean?" Vassil asked, his eyes focused on his high-school sweetheart. He had fallen for her hard during their first date and loved her with all his heart ever since. Even now, there were butterflies in his stomach and his worries were melting away. He suddenly felt an urge to kiss her passionately and remind her how much she meant to him.

She exhaled forcefully and brushed her disheveled hair back.

"Do you know how much diapers cost?" she asked, her tone a mixture of desperation and frustration. "Do you?" Her eyes were demanding an answer.

The dramatic repetition made Vassil visibly uncomfortable.

"Well—"

"Of course you don't!" his wife charged. "That is because you have not bought any recently." She blew a strand of loose hair away from her face and continued, "And you know what? I'm not going to buy any more!"

Vassil stood still, his pride wounded. On the day they got married, he had vowed to do everything in his power to care for his family and it profoundly pained him that he was not delivering on that promise.

His wife looked at him with visible sadness and spoke slowly.

"With this inflation and these prices," she stated, helplessly shaking her head in defeat, "we're really struggling, and I should not even be working so much, not five months pregnant."

Vassil leaned forward and caressed his wife's face, kissing her forehead. "I am doing all I can," he replied.

"I know you are," the woman responded, rigid and unmoved. "But it is not enough. All day, I'm shopping, cooking, cleaning. I have no free time, and we barely have enough money."

She abruptly took a step back and raised her voice again.

"And do you know what the worst part is?" She angrily pulled her purse off the hook and thrust it open. The large plastic bracelet on her wrist moved violently up and down.

"These are my maternity benefits," she said, producing a torn envelope with a piece of paper protruding from inside. "Not only are they virtually useless, but they are one month late." She sat down and leaned back against the wall.

She stared in silence, chest heaving and neck glistening with recent perspiration.

"Can you look for another job?" she asked quietly as she turned in the direction of her husband. "We can't survive like this."

Vassil rubbed his eyes and shot her a cross look. "You know that this is what I have wanted to do all my life," he said. "Being a commando is all I have trained for, all I know how to do."

His wife saw that one of her slippers had fallen off and extended her foot to catch it. Her socks appeared soiled and worn, needing a wash.

"Plus," Vassil continued, "what kind of job would I be able to find?"

She rubbed her forehead and sighed. "I know, I know."

Vassil sat down and extended his arm across her shoulders. "I will try to come up with something, okay?" With that, he kissed her temple and hugged her tightly. She leaned her tired head on his shoulder and cuddled into his muscular arm.

Vassil sensed resting in his embrace was the comfort Yulia needed. With one eye, he saw a picture on the wall, the two of them on a date before the wedding. It showed her in black leather boots and a skirt, a form-fitting but classy top, and a wide smile. Her hair fell halfway down her back as she hugged him. He was impeccably shaved and grinning with happiness. Vassil remembered how Yulia liked to enmesh her fingers with his and hold hands as they walked through the park and made plans for the future.

Vivacious, smart, and a tigress in bed, she enjoyed being tamed by the handsome military man.

The phone rang unexpectedly, rudely interrupting the moment. Yulia got up and walked into the living room.

"Alo?" she said impatiently. Surprise overwhelmed her as soon as she heard the person on the other side speak, and she immediately turned to face her husband.

"After all you've done," she began, looking into the eyes of the startled Vassil, who glanced at his watch, "you have a lot of nerve calling here."

Chapter Eight

"Who is it?" Vassil asked in surprise. They almost never got calls at this hour.

"Zhivko," his wife said plainly, handing him the receiver. "He wants to talk to you."

Vassil grabbed the phone and pressed it to his ear. His wife eyed him quizzically, arms folded in front of her chest.

"Hello?"

"It's me," Zhivko said, relieved to be talking to his best friend. "Can you talk?"

"Of course," Vassil replied. "How are you?"

"What can I say?" Zhivko began. "I don't know what the hell is going on. There were cops in front of my building this afternoon. They said they found drugs in my apartment!"

Vassil leaned against the wall and assumed a listening stance. He looked at his wife and gestured that everything was okay. She left and headed into the kitchen, slippers creating a slapping sound as she walked on the linoleum.

"Where are you?" he asked.

"I'm hiding," Zhivko replied.

"Are you okay?"

Zhivko sighed and exhaled meaningfully.

"No, my friend, I'm not," he admitted, sorrow mixed with anger in his voice. "I have no idea what is going on, everything is falling apart." Zhivko breathed heavily into the phone, nearly overpowered by emotion. He was sitting on the edge of the bed, stretching the cord. A little more, and the phone would fall off its stand.

"I'm sorry, my friend," Vassil attempted to comfort the man he had known since the first day he joined the elite unit. "I really am."

"Listen," Zhivko said cautiously, scratching his temple and forehead. "Can I count on your help?"

"What do you mean?"

"I need to figure out who did this, who is trying to set me up." He paused, but his friend did not come back with a response. "Can you help me?" Zhivko asked again.

Vassil paused in thought and looked around the room. "I don't really know what you want me to do," he began. "Why don't you just turn yourself in to the police?"

"I can't!" Zhivko replied loudly, the anger palpable in his voice. "They are leveling insane accusations at me. They want to arrest me!"

"Because they found cocaine in your apartment?" Vassil asked.

"And wads of cash, apparently," Zhivko added.

"How did that happen?"

"The hell if I know!" Zhivko yelled. "Someone must have framed me," he said after a pause to think. "I don't have any other explanation."

Vassil's wife walked in, stopping at the door.

"What is going on?" Yulia asked, hands first in the air and then on her hips. "What does he want?"

Vassil gestured for her to wait.

"Come on," she implored, nodding toward the bedroom. "I'm tired."

"Hello?" Zhivko asked. "You there?"

"I'm here," Vassil replied impatiently, looking at his wife.

"You are my best friend, and I don't know who else to turn to," Zhivko said, his voice somber and soft. "I need to see you so that we can find a way out of this."

Vassil bit his lip and brought his hand to his head. The situation was untenable, one that left him with no good options and many bad choices. He wanted to honor his friendship—he really did. But not now. There were other, more pressing issues to take care of.

His wife turned around and walked out in the direction of the bedroom.

"I can't get involved," Vassil said icily, sadness showing on his face.

"What?" The blow was unexpected and deeply personal. Zhivko was not sure he had heard correctly but feared he had. Confirmation came quickly.

"I'm sorry. You are on your own."

The line went dead. Zhivko leaned back and let the receiver go limp on his open palm. He sat there motionless, letting the events sink into his consciousness.

He suddenly tightened his grip on the receiver, forcing his fingers into a fist, and launched it into the opposing wall. The receiver thumped violently against the barren wall, bouncing off and causing a small tear in the wallpaper. The cord stretched beyond its limit and pulled on the phone, sending it crashing to the floor.

Zhivko leaned forward and held his head in his hands, shaking in disbelief.

Chapter Nine

It was just past midnight when Mira walked into her building lobby and stopped beside a wall of wooden mailboxes. She opened hers and flyers and papers tumbled into her hands. She crumpled them in her fist and threw them in her bag. Most of her neighbors had thrown theirs into an improvised cardboard trash can in the corner.

The elevator stopped at the eighth floor, and Mira walked out, brushing her hand over the wall in the semidarkness to locate the light switch. She pressed it, and a solitary light bulb on the ceiling came on, spraying a soft yellowish light across the corridor. The building was quiet, the residents of the five other apartments on the floor presumably asleep.

It was a drab, reinforced-concrete building constructed as part of a large residential complex erected in the 1970s in response to an urban housing shortage. Utilitarian and unexciting, it mostly featured single-family units of approximately eighty square meters, as well as a minority of smaller apartments, approximately fifty square meters, intended for the childless. At night, it was eerily quiet except for when footsteps coming from the common space echoed throughout the building.

The ceiling light had a timer mechanism that plunged the corridor into darkness just as Mira was fumbling through her bag for the keys. She pulled out the key holder and raised it to her eyes, picked out the appropriate key, and brought it to the door. It took a few unsuccessful stabs before it went in properly, but when it clicked, Mira turned it forcefully and pushed open the door. She wiped her feet on the mat and closed the door behind her. The bolt slid into place with a turn of the wrist.

The small apartment was silent and dark, save for the glow of the city lights coming in from some of the windows and a few drops of water periodically dripping down from the shower onto the tiles below. The faulty showerhead had been leaking water for nearly a year now.

Mira kicked off her shoes and placed her bag on the coatrack. She reached across and pressed the light switch.

Nothing.

She pumped the square button a few more times, but the lights did not come on. Frustrated, she sat down and leaned her head against the wall.

It's true that I am behind with some bills ...

Fatigue was overwhelming her body, and she could feel a headache coming. She slid her feet across the floor until her toes located the pink slippers. Walking to the bathroom, she deliberately left the door open as wide as possible to let in whatever light there was. Still, she could barely see her hands as she diligently washed them. She bent over to splash water on her face, indifferent to the fact that some soapy water ran down her neck and onto her shirt. It was nearly pitch-black, and it took a couple of attempts to locate a towel.

The double bed was just a few centimeters off the ground and took up a lot of space in the small bedroom. Light from outside illuminated the tossed sheets. She wanted to be neat but usually had little time in the morning and left the bed unmade. The desk was crowded with books and handwritten notes, the papers frequently ripped out from their pads haphazardly. The nearby shelves contained even more books, some propped up against each other while others had fallen. Little clay statues she had made as a child were just barely visible on the top shelf, as was a large picture from her prom and a small Orthodox icon placed upright.

Mira took off her shirt and threw it in the corner. Her two socks landed in the same place.

The jeans came next, folded carefully and slung across the back of the chair. Mira unhooked her bra and placed it nearby. She tried the desk light in vain, but it predictably refused to produce light.

In search of a possible explanation, Mira walked back to the entryway and grabbed her duffel bag. She walked with it back to the bedroom and retrieved the mail. Standing next to the window to take advantage of the light, she raised the papers close to her eyes. The flyers and other advertisements she let fall to the floor. They weren't what she was looking for.

When she finally got to the envelope, she ripped it open and pulled out a single thin sheet of paper with mechanical writing. The utility was informing her it had cut off the electricity for failure to pay the July bill.

A combination of anger and sadness was bubbling inside her. She crumpled the paper and threw it away into the darkness. It fluttered and fell on the carpet.

The last item in her hands was a folded piece of paper with large ink letters on it.

It was from her fiancé.

Former fiancé.

He wanted to know when she would come by to pick up her stuff.

Mira crushed it in her hands and threw it away as well. She turned around and looked out the window, mindlessly observing the nearby buildings and the green spaces between them. No discernible movement anywhere.

Her body ached. She raised herself on her toes and stretched her hands while arching her back, forcing a discreet pop from one of her vertebrae. She hid her face with her hands and rubbed her eyes.

The tears came slowly at first, causing no more than a soft sound of crying. Mira tried to compose herself and leaned against the wall for balance. Yet the tears kept coming, faster and heavier with each sob. Soon, her body was convulsing as she brushed tears from her cheeks.

Mira threw herself facedown on the bed, her loud crying muffled somewhat by the pillow. She had never before felt so alone and so in need of someone who could understand, reach out, and comfort her.

Eventually, the pillow became so wet she had to turn it over. Sleep did not come easily that night.

Chapter Ten

September 4, 1997

Zhivko walked along the streets of Sofia with purpose, the light raindrops sinking into the thick hood of his new sweatshirt, purchased earlier that day. The constant drizzle was only a nuisance, but he needed the hood for more than protection. Not knowing whether his picture had been released to the media or not, he did not want to take any chances. And besides, police cars were on routine patrol, and there was the possibility that some acquaintance might recognize him. Better safe than sorry.

The gun was tucked in the pouch pocket in front of the sweatshirt. He kept one hand on the firearm and the other swinging loosely by his side. Ready. Always ready. *Stay focused, soldier.*

Shortly after he joined the military for his compulsory two-year service, he participated in a ceremonial march. Wearing their newest, cleanest uniforms and shiny boots, they paraded past a monument with the words "Bulgaria, for you they died" etched in stone.

On a similarly rainy day a couple of years ago at a military base, he stood next to his brothers-in-arms, thin fingers tightly wrapped around the rifle. They were barely men, but they stood proudly in formation, jaws confidently raised and thrust forward, chests puffed and shoulders expanded.

The entire battalion turned in lockstep and moved forward. Music played and then quieted, a commander giving succinct commands through a microphone. The uniforms were green, clean, and ironed, unusually bright and contrasting with the equally bright red military cap. The beating of drums filled the space.

The rain slid down the men's freshly shaved cheeks and followed the contours of their jaws before dripping down. The soldiers suddenly clicked their boots together with a bang and turned once more. Zhivko could now see the crowd assembled not far away. Mothers and fathers, brothers and sisters, aunts and uncles, girlfriends, and even a few wives were observing with enthusiasm. Many waved and smiled at the men, trying to draw their attention.

The soldiers' faces revealed nothing, but their hearts swelled with pride and a nervous anticipation. Stomachs tightened underneath the uniform.

Some of the family members had not succeeded in locating their loved one and were scanning the battalion with raised fingers, trying to pinpoint the man and not lose him among the sea of similarly dressed individuals. An old man with poor eyesight conferred with his wife for a few seconds before agreeing with a satisfied grin that he had indeed located his grandson.

The music stopped. The rain was heavier, pounding the pavement with the characteristic sound. The crowd of onlookers huddled more tightly underneath their umbrellas.

Zhivko looked at them carefully. He studied the people with interest, noting their clothing and faces, some smiling happily, other partially obscured by cameras taking pictures. A beautiful girl in the front was looking at someone with eyes full of wonder and joy at the prospect of a reunion a long time in the making.

The anthem began, loudspeakers carrying it across the base. One more quick formation change and then quiet once more. Each soldier broke away from his peers with an exaggerated and well-practiced march. Ten strides later, he stopped, saluted the commander, and leaned in to kiss the flag, which was held lowered at a forty-five-degree angle by another military officer. Some in the crowd were clicking their cameras, eager not to miss the moment.

Zhivko scanned the audience once more, knowing there was no one there for him. No one took pictures when it was his turn to march across. He did not know his parents, nor did he know anything about them. Was there someone in his family who once upon a time fought and died for his country? Should the words on the famous monument be of any personal significance for him? He thrust his leg forward in dramatic fashion and approached the flag.

A car sounded its horn and brought him back to reality. Zhivko looked out across the street and saw one driver angrily gesturing at another. The cars moved apart, speeding away in separate directions. He kept his head down and walked on. Intentionally avoiding public transportation, he stuck to the inside edge of the sidewalks, nearly trampling on the grass. The rain continued to come down, and the sky turned a dark gray, bringing out the green in the surrounding trees and bushes.

Zhivko kept to the narrow streets and took a circuitous path, zigzagging around the city's bustling center. He was approaching the military medical academy from the side, wanting to avoid the heavy foot traffic in front of the main entrance. He looked up at the large building, its multiple white stories forming an impressive facade. There were countless windows, some open, most closed.

He moved closer to a dry area underneath a nearby tree and checked his watch. It was a little past noon, and his friend would soon be taking his lunch break. There was a makeshift restaurant nearby, a modest wooden structure near one of the side entrances. Zhivko stood and waited. After the inexplicable refusal of his best friend to help him, Zhivko had but one option left.

The man emerged from the medical academy's entrance with the usual spring in his step. Bogdan was thin and tall, his figure accentuated by his awkward habit of walking on the tips of his toes, the heels of his feet just barely touching the ground. The twenty-eight-year-old skipped down the stairs and turned toward the restaurant, which was a makeshift wooden structure and some tables and chairs underneath a tent pitched in the hospital's courtyard. He characteristically stopped for a moment to chat with a woman going the opposite way before continuing.

Zhivko walked forward along the fence, observing through the cracks. The commuters paid him no attention. The light turned red, and a traffic jam was forming on the streets behind him.

Bogdan pulled a beer out of the freezer and walked toward the cashier. Three minutes later, he was walking away, balancing a plate of boiled potatoes and shish kebabs on one hand. A piece of bread was in his mouth, obscuring most of his face except a pointy nose and small glasses. He found a secluded high table toward the far end and put the food down. He uncapped the beer and took a deep swallow. Bogdan then wiped his mouth with his hand and burped loudly.

Zhivko studied the landscape in all directions before moving in with quick steps. Crossing the open space in front of the entrance, he chose a table at the very corner of the restaurant's open area, just barely beyond the raindrops and partially obscured by one of the pillars holding up the roof. Bogdan was a few meters away, trying to push a small piece of kebab meat off the metallic rod with a weak plastic fork.

Zhivko produced a cigarette and lit it, nearly gagging with the first inhalation. He brought it up to his mouth again and pulled on it with more confidence. No one would pay attention to a lone man out for a smoke. He forced himself to finish half the cigarette, trying to look as casual as possible.

"Excuse me," he said, loudly enough to be heard by Bogdan but no one else. A group of doctors were having a heated political discussion not far away. "Can you pass the ashtray?"

"Sure," Bogdan replied, putting the fork down and reaching for the ashtray in the middle of the table. "Here you—"

He had picked up the little piece of dirty plastic and was approaching Zhivko when he looked at him for the first time.

"Ahh!" Bogdan gasped in surprise, blinking to make sure he was seeing right. "What are you doing here?"

"Quiet!" Zhivko commanded with a hiss, waving his hands downward in a calming motion. "Come here."

Bogdan walked to him and put the ashtray on the table. He looked inside the hood to confirm his friend's identity. Zhivko looked around, eyes scanning the premises. No one was paying them any attention. He extinguished the cigarette, which he felt had already poisoned his mouth with a nasty taste, and looked at Bogdan.

"Why are you here?" Bogdan asked, still struggling to comprehend the situation while looking into his troubled green eyes. "Aren't they looking for you? I thought you were in some kind of trouble."

"I am," Zhivko responded. "That's why I need your help."

"Me?" Bogdan asked with confusion, the small spectacles sliding down his pointy nose. "I don't understand—"

"Please," Zhivko began, reaching out and placing a hand on his friend's shoulder. "You gotta believe me. I don't know what they are accusing me of, but it's not true. I didn't do anything. I have been set up."

He was almost pleading now.

"Sure thing, buddy, hold on," Bogdan replied, looking rather uncomfortable. He walked over to his table and picked up the plate and fork, beer, napkin, and the chewed-on piece of bread. He returned to Zhivko and placed the items on the table. He moved in closer, making sure to tightly tuck in the blue shirt and push up his glasses. A laminated medical pass hung from his neck, threaded between the buttons on the shirt so as not to sway beneath his chin while he was eating.

A recent graduate of a medical university, Bogdan was an assistant in one of the police forensics labs. He was sometimes part of the crew that went to crime scenes, including after raids conducted by the commandos. He also put in part-time duty in the military medical academy, mostly examining the new conscripts and tending to those injured during the tedious service. He supplemented his meager income by using his skills as a card player. The activity earned him a constant stream of additional funds, as well as a beating just over a year ago.

Zhivko remembered coming to his rescue.

"You want to eat?" Bogdan asked. "There are some forks over there."

"No, thanks," Zhivko replied.

Bogdan nodded and put a piece of grilled beef in his mouth. He chewed noisily.

"Tell me what's going on."

Zhivko tensed immediately. "I don't know," he began, shaking his head and gripping the table for support. "I came home yesterday, and the police were there. They wanted to arrest me. Supposedly, there were drugs in my house."

Bogdan put a finger in his mouth to dislodge a piece of meat stuck between his teeth.

"I read the report," he said. "It was prepared late last night, except for some of the details."

"And?"

"They did find drugs," Bogdan said matter-of-factly. "As well as ten thousand dollars stashed in one of the drawers."

Zhivko raised his hands in protest.

"I assume you don't know how they got there …" Bogdan swallowed and quickly stuffed his mouth with mashed potatoes.

"Of course not!" Zhivko protested, angrily raising his voice while trying to remain calm. "Why were they searching my apartment in the first place?"

Bogdan put down the fork and leaned closer.

"Listen," he said. "There has been a lot of talk that people on the inside are helping organized crime bosses, okay?" He bit off a piece of bread and continued, "The minister authorized unannounced checks of the residences of crucial personnel."

"Is that even legal?"

"Hell if I know," Bogdan responded, reaching for a napkin. "Some of the other guys on your squad also got surprise visits. I can only imagine how Vassil's wife reacted." The forensic assistant laughed, revealing a strangely charming gap-toothed smile. "That woman is intense," Bogdan added.

Zhivko made a rolling motion with his hand, urging him to continue.

"Anyway, you were on the list as well. I think they got into your flat by taking the spare key, the one you've apparently given your neighbor in case of emergencies."

"Someone must have set me up," Zhivko said, searching his mind for a possible explanation. "I don't know how that stuff ended up in my apartment."

Bogdan took a sip of beer and scratched his chin.

"Are you suggesting it was an inside job?" he asked, his tone suddenly serious and face stern.

Zhivko did not answer right away. "I see no other explanation," he finally said. Bogdan was silent, slowly moving the remaining potatoes around the plate with his fork.

"Listen," he said. "They keep you guys somewhat secluded from the rest, so I don't know if you have heard any of the rumors or not."

"Rumors?"

Bogdan pushed the glasses higher and trained his little brown eyes on Zhivko. "Yeah, the rumors," he said and sucked in the saliva creeping toward the corners of his mouth. "No one dares to say anything directly, but people are suggesting that insiders are cooperating with the criminals."

"Corrupt cops?"

Bogdan wagged his finger. "It's bigger than that. We are not just talking about people getting away with traffic violations. All kinds of shit is being smuggled into Serbia daily. There is no way people across all branches and levels aren't involved."

Zhivko leaned back against the wooden pillar. "Is there any proof?"

Bogdan shook his head and ate the last of the bread.

"No, none." He swallowed and cleared his throat. "But I tell you, there have been reporters snooping around, asking questions. Trying to talk to people off the record." He scooped up the last remaining potato and looked up. "One reporter in particular."

"Which one?"

"I forget the name," Bogdan replied and waved his hand. "But look at today's *Trud*; she has an article in there."

"Thanks."

"Sure thing." With that, Bogdan burped again and punched his chest for relief. "But listen, I have to head back to work." He took a quick look around and then trained his eyes on Zhivko. "You can count on me, okay?" He intentionally prolonged their eye contact.

Zhivko felt as if a giant load had been lifted off his shoulder, and for a second, he wanted to hug the silly-looking man in front of him.

"Thanks, buddy. I appreciate it."

"No problem." Bogdan wiped his mouth with a napkin and pulled the ID out from underneath his shirt.

"Oh, and by the way, you're not a very convincing smoker."

Zhivko finally relaxed enough to crack a smile. "You're probably right," he said. "I can't stand it either."

"Yeah, nasty habit. My girlfriend smokes from time to time. It's the only thing we don't agree about."

"You and Inna still together?" Zhivko asked, referring to a soft-spoken chemist who was one of the few women who had responded favorably to Bogdan's incessant advances. "How long has it been now?"

"About a year and a half," Bogdan replied with a devilish smile. "We're quite serious too. I'm fucking almost every night." He punctuated the remark with an exaggerated hip thrusting and a proud grin.

"You getting married?"

"Thinking about it."

"Nice."

Bogdan smiled. "Thank you. If you don't get arrested and sent to jail, I will invite you to the wedding."

"The Inna and Bobo wedding," Zhivko teased with a smile. "I would not want to miss that."

"Hey," Bogdan began, "I told you never to call me that!" His last name was Borisov, and Zhivko enjoyed teasing him by taking the first two letters of his first and last name and combining them.

"Sorry."

Bogdan looked at his watch. "Good luck, my friend," he said with a pat on the shoulder. "Stay safe."

The two men separated. Zhivko felt a sense of relief as he pulled the hood over his head and walked out onto the sidewalk, throwing the box of cigarettes into the first trash can he saw. The drizzle had nearly stopped, but the sky was still overcast.

Chapter Eleven

The kiosk was overloaded with newspapers, folded neatly and arranged one over the other to conserve space. Magazines for all tastes were laid out on the sides and along the panels holding up the roof. A vibrant and colorful free press had been established virtually overnight following the collapse of communism.

"Anything for you?" the middle-aged man behind the kiosk asked.

"*Trud*," Zhivko replied, taking out his wallet. He picked up the newspaper and walked away. The soft drizzle prevented him from reading the newspaper right away, so he continued along the sidewalk, passing by the residential buildings until he saw a first-floor apartment that had been converted into a small pharmacy. He took shelter under its thin metallic roof, opened the newspaper, and began flipping quickly through its pages.

The headline read: "Interior Ministry Attempts Crackdown on Corruption but Questions Remain."

It was a page-length article illustrated with a photograph of Minister Stoyanov striking a power pose by leaning over the podium and waving his finger. Zhivko read as quickly as he could.

The interior minister's promise to crack down on alleged corruption within the ranks of the police and the units charged with fighting organized crime led to a series of unannounced property searches conducted yesterday. The homes of commandos and police sergeants and lieutenants were inspected. Investigators knocked on doors and proceeded to search for drugs, money, weapons, cigarettes, or any other materials that could indicate involvement in a smuggling operation. Even though the investigators did not enter the citizens' private property without consent, an exception was made in one case. Following an anonymous tip, police and investigators entered the apartment of special forces member Zhivko Mladenov, suspected of assisting drug smugglers. They found numerous hundred-dollar bills and small plastic bags of drugs hidden in the apartment. Despite the presence of police officers, who attempted to arrest Mladenov, the suspect escaped in dramatic fashion, with one police officer currently hospitalized with a concussion as a result of the fight. Police are still looking for the suspect, described as armed and dangerous. His whereabouts are unknown at this time.

That was followed by a couple of irrelevant paragraphs, mostly quotes from Stoyanov's many press conferences as well as neighbors and police present at the scene of Zhivko's attempted arrest. He stepped aside as someone left the pharmacy and then continued reading the last two paragraphs of the article.

These searches come at a time when the government is under increasing pressure to react to what many observers say are organized criminal networks that sprang up following the sanctions the United Nations imposed on the former Yugoslavia. Anecdotal evidence suggests that smuggling channels set up by the former State Security are currently in the hands of well-connected criminals. The few smugglers who have been jailed have said successful smuggling requires the participation of numerous parties along the supply chain and neglect, if not outright cooperation, on the part of certain officials. Analyzing the recent events, yesterday's unsuccessful arrest raises more questions than answers.

Security experts and foreign observers say the criminal networks would most certainly need to have their tentacles spread among the higher levels and have access to officials with the authority to pull strings and exercise operational control. Opposition parties are saying the Ministry of Internal Affairs is trying to score PR points by taking out a low-level employee in a hastily organized and poorly executed operation instead of investigating possible corruption at the higher levels.

That was it. Zhivko folded the newspaper and scratched his chin. Instead of things becoming clearer, the picture was getting even more complicated. He was a pawn in someone's chess game, apparently. The enemies were many and unknown. He shook his head in disgust.

Yet, he admired the reporter's courage. Was she the one Bogdan had been talking about? The one who was surreptitiously asking questions, mining sources, and probing for inside information? He opened the newspaper again.

Mira Lyubenova. The name was written in small letters underneath the headline. Her picture was at the start of the article, indenting the first three lines of the first paragraph. Lyubenova's hair was pulled back, and her eyebrows were highly arched over her eyes. The face was youthful, the thin lips sealed. It looked like a passport photo. Zhivko tore it out, folded it carefully, and placed it in the pocket of his jeans. The rest of the newspaper he threw away.

Chapter Twelve

Kiril folded the newspaper with anger, crumpling the pages. He threw it down on the ground and reclined in the leather chair, placing both feet on the desk. He liked to partially open the window, believing that the pure mountain air performed a cleansing function. The luxurious wooded residential areas to Sofia's south were popular with diplomats, foreign businessmen, and some of Bulgaria's newly rich.

He poured himself a glass of expensive whiskey and swirled it in the air before taking a sip. The aroma filled his nostrils and temporarily soothed him. He put the glass back on the table and capped the bottle. He had woken up just past ten o'clock and fooled around with Ivanka for a while before asking the maid to prepare a delicious lunch.

Earlier that day, Kiril had sent Nikolai and the two bodyguards away to a shooting range for their routine training. They didn't really need the extra practice and hoped there would never be any need to shoot someone. They could not rule it out, of course, but intimidation and the occasional use of brute physical force usually worked just fine.

The lunch consisted of steak with steamed vegetables and some juice. Kiril wiped his mouth with the expensive napkin and walked back up to the second floor to enter his study, where he was planning a leisurely read through of the newspapers.

His plans went to hell when he saw page eleven of *Trud*. A few months ago, his bodyguards cornered a particularly nefarious journalist from some other newspaper and proceeded with a savage beating that left more than one broken bone. He had been hopeful that had sent a clear message.

It obviously had not.

He picked up his mobile phone and dialed. Nikolai answered after the second ring.

"Hello?" There was an intense banging noise in the background, and the words were barely audible.

"Hello, friend," Kiril said, raising his voice to be heard. "Your colleague is calling."

Nikolai smiled and headed for the exit. He walked down the air-locked corridor and pushed through the soundproof doors. He was wearing the standard uniform for someone in his line of work. The tight and black short-sleeved shirt stretched over his muscles. Combined with dark jeans and metallic bracelets on the wrists, it created a distinct and intimidating appearance.

"Hello, colleague. What can I do for you?"

"Our favorite investigative reporter has written another article," Kiril began. "I just read it in the paper."

Nikolai looked around to make sure there was no one within earshot. The muffled sounds of firearms discharging could be heard through the doors.

"I see," he replied, waiting for his boss to take the initiative.

"She's relentless, and she is getting close," Kiril said sternly, controlling his annoyance. "She hasn't yet put together all the pieces, but she might."

"That's a problem."

"I agree." The instructions that followed were delivered with the usual purpose and directness. "Why don't you and the boys pay her a visit? Show her just how much we appreciate her work."

Kiril was confident Nikolai immediately understood what was being asked of him. If he had moral qualms about such assignments, he kept his misgivings to himself. Kiril knew Nikolai did not want to seem weak in front of the two grunts under his control and he definitely did not want to appear unreliable. Such people could be easily replaced.

"Of course," Nikolai replied. "We'll take care of it."

"Thank you, friend."

"Have a good day, colleague."

Nikolai hung up and put the phone in his pocket. It was time to get to work. He returned to the shooting range to round up the other two. The targets they were shooting at were riddled with bullet holes.

Meanwhile, Kiril thoughtfully emptied the remaining contents of the glass and poured himself some more whiskey. He ran his hands over his subtle morning stubble and decided it was time to shave.

He downed the whiskey in one gulp and returned the glass to the desk with a slam.

This reporter was really starting to piss him off. His people at the border control agency had said that she had made numerous visits, looking for information and asking questions. Moreover, she had apparently been seen at the Ministry of Interior and various police departments. His conclusion was an obvious one.

She needed to be taken care of. Perhaps some intimidation would do. Nothing serious, of course. There was no need to inflict a lot of damage. Just a few bruises to give her a scare. Nikolai and his men would know what to do.

Kiril tapped his fingers on the desk. He did his best thinking when alone, surrounded by shelves of books and expensive souvenirs. The next couple of days were crucial, and he needed everything to go well. Afterward, he would have time to plan his next steps and consolidate his control. He did not want to get caught up in the rush to make illicit profits and get sloppy.

Feeling dirty, Kiril got up and went to the bathroom for a shower.

Chapter Thirteen

"Mira!" Hubchev yelled, the deep and raspy voice piercing through the newsroom. "Mira!" he thundered again, leaning farther out of his office while still holding on to the doorframe.

Mira heard her name and turned around. Hubchev was waving for her to come in. She put the pen down on her notebook and got up, using her hands to stretch the creases of her bright-blue cotton shirt as she walked.

"Yes?" she asked.

"We need to talk," Hubchev said, gesturing for her to enter the office. Large, spacious, and located near the stairway, the editor's office contained a plain rectangular carpet with two padded chairs positioned in front of a large oak desk. Piles of newspapers, notes, and an oversized cup were spread across the desk. Part of the keyboard appeared from underneath the papers, and the monitor was near the edge. The walls were adorned with framed clippings of memorable headlines and pictures of the editor with politicians and celebrities. A damaged fan, its dusty head lowered like that of a dying bird, stood in one corner.

Mira walked in and took a seat.

Still by the door, Hubchev looked around impatiently and sighed. He didn't like it when something needed to be done and there was no one to bark at. He grabbed a young man walking by.

"Are you the new intern?" he asked.

"Excuse me?" the boy replied, looking confused and a tad scared. His narrow shoulders felt crushed by the editor's large hands.

"The new intern," Hubchev insisted. "Are you the intern?"

The guy cleared his throat. "No, I'm the new assistant weather forecaster." He looked nervous.

Hubchev frowned. "The *assistant* weather guy?" he asked incredulously. "It takes more than one person to read the report from the meteorological agency and then type a few sentences?"

The college kid stood speechless.

"Fine, whatever," Hubchev continued, speaking quickly. "Find the intern and tell him to bring coffee." He looked at Mira, who shook her finger no. "Just one," he said, "and get me some cigarettes as well. Mine have run out."

The guy nodded, and Hubchev let him go. He walked in and shut the door behind him. His pants made a swishing sound as his thick legs moved. His hulking figure looked just as big behind the desk, large arms placed on its surface.

"Nice article," he said, pulling a copy of the paper out. It was folded to the appropriate page. "Just what I expect from you."

"Thank you," Mira said. "It's an interesting story."

"Sure is," the editor replied, glancing over the page. "I have been getting heat about it all morning." He put the paper down and looked directly at Mira. "Seems the government is not happy we're not congratulating the police for exposing the mole and attempting to arrest him."

Mira shook her head, the ponytail gently swinging behind her. She had had just six hours of sleep.

"I think there might be more to the story, sir."

"I know," Hubchev responded, hands raised to his chin in a pensive pose. "I have your back."

"Thank you."

"Is there something in particular that bothers you?" he asked, intense eyes trained on the woman in the chair. He needed to know what kind of puzzle she was uncovering and how the pieces fit together.

Mira took a moment to think.

"Don't you think it's strange that they immediately found someone to blame?" she asked. "Stoyanov promises action, and the next day they find incriminating evidence in the apartment of some commando?" Picking up speed, Mira raised her voice and lowered its pitch. "Something doesn't quite make sense."

Hubchev rubbed his lips together.

"Is that all you have?" he asked.

"No," Mira responded. "I have talked to plenty of people, particularly over the past year or so. There is a lot going on beneath the surface that we don't see."

"And you are sure about that?"

"Absolutely."

"Good," Hubchev said. "I don't want us to be seen as criticizing the government based solely on hunches."

"We're not," Mira said firmly.

There was a loud knock on the door.

"Come in!"

A young woman with a pot of coffee walked in. A first-year journalism student, she was charming but lacking ambition. Hubchev intentionally gave her tedious administrative duties to keep her out of the way. She wore a knee-length dress and an eager smile.

"Your coffee," she said and approached the desk, clearing a spot for the pitcher.

"Thank you," Hubchev said with a quick smile. "And the cigarettes?"

"Oh," the girl replied, instantly embarrassed by her forgetfulness. "I'm sorry."

Hubchev frowned. "Get them," he instructed, angrily pointing at the door with a shaking finger. "Please!"

"Right away."

The intern walked out without looking at Mira.

"Today's youth," Hubchev said with a tone of resigned disappointment. Steam and aroma rose from the large cup as he poured himself coffee. "Where were we?"

"Talking about my article," Mira reminded him.

"Right," the editor said and gulped down some coffee. "Your article." He scratched his nose and continued, "Keep doing what you're doing, but I want you to be very careful about this. This topic is a political minefield, and a wrong step could be bad for all of us."

"I understand," Mira agreed with a nod.

There was another loud knock, and the door opened before Hubchev had an opportunity to react. Martina popped her head in, curly hair falling to one side.

"You got my cigarettes?" Hubchev asked.

"No …" Martina replied slowly, momentarily looking confused before addressing Mira. "There is a phone call for you."

"Who is it?" Mira asked.

"He would not say," Martina replied, taking a step inside. "But he said it's urgent and that he will talk only to you."

Hubchev watched as a perplexed Mira glanced back and forth between him and Martina before getting up.

"Excuse me," she said and left the editor's office, sprinting to her desk. The receiver was placed on her desk, the cord snaking over the keyboard.

"Alo?" she said, instinctively grabbing her pen and activating it with a push of its top.

"Is this Mira Lyubenova?" the male voice asked. Mira could hear breathing and a mixture of background noises.

"Yes," she answered. "It's me. Who's calling?"

Martina took her seat behind the opposite desk and observed with heightened curiosity.

"This is Zhivko Mladenov," the voice said. "You wrote an article about me." The words were enunciated carefully and with a serious tone.

A surge of adrenaline coursed through Mira's veins. It was moments like these that made the job exciting. Her heart rate accelerated.

"What do you want?" she asked, putting a finger in her free ear to block out the sounds of the newsroom.

"Meet me in half an hour in front of the pillars of the National Palace of Culture," Zhivko instructed. "Don't tell anyone. Come alone."

Mira swallowed. "Okay."

The line went dead. She replaced the receiver and glanced at her watch. She spent some time chewing nervously on her pen, thinking in silence.

"I gotta go," she said to Martina and threw pen, notebook, and recorder in her bag. "There is something I have to take care of."

"Fine," Martina said. "See you later."

Mira threaded her arms through the straps of the bag and made for the exit. She eschewed the elevator for the stairs and a minute later breezed across the marble floor of the lobby, giving the bored security guard the customary quick wave.

It was still somewhat cloudy but warm outside, the sidewalks full of rushed pedestrians while cars competed with each other for advantage and position.

Mira exited the building and joined the fray.

Across the street, Stefan observed her closely from his seat at a café. He put down his drink and placed a bill beneath it, using the glass as a weight to keep it from blowing away. The waiter would appreciate the sizeable tip.

Never letting Mira out of his sight, the man pushed chairs out of his way and walked out. He was about thirty meters away from Mira when he stepped onto the sidewalk and she turned the corner ahead, briefly disappearing from view.

He accelerated and was no more than fifteen meters away when he too rounded the corner and saw Mira's back, the black bag clearly visible against the blue shirt. *It's unusual for a woman to carry a bag instead of a purse.* He followed her down the sidewalk, careful to avoid looking directly at her for fear they might make eye contact should she suddenly decide to turn around. The man removed his mobile phone from a small plastic holder attached to his belt and dialed.

"She's on the move," Stefan said, cupping his hand over his mouth. "I'm behind her."

Chapter Fourteen

Located in the center of the city with the beautiful Vitosha Mountain rising in the background behind it, the National Palace of Culture was a multifunctional building and the largest exhibition center in Southeastern Europe. Erected in 1981 to a height of eight stories and a total area of more than 120,000 square meters, its black-and-white facade quickly became a readily recognizable symbol of Sofia.

Zhivko positioned himself on the terrace of the Panorama Restaurant located on the top floor and waited. A large part of the city unfolded before him, the red roofs of the buildings almost indistinguishable from each other. Bright neon advertisements were present on some of them, mounted haphazardly as the nation rushed to adopt capitalism.

There was a light breeze, and the air was fresher. Zhivko looked to his left at the three giant flag pillars. He had a clear view in all directions, an ideal platform for his trained eyes. He looked at his watch.

It was 2:35 p.m. *Would she be punctual?*

She was. He spotted Mira walking along the path by the long row of fountains leading up to the National Palace of Culture. She made a right toward the pillars just before reaching the building. She reached the large metallic columns and waited, looking around. Zhivko spotted her almost immediately.

He took out the ripped newspaper picture for confirmation. The plan was to approach Mira and whisk her away to a secluded location for a brief conversation. There was a school just a few steps away, and nobody would pay any attention if two people sat down on one of the benches in the yard. The wide-open area provided clear views in all directions and a choice of quick escape routes.

Zhivko was about to pull away from the ledge when something caught his eye.

Across from the pillars was a concrete island with a tram stop fenced off, traffic along the boulevard diverted into two streams around it. An auxiliary street fed into the main boulevard. There was a black Mercedes on the street about to make a right turn.

But it was not making the turn. It was not parked either. It just sat and idled.

Something is wrong here.

He could not see the model, but it was obviously new and very expensive. The car just waited there, its shiny frame glistening in the sunlight as the clouds above dissipated.

Its positioning was a traffic violation. But the driver did not seem to care. Looking through the windshield, Zhivko could make out the silhouette of a man. There did not seem to be anyone in the passenger's side. It was partially blocking traffic, making it difficult for the other cars to turn.

Something is very wrong.

Mira was still pacing back and forth in front of the pillars, her demeanor revealing a heightened level of anxiety. Zhivko looked at her and then focused back on the Mercedes. The car was still there, but suddenly, another vehicle moved in front of it, preparing to make a right turn. A second vehicle followed soon after and then a third. A large yellow tram pulled to a stop, unloading a group of passengers, who scattered in all directions. The other cars made their right turns and disappeared.

All of a sudden, the back right-side door of the Mercedes opened and a man got out, his head bopping from side to side for a better view. Apparently frustrated, the man walked away from the car and onto the sidewalk, all the while looking across the boulevard. He stopped by the kiosk but showed no signs of buying anything.

The man fixed his gaze and was watching something intently.

Mira! A shot of electricity went up and down Zhivko's spine.

The tram closed its doors and rumbled and screeched away toward the next stop. The man promptly returned to the black Mercedes.

Zhivko breathed in and searched his mind. The plan had changed, and now he had to come up with another one. He turned around and headed into the restaurant, swiftly moving toward the exit. The colder air of the stairwell washed over Zhivko's face as he hurried down the stairs, passing by what looked like a group of people preparing to celebrate a wedding.

He reached the bottom floor and walked out, staying near the building. The spray of nearby water fountains made the air refreshingly moist.

"Hey, kid," he said, gesturing at a teenager attempting a trick with his skateboard. A buddy of his was sitting astride a bicycle watching with interest.

"Yeah?" the kid asked, stepping on one edge of the skateboard to pick it up.

"My girlfriend is over there, waiting for me," Zhivko lied, hoping he was a good actor. "I will pay you five leva if you go tell her to meet me on the other side, by the ticket center." He smiled like an idiot in love. "I want to surprise her."

The kid laughed. "Sure, dude. Give me the cash, and I'm off."

Zhivko reached inside his wallet and handed the skinny, long-haired kid the money.

Chapter Fifteen

"Do you see us now?" Nikolai asked, looking through the window.

"I do," Stefan said. "I am coming toward you." He was approaching the National Palace of Culture from the west side, heading up the sidewalk and observing Mira, who was walking along the row of water fountains. Soon, she would have to turn right, toward the flagpoles, which meant her path would converge with that of her follower.

Stefan took evasive action and crossed the boulevard, first to the tram stop and then around the fence toward the black Mercedes. He opened the right back door and got in.

"Well done," Nikolai said, glancing back at the hefty, somewhat dark-skinned man.

"Thanks," Stefan said, placing the mobile phone down and sinking into the cushioned seats. "This chick walks fast."

Stefan had been tailing the reporter ever since she left the office, periodically calling Nikolai with updates on her movements so that he could drive the car accordingly. The goal was to always keep track of Mira and her whereabouts. If she was meeting with a secret informer, the big boss wanted to know who it was so that measures could be taken. The closer she got, the closer they got.

Sitting on the opposite side of Stefan, Ahmed smiled and said nothing. The third member of the team, he felt underutilized and unappreciated. He wondered if it was because of his age—at just twenty-three, he was a provincial kid who had come to the big city to earn money and send it back home—or because of his ethnicity. He was from the country's ethnic Turkish minority, and he sometimes felt as if the dominant ethnic Bulgarians disliked him for it. He leaned over and scratched his scalp. His hair was thinning, and that was a source of worry as well.

"Is that her right there?" Nikolai asked, pointing forward. "In the blue shirt …"

"Yeah," Stefan answered. "I've been tracking her for the past few days."

Nikolai's expression remained unchanged. Jaw clenched, he stared ahead. Hidden by the occasional passing car or pedestrian, Mira was nevertheless visible as she stood by the giant pillars.

The engine of the Mercedes hummed softly. The three men sat in silence.

"Is she waiting for someone?" Nikolai asked, glancing up in the rearview mirror at his two subordinates.

"It's possible," Stefan said. "She left the office in a hurry."

"What exactly are we going to do to her?" Stefan asked. He vividly remembered the visit they paid the other journalist. In a strange, animalistic sort of way, it was an enjoyable experience. He felt powerful and intoxicated by his crushing strength as he rained blows on the helpless man, who after awhile didn't even have the sense to scream. It was a memorable thrill. He just wasn't sure he was willing to do it to a woman.

"I can tell you what I would like to do to her," Ahmed said, a mischievous grin on his face. "Her ass looks—"

"Shut up!" Nikolai barked. "Look ahead and stay focused."

Stefan raised his eyebrows disapprovingly at Ahmed and did as instructed. Mira was still there, now pacing back and forth.

A car pulled up in front of them and signaled a right turn. Mira briefly disappeared from view. The car turned, and Mira reappeared, only to disappear again as another car prepared for a turn. Pedestrians rushing to the tram stop prevented it from moving away.

Nikolai anxiously tightened his grip on the steering wheel and frowned.

The car finally turned, but an even bigger obstruction arrived. The yellow tram stopped and opened its doors with a thump. Its long, rectangular body completely hid Mira and the surrounding area.

"Motherfucker!" Nikolai yelled and hit the dashboard with his palm. The tram was not moving, as commuters were still exiting down its steep stairs.

"Stefan, get out and try to get a view of the woman," he ordered. "I don't want to lose her now."

Stefan flung the door open and exited. Holding the door and the car frame for balance, he raised himself on his toes, but the tram was too large.

"Hold on," he said and shut the door. He walked onto the sidewalk and around the newspaper stand for a better view. Now the pillars were clearly visible across the boulevard. The woman was still there, her blue shirt unmistakable.

"She hasn't moved," Stefan said and returned to the car.

"Right," Nikolai said. "I can see her now as well."

"Wait!" Ahmed said suddenly, pointing. "She is walking away."

The three men watched as Mira moved away from the flagpoles, heading across the face of the building and toward its opposite side. She was quickly disappearing from view.

"Get out!" Nikolai barked, shifting the Mercedes into first gear. "Both of you. Follow her, and tell me what's going on. I'm going to make a circle around the palace to the other side."

Stefan grabbed the mobile phone and left, slamming the door shut. Ahmed left the car as well, and the two men crossed the boulevard in a hurry. Nikolai drove by behind them. Driving to the other side of the largest building in the country entailed going through a number of lights. The engine roared at the other cars.

Nikolai held the mobile phone uncomfortably, gripping it between his hand and the steering wheel. Ahmed and Stefan were now on the square, their eyes searching the large open area.

Chapter Sixteen

"Miss," the teenager said, trying to draw Mira's attention as he approached her, skateboard in hand. "Miss!"

"Excuse me?" Mira replied. "What do you want?" Her eyes studied the face of the skinny teenager, instinctively raising her guard and trying to ascertain if he was a threat.

"Your boyfriend wanted me to tell you that he's waiting for you by the ticket center on the other side," the boy said, looking directly at Mira.

"Who?" Mira asked, still confused. She looked at the boy, whose face was partially obscured by uncombed wavy hair. He looked honest enough.

"My boyfriend?" Mira asked, quickly turning her head in all directions.

"Yes," the teenager answered. He pointed behind him. "He was right there, and he told me to tell you to meet him in front of the ticket center. Said it's a surprise."

Mira nodded. *It has to be Mladenov.*

A wave of nervousness swept over her, her heart rate suddenly rising.

"Thank you," she said to the kid, managing a smile. "I'll go see him."

With that, she walked away, trying to remain calm as her eyes darted from person to person. There were kids chasing each other, young couples on a lazy stroll, businessmen in a hurry, retirees walking slowly. *Is he among them?*

She realized that she didn't have a clue what he looked like, and that was now beginning to frighten her a little. Mira left the two kids to their skateboarding and walked across the main entrance of the palace, not knowing what to expect. The spray from the nearby fountains moistened the air, which was pleasantly caressing her face. She could almost see the ticket office now. Shouts from the nearby bumper cars were discernible.

Mira suddenly felt a powerful hand grip her elbow, virtually immobilizing her right arm. The sharp pain dug deeply through her flesh. She felt scared.

"Walk," the voice instructed. "Keep moving."

The man who had appeared beside her was taller, probably just over 180 centimeters and with an imposing physique. She could only see the side of his face. The hair was neatly cropped and dark.

"Don't look at me," the man said sternly, briefly shifting his eyes to the woman. "Look forward and walk."

Mira had no choice. The man was using his grip of her elbow to steer her and control her movements. She started breathing heavily. Yet she forced herself to stay in control of her mind. She was a tough girl.

"Walk quickly," the man instructed, pushing her forward. "Stay close, and don't draw attention." Mira did as she was told. The two of them were walking away from the Palace of Culture, following a path of white tiles that would lead them toward Vassil Levsky Boulevard, one of the city's main thoroughfares.

Her elbow was growing numb, the clenched grip of the large man inescapable. She was beginning to sweat.

Zhivko looked over his shoulder toward the flagpoles in the distance. His eyes scanned the landscape for something out of the ordinary, something threatening. He noticed them almost immediately.

The two men were walking side by side, a sense of purpose in their quick footsteps. Their demeanor indicated they were not out for a leisurely stroll, and they weren't like the rest of the random pedestrians. No, they were out on the hunt for something, someone.

The two men saw Zhivko eyeing them and stopped. There was an instant flash of recognition as prey and predator made unwilling eye contact. The two men halted and stood still. The commando appeared heavier than either of them—muscle, not fat. His movements were quick and deliberate, a forceful economy of motion. The two men looked at each other for a moment and then continued walking, their stride now quicker.

Mira remained oblivious, but she saw the concern etched in Mladenov's otherwise expressionless face.

"Go faster," he commanded stiffly. "Move!"

He pushed her elbow forward, causing her to wince. They were approaching the end of the path, where it merged with a sidewalk and a makeshift taxi stand. Mira observed their trajectory with a heightened sense of urgency.

She had met criminals and dangerous men before, but she had always exercised at least some level of control over the situation. Now she felt completely helpless and vulnerable. The voice inside her told her to find a way out.

Walking along the sidewalk was a police officer in dark trousers and a light-blue shirt. He wasn't too far away, at most twenty meters. He turned along the path and headed in their direction.

Now fifteen meters away. The two men were still coming from behind.

Mira expected the cop to pass by her when something apparently caught his eye. She and Zhivko did not look like casual friends, but they certainly were not lovers either. Men didn't hold their girlfriends that way.

The cop stopped. Zhivko did as well, tugging Mira back into position by her elbow.

"Sir," the cop began, his voice polite but firm, "why are you holding her that way?"

Zhivko said nothing. His mind was racing for a solution, a way out, as the cop neared.

"Are you okay, ma'am?" the police officer asked. "Is this man hurting you?"

Mira did not say anything but grimaced with discomfort. Some of the pedestrians turned in her direction as the awkward standoff continued. Zhivko did not relax his grip on her elbow. He turned to look at the two men following them. They stood approximately twenty meters away, observing the situation. They stopped, one gesturing to the other to stay back.

The police officer approached with increasing determination as curious bystanders looked on. "What is the problem, miss?" the cop asked, eyes darting from Zhivko to Mira.

"Leave us alone," Zhivko said with an impolite hiss. "We're walking home."

The cop was not buying it.

"Let go of her arm, sir!" he ordered, looking directly at Zhivko. The commando did not respond, except to look down and position his body so that his shoulders were level with those of the sergeant.

The two men were standing still, observing the unexpected situation. Zhivko quickly turned his head to verify their position and then assumed his previous stance. Drops of sweat began to collect at his temples.

"Sir!" the cop commanded loudly, drawing the attention of even more bystanders. "Let her go!"

Zhivko inhaled deeply. He did not know who the goons following the reporter were, but he knew he had to remove her to a safe location. He needed to speak with her and find out more information so he could clear his name. Violence was not his intention, but as far as he was now concerned, fighting his way out was the only option available.

"I said," the cop repeated through his teeth, his tone clearly affected by Zhivko's insolence, "to let her go!" He moved forward and reached for Zhivko's left arm. It was just the opening the commando needed. He sprang to life, letting go of Mira's elbow and taking a step forward. He grabbed the cop's wrist and moved in with his right arm.

The first elbow strike accelerated with lightning speed and smashed into the cop's chin. A split second later, the initial strike was followed by another. The movements were blindingly fast and devastatingly forceful. The bony tip of the elbow was capable of inflicting a lot of damage.

The cop gasped in pain and stumbled backward a few steps, eventually losing his balance and falling. There was blood on his face. Mira watched in silent disbelief.

Zhivko reached for her wrist and grabbed it. Careful not to twist or cause unnecessary pain, he nevertheless pulled her forward sharply, effortlessly throwing her on the grassy meadow near the downed cop. She screamed, as did one bystander. There was a crowd of onlookers now, but no one dared intervene.

The cop was beginning to get up when Zhivko circled behind him and grabbed him, wrapping a muscular arm around his neck, placing an elbow beneath the chin. Clasping his hands behind the man's head, Zhivko's bicep and forearm applied pressure on the vulnerable carotid arteries. Almost immediately, the rear choke stopped the flow of blood to the head.

One second …

Mira saw the cop was trying to say something but had no air.

Two seconds …

The victim would already be seeing stars. Everything would be blurry, so blurry. Soon the world went dark and quiet for the cop. The dazed man put up a feeble resistance, but with no blood flow, he went limp within seconds.

Zhivko put him down on the ground. People gasped and raised their hands to their mouths. The two goons had not moved, unsure of what to do.

Zhivko reached for Mira again and pulled her off the ground.

"No!" she tried to push away but was helpless. Applying the now-familiar elbow hold, Zhivko pushed her in front of him. She was stumbling, but he would not let her fall. Her shoes kicked against the grass, and she attempted to punch with her free hand. The weak blow from the small fist elicited no response from her captor. She glanced back in horror at the motionless police officer, now slumped over to one side.

"Walk!" Zhivko commanded, looking back over his shoulder. "You're in danger."

Ahmed and Stefan were following but keeping their distance. Mira and Zhivko were now on the sidewalk, approaching the row of cabs on the street ahead. There were four cars, all unmanned. The drivers were outside; until a few seconds ago, they had been talking among themselves in anticipation of clients.

Zhivko neared one of the cars and stopped. It was an Opel. A reliable if unimpressive vehicle, it was a step above the other three Ladas. The key was in the ignition. Zhivko opened the door and pulled at Mira's elbow. She sensed the hopelessness of the situation and got in.

"Hey!" the young driver yelled, breaking from the group of cabbies. "What the hell do you think you're doing?" the veins on his neck were swollen with anger.

Zhivko was not about to waste time. He reached under his belt and pulled out his gun, pointing it directly at the driver.

"I'm sorry, I really am," he said. The man raised his hands and backed off slowly. The other cabbies watched in disbelief. Zhivko slammed the door and circled around the car to the driver's seat. He turned the key and brought the engine to life, quickly shifting into reverse and then back into first gear.

Mira sat terrified, her rosy cheeks turned pale.

"Why are you kidnapping me?" she asked with a gasp as the car pulled away.

"Kidnapping?" he hissed, looking at Mira. Strands of hair were crisscrossing her face. "I am protecting you from them," he replied and pointed toward the sidewalk at Ahmed and Stefan, who were standing with eyes fixed on the car.

Mira turned her head and caught a momentary glimpse of the two men before Zhivko shifted into second gear and then madly into third, pressing his foot down on the accelerator. He glanced into the mirror, relieved that the other cabs were not following him.

Everything was happening too fast for comprehension. The car was gaining speed, catching a break and flying through an intersection while the light was still yellow. Mira leaned back into the seat.

"Why are they after us?" she asked, relieved that her professional inquisitive instincts were still with her. They were now on a straight stretch of road. Zhivko maneuvered the car into the left lane and kept his foot on the gas. "They're not," he responded and looked at her. "They're after you!"

His eyes showed his exasperation. "All I wanted to do was talk."

Chapter Seventeen

Mira tried to speak but could not. She looked out the window instead. Mladenov was driving as fast as traffic allowed, aggressively weaving in and out of lanes. The Opel handled well. Another driver honked loudly, a reaction to being cut off. Mladenov saw the light turn red and brought the car to a halt, his tension evident in the intensity with which he gripped the steering wheel. He saw Mira jerk forward and put her arm out as protection.

"How do you know I was being followed?" Mira asked, turning to face him. She swallowed heavily and with trepidation.

Zhivko looked ahead and then checked the mirrors, surveying his surroundings. No sirens blaring, no police. At least not yet. But at this point, he was more worried about the other cabbies.

Bulgarian taxi drivers were famously loyal to each other. A few years earlier, when a drug addict stabbed a driver and ran away, the dispatcher radioed everyone in the area and shortly afterward, the other drivers were helping the police blockade the city's exit routes and patrolling streets large and small. The irate drivers quickly apprehended the suspect and nearly lynched him before the police whisked him away.

Zhivko turned on the meter, thus activating a little red light on the top right of the windshield. Now everyone seeing the car would know that it was occupied.

"I saw them watching you while you were waiting for me," he replied, not taking his eyes off the road. "They were across the street in a black Mercedes. I saw a man get out of the car to get a better view. He was one of the two men who followed us to the taxis."

Mira breathed deeply and cupped her hands over her face. A chill rippled through her body.

"My God," she said, intensely worried. "Are you sure?"

"Yes," Zhivko replied. "I had that kid get you because I didn't want them to see me."

The light turned green, and Zhivko returned his foot to the accelerator, tightly tailgating the car in front. The events of the past few minutes were beginning to make sense to Mira, but the questions in her mind still outnumbered the answers.

"Do you have any idea who they could be?" Zhivko asked, finally succeeding in convincing the car in front to change lanes and make way.

"No," Mira said. "I have no idea."

"What kind of articles do you write?"

"Organized crime, political corruption, that kind of stuff."

Zhivko gave her a knowing glance, holding her eyes for a second.

"You think that ..." She looked scared.

He pressed his palm into the horn as the Opel hugged a tight turn, forcing Mira to grab the door handle for stability. Her hands were shaking, and her knuckles looked white. Zhivko assumed she wouldn't attempt an escape at these speeds, but when the car slowed down for another red light ...

"Have you ever received any death threats?" he asked, looking over at the journalist, who was still visibly overwhelmed by the recent events. "Come on! Think!"

She took a moment.

"I don't think so," she replied. "People tell me my work is dangerous and I shouldn't do it, but I have never been threatened."

"I think you just have."

Mira looked into Mladenov's green eyes. She apparently noticed a trace of concern and compassion in his voice because she relaxed a little.

"I never thought something like this would actually happen," she replied, shaking her head.

"Why do you think they were tracking you?" Zhivko asked firmly. "What do you think they were going to do to you because of your articles?"

"I don't know." She snorted and shook her head. "I don't even know who *they* are!"

"I don't either," Zhivko said. "But they must have been tracking you for a while. It's not safe for you to go home." He glanced at the mirror, relieved they were not being followed.

"Where am I supposed to go?" she asked incredulously.

"I don't know," he replied, biting his lower lip. "But I need to talk to you. You seem to have inside information, and I need to know what it is." He was giving orders, commands. Her cooperation was essential, and he was not about to negotiate for it.

"You've been talking to people, and I need to know who they are and what they are saying. Someone framed me, and I need to clear my name."

Zhivko's face revealed raw emotion, a genuine deep-seated anger, and commitment.

The intercom suddenly crackled, a clear female voice replacing the initial static.

"Attention all colleagues," the dispatcher said. "This is a message that goes out to all vehicles, regardless of location."

Zhivko turned up the volume.

"A few minutes ago, an armed man stole a cab parked near the National Palace of Culture. The car is an Opel, 1993 model. The license plate is C-A-five-six-eight-seven-D-D. If you see this vehicle, please call the police immediately."

"I'm on it," someone replied.

"Understood. I'll keep my eyes open," another cabbie added.

Zhivko searched his mind for options. What was the fastest way out of the city without being noticed?

The light turned red, and Zhivko pulled to a stop. The yellow Opel was second in line. A stream of pedestrians took to the crosswalk. He looked around and established there weren't any taxis visible in the rows of cars behind.

They were near another park, complete with a man-made lake just next to the boulevard. Young people were enjoying the paddleboats, chopping the water while laughter filled the air. Mira scooted her body toward the window and eased her hand onto the door handle.

"Don't even think about it," Zhivko said in a stern voice, letting go of the gear shift to grab her arm.

Mira hesitated, apparently unsure of what to do or say.

"I still need you," he said. "And with those men following you, you might need me."

Zhivko did not relax his grip on her arm, just in case she needed extra persuasion.

Mira released the door handle, her eyes still studying him. He reached across and locked the door.

"When we escape, if you want, I'll let you go. But not here, not now." His tone demanded obedience.

"Has anyone seen him?" a voice over the intercom asked.

Zhivko picked up the transceiver.

"Tell them you saw me near Hotel Kempinski," he instructed and put the transceiver in front of Mira's mouth. "Go ahead," he prodded, nodding his head.

Mira took two seconds to collect herself as Zhivko pressed the transmitter button.

"I just saw him near Kempinski," she said in a flat voice. The hotel, one of the tallest and most luxurious in the city, was located in the opposite direction.

Zhivko nodded approvingly. "That should buy us some time."

The light turned green. He handed her the transceiver.

"Keep it away from your mouth and press the button down."

Mira did as she was told, putting her hand between her knees. She looked confused.

"We're jamming the line," he explained. The Opel accelerated through the intersection and past the taxi stand. None of the vehicles paid them any attention.

Zhivko wiped the side of his face with a shrug of his shoulder and breathed a sigh of relief.

"Where are we going?" Mira asked.

"We need to leave the city," he replied. "Do you have a place somewhere?"

Mira hesitated, apparently uneasy about the escalating level of commitment that was suddenly required of her.

"We have a villa near Pleven," she said, referencing a town in the Bulgarian north. "Right now, there is no one there; my parents are on holiday on the Black Sea."

A plan immediately formed in Zhivko's mind.

"We are going to the train station," he announced. "Driving is out of the question; it's too risky."

They reached another intersection, clearing it with ease and without arousing suspicion. They were soon driving alongside the Vladaya River, a small tributary to the much larger Iskar River. Traffic slowed down as large red public transportation buses appeared, their heavy exhaust fumes poisoning the air.

Zhivko again moved into the farthest left lane. Without the air conditioner on, the heat inside the vehicle was rising and becoming more noticeable. They inched forward in silence.

Just as they reached Lion's Bridge, Zhivko suddenly jerked the car right across several lanes, turning onto the final stretch leading to the Central Railway Station. The maneuver did not go unnoticed.

Looking into the rearview mirror, Zhivko saw two yellow cars accelerating in the distance. One was blaring its horn, urging the other vehicles to get out of the way. Mira looked over her shoulder.

Zhivko pressed his foot to the pedal, going through a red light and speeding past an oncoming tram in the nick of time. The driver rang a distinct siren in protest. The cabs got caught by the light and stopped. But that hardly mattered, because the railway station, its vast gray building now within view, was located just meters away from the central bus station. The area was a hornet's nest of taxis. Mira had successfully jammed one radio frequency, but bigger taxi companies usually needed two.

Surely the cabs ahead had been alerted by now.

He saw an opening and turned left, crossing the tram tracks and veering into the opposite lanes. The wheels bounced over the rails with four quick thuds. An oncoming tourist bus blared its horn loudly. Zhivko brought the car to a cab stand near the sidewalk and killed the engine. He looked in all directions.

"Get out," he ordered. "We're going on foot."

He popped the trunk and got out, slamming the door behind him. Mira got out from the other side.

Inside the trunk were tools, a spare tire, some rags, and a jug of antifreeze. Zhivko sifted through the contents in a frantic hurry. The light behind them had turned green, and the two cabs were approaching.

Zhivko found a plain, beaten-up white shirt; he pulled it out and closed the trunk.

"Let's go," he said and grabbed Mira's hand. The sidewalk was fenced off by thick bushes and partially obscured by trees. They found a place where the bushes were not as thick and pushed through.

The sidewalk was empty, except for some pedestrians at the far end.

"Take your shirt off," Zhivko said.

"Excuse me?" Mira replied indignantly yet unexpectedly excited by the command. "What do you want me to do?"

"You are too recognizable," he explained and raised his hand, holding the fisted white shirt. "Put this on."

Mira still looked outraged and uncompromising.

"Go ahead," he urged. "We don't have time. I'll turn around." He pushed the white shirt into her hands. Mira quickly looked up and down the sidewalk and took it. Zhivko turned around, and she did the same, taking off her bag and replacing her blue shirt with the white one found in the trunk of the cab. It had very short sleeves, barely a few centimeters hanging off the shoulders. *Do I look okay?* Why was she thinking about this now? The shirt was crumpled and had an oil stain on the back.

"Good," Zhivko said a few seconds later, turning around to see Mira in her new attire. "Now walk with me." He pretended not to notice how the new shirt hugged her breasts.

They walked briskly down the sidewalk, partially hidden from view by the trees and bushes. There was another tram line ahead; a rectangular two-part tram was pulling in for a stop. The driver stopped with a loud hissing of the brakes and opened the doors. A handful of people exited and disappeared along the small side street.

Perfect.

Zhivko and Mira climbed on board and grabbed hold of the railings. There were just four other people, three oblivious teenagers and one old woman lugging a large plastic bag with vegetables. She took a seat and left the produce at her feet.

"Two tickets," Zhivko said to the driver, who ripped them out of a pack placed next to a jar with money and handed them over without looking up. Zhivko gave one ticket to Mira and looked out the windows. There was no one coming—yet.

The tram closed its doors and took off. This was its last stop, the tracks encircling a large parking lot and an abandoned building. The tram emerged on the main boulevard, suddenly engulfed by noise. It followed the path of a large arch and within seconds stopped directly in front of the train station. The brakes hissed once again, and the doors flew open.

Zhivko and Mira jumped down. In front of the railway station was a large monument reaching into the sky, surrounded by a tentlike roof structure. Underneath were an improvised bazaar and a series of small, one-story buildings housing tourist companies and souvenir shops. He grabbed Mira by the wrist, this time more gently.

"Sorry if last time I squeezed too hard and hurt you," he said with a look of concern. "But the circumstances were different."

"That's fine," Mira replied. "I understand."

In fact, the feeling that a man genuinely cared for her gave her butterflies.

Zhivko surveyed the landscape and noticed a police car pulling up in the driveway directly in front of one of the station entrances.

"Hurry," he said, weaving his way through the crowds with Mira behind him. They took the stairs down toward the foot of the monument. Gypsies manned improvised stands and kiosks, trying to get the attention of the commuters. Zhivko abruptly stopped.

"How much for a hat?" he asked a dark-skinned young man and pointed to a heap of folded cheap baseball caps.

"Five leva each," the man responded eagerly, revealing a large golden tooth.

"Fine," Zhivko said quickly. "Give me two." He took out his wallet and handed over the money. "Do you have any bags?"

"There are plenty of purses for the lady; this one here—"

"Not purses," Zhivko corrected impatiently. "Hiking bags, big ones."

"No," the gypsy said. "But hold on." He put two fingers in his mouth and whistled, getting the attention of a seller two kiosks away. The man turned around.

"You got bags, Pesho?" the gypsy asked. "Big ones, for hiking."

The man put down his cigarette and smiled. "Right here," he said, waving them over. Mira looked at Zhivko and began to speak.

"Quiet," he instructed under his breath, gently pulling on her hand to follow him.

"We got all kinds of bags here," the man said, taking a puff of his cigarette and waving his hand over an assortment of hiking bags arranged from largest to smallest. "All kinds of colors too."

He rubbed his hands together and beamed with joy at the impending sale.

Zhivko picked up the largest one, which stood at more than one meter and had straps for the shoulders and straps to be tied around the waist.

"How much?"

"One hundred."

Zhivko frowned.

"It's big," the man retorted, shrugging his shoulders. "One hundred."

Zhivko produced the bills from his wallet and handed them over. Without waiting, he grabbed the bag and continued walking toward the station. Mira followed obediently.

"Put this on," he said and handed her the black baseball cap. Mira put the hat on, threading her ponytail through the opening in the back. Zhivko put on his hat as well. He then ripped the plastic wrapping from the bag and threw it aside. Next, he took off his sweatshirt and crumpled it into a ball. The wallet he placed in his jeans. He put his arms through the straps of the bag and heaved it onto his shoulders. Muscles stretched and pulled impressively.

Even empty, it was heavy and bulky. It towered over his head, so that from behind, there was nothing visible except the legs from the thighs down. It was as good a disguise as he could come up with on the fly.

Now they looked like any two poor travelers about to embark on a trip to explore the country. They continued walking and soon found themselves on the sidewalk in front of the main train station building. There were kiosks everywhere, passengers moving in and out, lugging their bags behind them. The long rectangular face of the building was glass, the roof supported by large H-shaped concrete pillars. An empty police car was parked in front, two officers standing nearby, scanning the pedestrians.

Mira and Zhivko saw them.

"Don't look at them," Zhivko instructed. "Keep your head down, and look at the exit."

They walked quickly. One of the cops took notice. They continued walking, the entrance just a few steps away. The cop seemed suspicious.

And then he turned away. They had fooled him.

Inside the railway station, it was cooler and slightly darker. The high ceiling was about ten meters above the floor, giving the place a spacious feeling and creating an echo effect. Passengers of all ages were sitting on the benches.

Zhivko looked at the large electronic timetable display on the wall for trains heading to northern Bulgaria. There was one leaving soon.

"Go in front of me," he said. The two of them made their way downstairs toward the ticket offices, Zhivko awkwardly handling the steps with the oversized bag on his back. Of the thirty ticket windows, only ten were working. In front of some, there were queues. Zhivko gestured in the direction of window twelve, and Mira walked up.

A thin woman pushing fifty looked up and closed the tabloid magazine she had been reading, pushing up her glasses before speaking.

"Da," she said, voice betraying her utter boredom.

Mira looked behind her at Zhivko, who nodded. "Two tickets to Pleven."

"Private salon," Zhivko added. He heard rapid footsteps coming from the stairs behind him and turned around, relieved to see that the noise was coming from two men running to catch a train.

The woman reached for a pack of tickets and ripped out two. She signed the bottom of each and stamped them.

"There you go," she said dryly. "Platform eight."

Mira grabbed the tickets and left. She and Zhivko made their way down through the narrow tunnel underneath the tracks until he saw a large, crooked sign nailed to the wall. The platform was ahead, just up a flight of steps. He looked behind him but still no police.

When they got to the top, he intentionally turned his back to the station, counting on the giant red bag to shield him and Mira from prying eyes. There were many platforms one after the other, like little islands separated by rail tracks. An international train had just left for Serbia, the bluish passenger cars receding in the west where a web of tracks converged.

Their train was pulled by a DR Class 132 locomotive, a diesel electric behemoth with two large, square windows on the front. The eagle-like logo of the Bulgarian State Railways was emblazoned in the middle of each car. Zhivko helped Mira into the nearest one.

The inside corridor was narrow and hot. The bag nearly brushed up against the ceiling as Zhivko walked. This was obviously the wrong car, but he did not want to take the risk of going outside. They made their way along the corridors, the large bag commanding the respect of the other passengers, who ducked out of the way to let Mira and Zhivko walk by.

Their private cabin was toward the end of the third car and consisted of the standard arrangement—two bunk beds on each side of the room and a small table in the middle. Zhivko slid the firm wooden door closed and took off the cumbersome bag, relaxing his shoulders. The window looked out to the side opposite the train station, for which he was grateful.

He retrieved his gun. Mira sat down, looking worried. She had been around firearms many times, but they always made her uneasy. She once had to go to a hospital and interview a bodyguard shot while shielding his boss from a rival criminal, and the image of the man's grotesquely damaged body was seared into her brain.

"Relax," the commando said calmly. "It's just a precaution."

The cabin was more or less level with the platform outside, so people walking by could look in with ease. Zhivko pulled the thin curtains across. The cabin became darker, sunshine just creeping in from the space along the edges of the window.

Zhivko sat down on the bed, close to the sliding door and as far as possible from the window. He instructed Mira to do the same and put his hand over the gun.

"Be still," he instructed. "We are not safe yet."

They sat in silence, listening to the other passengers walking about and moving into their cabins. Bags bumped against the floor and the walls outside.

Mira took the opportunity to study the man. He looked to be in his early thirties, and his hair did not have even a hint of gray. His dark jeans were slightly dirty and worn out, the short-sleeved dark-blue shirt extending to just below the belt. His cheekbones were wide and his face sweaty near the jawline and temples.

The broad shoulders and thick arms indicated strength. The green eyes were unsettled, periodically darting around the cabin. A versatile but unimpressive watch rested on the left hand. Mouth closed and jaw clenched, he looked serious and tense. They were close, yet she sensed the distance between them was great. She considered herself a good judge of character, but making sense of this situation was unusually challenging. All she was sure of was that the man posed no threat to her.

At least for the moment.

The operator relaxed the brakes, and the train lurched forward softly, leaving the station at a pace roughly equivalent to jogging. Mira slid across the bed and peered through the drapes. The train settled into its track and picked up speed; the soothing click-clocking of the wheels against the tracks soon became the only noise heard. Zhivko let go of the gun and rubbed his eyes in relief.

He saw Mira give him a faint smile, but he chose to stare back blankly.

Mira pulled open the curtains and looked outside. The countryside unfolded as picturesque trees and long fields of grass quickly replaced the urban landscape. She slid the top half of the window down and a blast of cool air rushed in. They were soon passing through mountains, steep ravines and ominous-looking cliffs surrounding the train as it weaved its way through nature.

The rhythmic clicking of the train wheels provided Zhivko with a sense of calm.

Chapter Eighteen

Nikolai finally saw some open road in front of him and stepped on the accelerator, momentarily turning his head to the sidewalk. A bunch of cabdrivers were having a heated discussion, one man wildly gesturing with his hands in the air while the other had the intercom cord extended out through the window of the car and was speaking into the transmitter with urgency.

Not far away, a young man and his girlfriend were helping a police officer get up. The woman was holding him by the arm and elbow, while the man was tugging on his other arm. The cop's mouth was bloodied, drawing the curious stares of a group of teenagers. Bystanders whisked their children away.

Nikolai did not have an explanation for what he was seeing, but the plausible scenarios that were forming in his mind were not giving him cause for optimism. If they had screwed up, he would look bad in front of the boss.

It would be very bad if the boss got angry and decided to replace him. What would he do then? A normal office job was not for someone like him, with his background and skills. He could try some sort of security work, but the pay would be a fraction of what he was earning now—not to mention he would have to pay taxes.

No, for the time being, Nikolai needed this job. He saw Ahmed and Stefan on the sidewalk, one observing the unfolding drama while the other was looking at the passing cars.

Nikolai turned sharply and decelerated, easing off the brakes in the last minute to avoid a screeching sound. Stefan opened the back door while Ahmed rushed to the other side. They got in quickly and closed the doors. Nikolai drove a few meters forward, stopped the car, and turned on the emergency lights. The engine kept running.

"What the hell happened?" he asked swiftly, turning around to face the two grunts. "Where is she?"

"She got away," Stefan replied, raising his eyebrows.

"What?" Nikolai asked, eyes darting back and forth between the two of them. "How did this happen?"

Ahmed and Stefan looked at each other and gave their boss a recap of the recent events.

Nikolai smashed his hand against his head and gripped his forehead in anger. He messed up his hair and then immediately ran his hand over his head in a makeshift attempt at grooming.

"Where did they go?" he asked, again looking at the two men in the backseat.

"That way," Stefan replied, pointing. "They turned left in the direction of the national stadium."

Nikolai nodded. "It's pointless to follow now," he said with disappointment. "They're gone." He sighed deeply and slammed his hand into the passenger seat. The black leather let out a dull thud. "Did you get a good look at the man?"

"We did," Ahmed responded, proud of his accomplishment. "We got a good look at his face when he turned around to strangle the cop." He paused to think. "Have not seen him before, though."

"It's that guy … Mladenov," Nikolai said. "He is the one the police are looking for and the one the reporter wrote about. He is the only one other than us who has a reason to go after this woman. He must have read about himself in the paper."

The boss is not going to like this at all.

There was silence in the car. The engine hummed while the traffic outside continued unabated, vehicles periodically whizzing by.

"What do we do now?" Stefan asked.

"I don't know," Nikolai responded. "This was not supposed to happen." He reached for the belt and freed the mobile phone from its holder.

"Hello?" the familiar authoritative voice said.

"Hi, colleague," Nikolai began. "It's your old friend calling." He saw Ahmed and Stefan leaning forward in the seats and decided to press the phone tighter against his ear. He didn't need those two hearing the conversation. He depended on the boss, and they in turn depended on him. Nikolai did not see any benefit to breaking the chain of command.

There was always the risk that those two might start thinking too much on their own and begin to contradict him, thus eroding his standing and authority.

"It is good to hear from you," Kiril replied. "How is the day going?"

Nikolai paused, but there was no subtle way of delivering the news.

"Not well," he answered. "We were tracking the girl when she was kidnapped."

There was silence on the line, which Nikolai took as a bad sign.

"Kidnapped?" the boss asked incredulously.

"Yes. The commando came out of nowhere and forced her into a cab. There were too many people around for us to do anything."

Another pause, this time longer.

"I'm disappointed," Kiril said. "This is certainly not according to plan."

Nikolai did not need the reminder. "What do we do now?" he asked, clenching his free hand into a fist.

"Listen closely," Kiril said. Nikolai pressed the phone firmly against his ear.

"Our smuggling depends on the ... shall we say, *cooperation* of certain people in key positions," the boss said with unintentional condescension that Nikolai pretended did not bother him. "I pay those people good money for their efforts, and it's vital they remain in place and their activities clandestine."

"I know," Nikolai acknowledged.

"That's good," Kiril replied. "Because the whole operation could fall apart if the people working for me on the inside get discovered ... unless we can blame someone else and throw that person to the wolves." A harsh tone crept into his voice. "Got it?"

"Yes."

"That's why I can't have this commando walking around freely, and I certainly can't have him hook up with some investigative reporter who makes a career out of investigating crime and corruption."

Nikolai felt as if the spit from Kiril's lips had traveled through the phone and splashed on his face.

The sound of a police siren wailing in the distance suddenly reached the ears of the men inside the car. Nikolai plugged his ear with a finger. "I'm listening," he said. Behind him, Stefan and Ahmed were waiting anxiously.

For a few seconds, Nikolai said nothing as his boss gave him instructions. He vowed to himself that he would not allow any more mistakes.

"Do you understand everything, my friend?" Kiril asked curtly.

"Of course, colleague."

"That's good," the boss replied. "Make sure this is the last time you have a bad day!"

"I promise."

Nikolai hung up the mobile phone and put it away. His hands shook a little as his eyebrows bunched together and his brow wrinkled. The wailing of the police siren was getting louder and closer.

"What happened?" Stefan asked anxiously.

"The boss is going out tonight, so we have to be there with him," Nikolai responded.

"And the reporter?" Ahmed asked. Turning around, he could see the police car in the distance, lights flashing.

Nikolai turned off the emergency lights and gave a left turn signal. The Mercedes inched its way forward until the former wrestler saw an opening and took advantage by stepping on the gas.

"We have to take her out," he said matter-of-factly. "She knows too much."

The two men in the backseat looked at each other and then back at Nikolai. A lump was forming in Ahmed's throat.

"The commando as well," Nikolai added. "If we get the opportunity, we kill both."

In the rearview mirror, Nikolai's subordinates looked unconvinced and lacking in commitment. The young Turk was clearly in a state of disbelief, mouth agape as he shifted uneasily in his seat. Nikolai, on the contrary, made an extra effort to portray strength and resolution. His face showed no emotion, and his voice was firm. The only sound now was that of the key chain swinging back and forth.

"Both of them," he repeated.

Chapter Nineteen

The railway station at Pleven was small, a white two-story building with a sloping burgundy roof and an unimpressive concrete slab covering most of the platform. On top, the word "Pleven" was written, both in the Cyrillic and Roman scripts. There was a closed kiosk on one end and a water fountain gushing mineral water, which Zhivko and Mira splashed on their faces to freshen up.

By this time, she did not consider the quiet commando a threat, but she did wonder what was hidden behind the ever-observant green eyes. It struck her as unusual that he avoided eye contact, but she attributed that peculiarity to his professional training. When they stepped onto the platform along with a handful of other people, she noticed that he was just as alert as he had been back in Sofia.

He possessed an economy of motion, walking with a purpose and always toward a specific target. Acutely aware of his surroundings, he scanned for information and assessed its relevance. He did not pay attention to the peeling ads on the walls or glance through magazines. At the station, he stopped to purchase a bottle of water, a traveler's kit, and a map.

It was a few minutes past five o'clock when they exited the train station, and the air was noticeably cooler and cleaner. A red trolley made a U-turn in front of the station and came to a stop, spilling a handful of passengers. Zhivko scoped the scene for possible threats, but it was tranquil. Nothing looked out of the ordinary, and none of the people appeared out of place.

Mira looked at the cabs, but Zhivko waved his disapproval.

"Not here," he said. "It's too risky. Let's walk around and find another stop."

"Fine."

"Do you know anyone here?" he asked, trying to figure out the most suitable plan of action.

"Not in the city, no," Mira replied.

"So there is no chance of you being recognized by someone?"

Mira shook her head. "I don't think so."

"Good," he said with an approving half smile. "Then lead the way."

Pleven was a city of low buildings with a wide and long pedestrian street meandering through the downtown area. The buildings were a mixture of drab Communist concrete and older, pre–World War II architecture. Most of the older buildings were elaborately decorated. Walls, ceilings, and parts of the facade featured floral motifs: ceilings, porches, doors, and furniture were carved out of wood and painted. The city was dotted with monuments, many relating to the Russo-Turkish War in the late nineteenth century. Zhivko kept his head down and set a brisk pace, but even he had to slow down and look up when they reached the end of the street and came within view of the St. George the Conqueror Chapel Mausoleum.

A magnificent chapel, it was the city's landmark and surrounded by a park. Its facade was red and white, its roofs domed by large green cupolas. The chapel was surrounded by a thick white wall and stately trees, old steel cannons placed at the corners. The area beyond the wall was wide open, with children playing as their parents urged them to be careful. A series of water fountains were splashing nearby. A little girl was intrepidly pushing her hand into one jet of water and then stepping back with a joyous yell.

As they exited the park, they passed another monument, this one depicting a man triumphantly holding his rifle in the air. They found themselves at a small intersection and at the beginning of a residential neighborhood. Mira saw a cab and waved.

After a ten-minute drive, they were in a nearby village, left alone in the central city square. There was a valley to their right, and he could make out the soft sounds of streaming water coming from somewhere beneath the thick vegetation. He wiped sweat off his brow and continued. The sun was low on the horizon, periodically obscured by the rolling hills in the distance. Soon, it would disappear for the day.

"We're here," Mira announced, stopping by one of the houses on the left side of the road and turning to Zhivko. She stretched her arms and exhaled. He walked up to her and looked around.

Houses were lined up one next to the other on this side of the road, each property about twenty meters in width. The villa had a brown fence extending about a meter and a half above the ground, a concrete path leading toward the house. Some of the flowers in the garden were dead while the rest grew wildly in all directions.

Mira put her arm through the bars of the fence and spent a few seconds feeling the other side of the door before finding the lever and pulling it. The door creaked and swung open.

The other three sides to the rectangular property consisted of thick stone walls painted white. The area on the other side of the house was flat, dotted with apple trees whose branches arched down, weighted down by fruit. The lawn had not been mowed, and the grass was knee high.

Zhivko took the backpack off and gave his shoulders some much-needed relief.

"Do you have the key?" he asked.

Mira walked to the edge of the two-story house, as if to turn the corner. In the dirt by the path was a large rectangular metal cover. She heaved it off. The brick walls of the shallow hole sheltered two pipes and a water meter. Mira turned a valve and then reached underneath it, using her fingers to feel along the length of pipe. She removed a key and got up, placing the cover back in its position.

"That's where we hide the spare key," she announced triumphantly, looking at Zhivko.

Mira walked over and placed the key in the keyhole. She briefly played with the lock before the thick wooden door let her push it open with a cracking sound. The foyer was dark and the air cool. She walked in and took her bag off, placing it on the rack. Zhivko carried the massive backpack in and placed it on the floor.

Mira took her shoes off and stretched her toes. Zhivko walked outside again, nearing the gate in the middle of the fence. He opened it, knelt down, and scooped up two handfuls of gravel. He managed to close the gate slowly and slide the bolt and then carefully spread the gravel along the paved path so that his hands were empty when he reached the door.

"In case of intruders," he explained, catching Mira's inquisitive look. He walked in and locked the door. There were no windows in the foyer for natural light to come in, so Mira flipped a switch on the wall, and a solitary light bulb on the ceiling came on.

Zhivko found a seat at the base of the steps and looked around. The beams supporting the second floor featured intricate wooden handiwork. He could see into the kitchen and living room, where thick ornate rugs lined the floors. The walls were built in the old style, with river rocks instead of bricks. A discreet Orthodox icon hung on one wall.

"The bedrooms and bathroom are on the second floor," Mira said, reaching for a pair of slippers and tossing them at Zhivko.

"Are we safe?" he asked.

"We should be," she said. "Hardly anyone outside my family knows about this place, and only my parents have a key."

"Thank you," Zhivko replied warmly. "I need to get my thoughts together, and we have a lot to talk about."

"You have to tell me what you know," Mira responded. "From where I stand, there are a lot of things that look fishy."

Zhivko raised his eyebrows and shook his head. "It would appear so."

There was an awkward pause that desperately needed to be filled.

"You hungry?" Mira asked, noticing that Zhivko finally looked at ease.

"Yeah," he responded, cautiously displaying a charming smile. "Very."

"I have not been here in a while," Mira began, "but there are bottles of mineral water beneath the stairs." She gestured with her hand. "There are beers in the fridge and some eggs." She thought some more and scratched her head. "My dad was here last week, and I am sure he bought groceries. There should be butter and cheese. We can make spaghetti and drink tea."

Zhivko took off the baseball hat and brushed his hair with his fingers.

"That sounds fine," he said. "Let's get started."

Mira got up. "Okay, come with me and wash your hands. Dishes and utensils are in the cupboards."

The kitchen was small and had an old stove in one corner. The sink was narrow, and there was no dishwasher. A round table with an ornate black-and-red tablecloth took up more than half the floor space. Mira poured water into the teakettle and put it on the stove while Zhivko laid out the plates and utensils. She placed sticks of spaghetti in a pot with water.

They sat down opposite each other, Zhivko crossing his arms in front of him.

"Nice place," he commented. "It's evident you've put a lot of work into it."

"It was first built by my grandparents," she explained. "Over the years, we've made modifications and built new things. It's a work in progress really."

The kettle started whistling under a cloud of white steam. Mira used a towel to grab the handle and poured some into two cups. Zhivko dipped his tea bag into the hot water and moved it around with his spoon, softly blowing on the spoon every time he raised it.

"You don't talk much, do you?" Mira asked. Zhivko looked up, sipped his first spoon of tea, and said nothing. Mira was not one to give up quickly.

"Doesn't your family have a place like this somewhere?" she asked.

"I don't have parents," Zhivko replied curtly.

Mira was taken aback, momentarily struggling to find appropriate words. For the first time since they had met, she saw turmoil behind the man's eyes. Maybe even a hint of pain.

"I … uh …" she protested. "I'm sorry," she finally said. "I didn't know."

"Doesn't matter," Zhivko replied, letting the steam rise over his face. It was now time to change the subject. "How come you know so much?" he asked with vigor in his voice, now looking directly at the reporter. "Where do you get the information for your articles?"

Mira took a sip and put the cup down. "I do a lot of investigating," she said. "I talk to people. I have sources."

"What sources?" Zhivko inquired. "Who have you been talking to?"

"I know people in the customs agencies," she said. "Border guards, mostly midlevel. They talk to me anonymously, off the record." She saw he was interested and continued, "Despite public perception, most of them are good people who are not corrupt and want to make things right. But ever since sanctions were imposed on Yugoslavia in 1992, the problem has spread like a cancer and become deeply entrenched."

Mira squeezed lemon into her tea and took another sip.

"You're talking about smuggling?" Zhivko asked.

"Da."

He needed a moment to think.

"The guys and I have talked about stuff like that," he replied. "Our unit is kind of isolated, but we do hear what's going on. The entire ministry has become sloppy; people feel overwhelmed by the sudden rise in organized crime."

His eyes wandered across the room.

Zhivko looked uncomfortable discussing the subject. "I have never witnessed corruption, at least not among my colleagues. There are police officers alluding to it, but it's difficult to confirm."

"It's difficult to deny," Mira added.

Zhivko took a long sip and said nothing.

"Some of the customs agents and border guards are corrupt," she explained. "It's difficult to prove and hard to personalize the blame, but it's obvious. All kinds of goods are being smuggled."

"Over the past year, we've done raids on depots with drugs and illicit cigarettes," Zhivko said. "We arrested a number of people."

"Sure," Mira agreed. "I know. But it is not enough. And some of those arrests may have been staged." That made him pause.

"How so?"

"Do you remember a few months ago, when you guys caught a drug dealer bribing a customs agent?"

"I do."

Mira took a long sip and continued, "I did some investigating afterward. Turns out the dealer was a low-level guy who was cheating his boss by selling some of the stuff for his own profit. And the agent was getting greedy, wanting more and more money for his cooperation."

"It was a setup?"

"Most likely," Mira replied. "Nothing is what it seems anymore. That's why I was suspicious when they accused you almost immediately after the minister promised a crackdown on corruption."

"I'm innocent!" Zhivko said firmly, raising his voice. "I stepped out to buy some food, and when I came back, there were cops waiting for me."

Mira had spent years interviewing criminals, both petty and big-time, trying to understand their thoughts, motivations, and emotions. For her, the who, what, when, where, and how was easy. But she felt that only good investigators could answer the "why" question and always challenged herself to go a layer deeper. She wanted to understand, not just report. She could read people well. The man looked like he was trying to tell the truth. He was now making prolonged eye contact, which was an unusual occurrence in their brief acquaintance.

Hoping to draw him out, she said nothing.

Zhivko exhaled in frustration. "Do you think the customs agents are running a smuggling racket?"

Mira emphatically shook her head. "No, they are just participants."

"Who is at the top?"

"I wish I knew," Mira replied, her voice slightly dreamy. "It seems like there are a few people running it and a lot of people loosely involved. I have no access to the puppet masters, so it's like looking for separate pieces to a jigsaw puzzle and then trying to put them together."

Zhivko lost interest in his cup of tea. "What's your version?"

"It's more than a version." Mira sighed. "I have been investigating this stuff for years," she began and leaned forward, raising her hands in front of her. "You know of the channels the state security used in the Communist days to move things in and out of the country?"

"Vaguely," Zhivko replied. "We commandos arrest and shoot criminals; we don't do politics." A quick smile played on his face.

"It's very murky," Mira acknowledged. "But we know that in the late 1970s, the state-owned arms export company was smuggling weapons to various countries. The former state security service had extensive networks, including international shell companies used to cover their tracks and make things look legal. When communism collapsed in 1989, all that fell apart, but the people who set up the channels and know the secrets remain."

Zhivko listened with intense interest.

"So?" he asked.

"The government transformed its security structures after the collapse of the totalitarian system. The Ministry of the Interior is letting go of many officers, either because it can't pay them or because they suddenly have nothing to do. These guys have information on agents, connections, secret smuggling channels, and knowledge of how to evade the border police, all of it."

Mira ran her fingers across the table in a spiderlike fashion.

"Those channels are now used to meet the domestic demand for a wide range of products, especially since the Communist economy is gone but a real market economy has not yet developed. Bulgaria is also a transit route for goods smuggled in and then smuggled out to other places."

"Sounds plausible," Zhivko said after some thought.

"It's the reality, unfortunately," Mira corrected and took a breath. "The process was already underway when war broke out in the former Yugoslavia. However, the sanctions the United Nations imposed on the Yugoslav republics in 1992 gave a boost to organized crime in southeastern Europe because there was a high illicit demand for everything. Smuggling embargoed goods into Yugoslavia was a catalyst for organized crime in all the countries that border Yugoslavia, including us. I think it's safe to say that organized criminal groups have emerged, utilizing the previous networks. Even though the United Nations lifted the sanctions last year, the channels have reconstituted and there is a lot of money to be made if you know how to take advantage."

"But where do I fit in?" Zhivko asked poignantly. "Why was I set up?"

"You're an easy target," Mira explained, her words stinging him with a particular viciousness.

Chapter Twenty

Mira pushed her chair back and got up, interrupting the awkward silence.

"The spaghetti is ready," she said and turned off the stove. She picked up the pot with the help of a towel, wrapping it around her hands to avoid getting burned. Thick steam rose up. Mira tilted the pot over the sink and poured out the hot water. The sudden change in temperature made the cold steel siding of the sink expand with a cracking sound.

Mira walked over to the table and used the spoon to push half the spaghetti into Zhivko's plate before returning to her seat and putting the remainder onto hers. Zhivko sliced off a piece of butter and while it was still stuck to the knife, slid it onto Mira's spaghetti. He then gave himself some butter and proceeded to dice up some cheese.

"Why do you say that I'm an easy target?" he asked.

"There are a couple of reasons," she answered, waving the steam away with her hand. "You said you're an orphan, right?" she asked. "No parents."

Zhivko nodded.

"Not married?" Mira said more cautiously, looking down at his finger for a ring.

He nodded again. She felt relieved and then caught herself.

"That's one reason," she explained. "There is no one to stick up for you, and nobody will miss you. People like me interview relatives who speak in support of loved ones accused of crimes." Mira raised her eyebrows and pushed a loose strand of hair away from her temple.

Zhivko slid forward a small plate of diced cheese.

"Moreover," Mira continued, tentatively wrapping some spaghetti around her fork. "It's obvious what the perception will be. You are a poor young man who got tempted by greed. The public is already on edge about corruption in the police force, so it's not that big of a stretch."

Mira got up, reached deep inside one of the cupboards, and retrieved a jar of sauce. She attempted to open it, failed, and placed it in the middle of the table.

"I'm completely innocent," he said angrily, bringing his fist down on the table with a bang. "Someone must have set me up. I don't know how that stuff got into my apartment, but someone must have planted it." He unconsciously leaned forward, his wide shoulders crowding the table. "The special forces are my life," he said in a firm voice.

The intensity that Mira had not seen since the dramatic events in front of the National Palace of Culture had returned. He released one finger from the fist and pointed at her.

"I joined immediately after the military service and never regretted it," his eyebrows narrowed. "Some of the guys are like family to me. No way would I jeopardize all that just to assist some criminal network and make a quick buck."

Mira took in a forkful of spaghetti, sucking it in quickly so it wouldn't hang from her mouth. Zhivko was still waving his finger.

"No way," he repeated.

"Do you know how that stuff got into your apartment?" she asked.

"Not a clue," he replied. "I have been searching for an explanation ever since it happened, but I don't have an answer."

"If someone set you up, it would have to be someone close to you," Mira pontificated. "Do you suspect anyone?"

Zhivko took a moment to think. "No." He breathed in and sighed.

"A few weeks ago, there was a raid," he began. "It was supposed to be a drug depot and distribution center near the Turkish border, just outside Svilengrad." Zhivko chewed on some spaghetti. "Seizing the cargo and possibly a couple of the smugglers. We did everything right and followed procedure, as usual. The problem is there was nothing there. The place had been cleaned out, most likely in a hurry."

"Ever since, it has been kind of tense," Zhivko said. "No one has voiced it, and I don't think there has been a formal report prepared yet, but there is suspicion in the air."

"How so?" Mira asked.

Zhivko reached for the sauce, twisted the cap open, and poured some.

"It is unlikely the smugglers randomly decided to move all their illicit goods," he explained. "It was a big place, near a major road but somewhat secluded. It looked like they had been using it a lot. The unspoken fear among us is that someone is a mole passing along information."

"Anyone in particular?"

"Nah," Zhivko replied and shook his finger. "Truth is it's unpleasant even thinking about it."

"Now they probably suspect you."

"Yeah." He snorted bitterly. "Probably." He still could not believe the speed with which his life had been turned upside down.

"When do they usually tell you about these raids?"

"It varies," he answered. "Depends on the place, timing, difficulty of the job. For example, if we are doing a simple operation locally, they tell us just a few hours earlier, which is plenty of time to prepare."

"What about when you were in Svilengrad?"

"They told us a day earlier," Zhivko answered, lifting a fork heavy with spaghetti. "They told us a day before that we would be traveling. The next day, we woke up early and went to the city. We were briefed along the way, but we also did some last-minute preparing at a safe house nearby."

Mira finished her tea. "So there are a number of people who knew a day earlier that something was going to happen in Svilengrad?"

"Yes."

"It's possible then that someone tipped them off?"

"Sure," Zhivko replied thoughtfully. "Apparently, that is what happened. But it was not me."

At this point, Mira was convinced he was telling the truth.

Zhivko finished his spaghetti and pushed the remainder into the corner of the plate.

"Thank you," he said. "I really appreciate it. Sorry for the rude introduction earlier."

He looked at her cautiously, not sure if their brief relationship was ready for a friendlier approach.

Mira smiled. "No worries," she replied, a little charmed and trying to hide it. "You scared me, but I understand why you did it." The pinkish hue on her face exuded irresistible femininity, and the allure of the soft skin was making it difficult for him to maintain his cool demeanor.

"You say this is your parents' place?" he asked, a hint of suspicion in his voice.

"That's right."

"Then who is the guy in the picture?" Zhivko asked and pointed to a hand-sized photograph. It showed a young man, straight brown hair oiled back and lips sealed into a dignified expression.

Mira turned around in surprise, oblivious to the photograph. She got up and walked over to the counter.

"No one," she said and put the framed picture down on its face. "Just a former fiancé."

Her soft facial features suddenly became harsher, and the pink drained from her cheeks.

"I'm sorry I asked."

Mira walked back to her chair and sat down. It was dark outside, and night flies occasionally banged against the window. Light from the kitchen spilled out onto the front yard, illuminating the dying flowers in an eerie way.

"Are you finished?" she asked, gesturing at the plate.

"Yes," Zhivko answered, wiping his mouth with a napkin. "It was delicious."

"Thanks for helping out," Mira replied and got up, picking up her plate and placing it in the sink. The porcelain squeaked as it connected with the steel. She waved for Zhivko's empty plate, and he pushed it across the table.

"Can I …" he began and then stuttered before regaining his composure. "I need to take a shower," Zhivko announced, suddenly looking sheepish, his face carrying a boyish expression.

"It's been a long day," he explained, trying to bolster his claim.

Mira was about to turn on the faucet but did not. She turned around to face him. At that point, she realized that this was the first time she had seen him standing directly before her. The dark shirt extended to just above his elbows and fit tightly around his arms. His hands looked strong and rugged, like they could snap something in half at a moment's notice.

A slight stubble was appearing on his face. He looked ready for action, but the lines beneath his eyes indicated fatigue.

Mira looked away for a moment and then back at him. There was something handsome about the well-proportioned man with the wide cheekbones. She sensed he was not someone who opened up easily to people, and that intrigued her even more.

"No problem," she replied before it got awkward. "The shower is upstairs."

Zhivko stepped aside, and she walked out, leading him up the narrow staircase to the second floor. There were ornate nineteenth-century rugs on the stairway, while various old family photos decorated the walls. One was of a little girl with curly hair building a sand castle at the beach, holding a plastic shovel as she knelt before a pile of sand.

The corridor on the second floor was narrow and short, starting at the stairs and ending in front of two bedrooms positioned side by side, a shared wall between them. The bathroom was near the staircase, directly across from a third, smaller bedroom.

"This is the guest room," Mira said, opening the door. "You'll find towels in the closet."

Zhivko walked in. The sloping roof made one end of the room's ceiling noticeably lower than the other. The walls were spartanly decorated save for the plain white wallpaper. There was a bed and a nightstand with a dead windup clock.

"Thanks," he said. "This will do fine."

"That's all there is," Mira replied with a smile. "The next door down the corridor is the bathroom, just don't stay for too long because you'll use all the hot water and I don't want to wait for the water heater when it's my turn."

"Understood," he replied and moved toward the woman, grabbing hold of the door with one hand. "I'll make it quick." The humble smile made a fleeting appearance again.

"I will finish up in the kitchen," Mira said and stepped out of the room, watching Zhivko disappear through the crack as the door closed. The top third of the door contained a window, the glass intentionally misshaped and hazy. She could see the light bulb shining as a bright blob in the distance, periodically obscured by the moving silhouette of Zhivko's head.

Mira skipped down the stairs in a hurry.

Chapter Twenty-One

Martina stretched her thin arms and heard a soft cracking sound. That wasn't a good sign. She vowed to find the time for more aerobics. She had made similar promises to herself in the past, but this time, she swore it would be for real.

The plan for tonight was to spend a few hours observing the comings and goings of the disco's clientele. The patrons were no ordinary people, so there was the potential for some interesting pictures. Even better should a fight or a shooting break out.

The light-blue Skoda was parked discreetly across the street from the disco Planet, which was located in the very heart of downtown Sofia. Martina had positioned the vehicle as close as possible to the car behind it, so that the bumpers were almost touching, intentionally leaving as much space as possible between herself and the car in front. The lights were turned off, but the key was in the ignition, a precautionary measure in case Martina needed to make a quick dash.

She doubted that would be necessary. This was her third stakeout, and the previous two had been dreadfully boring. She yawned and opened her bag, searching around in the semidarkness to locate her recorder.

Martina raised the machine to her mouth and pressed a button.

"It's Thursday, September fourth, a little past eleven p.m.," she said clearly, making sure not to raise her voice above the minimum necessary volume. "I am across the street from the main entrance to Planet," she continued. "Nothing to report so far."

Martina clicked the off button and put the recorder down on the passenger's seat next to her messenger bag. She had left the office earlier than usual and had returned home for a quick dinner and a lazy few hours spent on the couch before grabbing her high-powered camera and leaving. She brought along a round black hat that normally served as a fashion accessory but tonight would double as a disguise. She was wearing it now—also making sure her curly hair was falling symmetrically along both sides of her face.

Just in case.

Martina looked across at the entrance to the disco. Nothing yet. There were two large, muscular men with thick necks standing in front of the double doors, both assuming a power stance with hands crossed at the crotch. They were wearing dark blazers over dark shirts, the wire from their earpieces disappearing down behind the collars. It was safe to assume they had guns as well. She wanted to take a picture but decided not to waste any frames.

The top prize in terms of celebrity pictures right then was Ivanka, who apparently occasionally visited the disco with her boyfriend. Rumors had it that her boyfriend, if that was even the word—Martina preferred *sponsor* or, more crudely, *pimp*—was some sort of mysterious underworld criminal boss. Pictures of him with the stunning blonde would surely be of interest. The young reporter prepared the camera and let it lay in her lap, the strap around her hand and the fingers on the appropriate buttons.

She waited in silence. Taxis occasionally drove by, and every once in a while the shadowy figures of pedestrians appeared on the sidewalk. A stray dog sniffed around a distant garbage can. Inside the car, Martina felt a little cold and buttoned up the white shirt she was wearing over her tight black top.

Across the street, the parking lot was beginning to fill up with expensive and shiny cars. Shortly before midnight, two young men and a woman walked up to the doors. They had a brief conversation with the bouncers, who did not move or speak much, coolly and decisively waving them away. One of the men argued his case, but the bouncers hardly acknowledged him.

Martina almost giggled. The threesome walked away and disappeared into the darkness. Another half hour passed.

It was about midnight when two impressive black Mercedes came down from the main boulevard at a fast speed, slowing down abruptly as they approached Planet. Martina readied her camera.

The first car pulled up in front of the entrance and stopped, its engine running. The second vehicle stopped just behind it, and two well-built men stepped out from each rear door. Both were dressed in dark suits and walked quickly to the passenger door of the first car. The men looked around in all directions, assessing possible threats. Confident there were none, one nodded to the other and reached for the door.

By this time, Martina had snapped about five pictures. She could sense her adrenaline rising.

The passenger door opened slowly, shielded from both sides by the two men. Martina could see a blonde woman, her golden hair flowing behind her over the top of a fur coat. High heels made her just as tall as the men guarding her.

Martina snapped some more pictures and adjusted the lens.

The blonde turned to the left and looked across the hood of the Mercedes. The driver's door opened, and a man stepped out. He was about 180 centimeters with a clear, aristocratic face and straight and thick black—though slightly graying—hair, which he had oiled back. He was smartly dressed in an expensive cotton suit, a shiny silk shirt, and an elegant blue tie, which he readjusted while standing near the opened door. It allowed for a perfect shot, and Martina took advantage.

The man, who looked to be in his early forties, walked around the car and gently put his arm across the woman's back. The two walked toward the entrance, the bouncers immediately acknowledging them with a nod and opening the doors. Martina could not get a good look at the woman's face, but she definitely looked like Ivanka. She held a white purse in her right hand and wore her coat with poise as she approached the entrance.

The two men closed the doors to the first car and followed Ivanka and her boyfriend. The second Mercedes moved away and sought a place in the parking lot. Martina continued snapping pictures in rapid succession until the figures passed through the entrance.

The scene inside the club was dark, with bright white lasers dancing across the floor and walls. The walls were a shiny reflective black, interrupted by thin lines of electric blue. The dance floor was relatively small and shaped like an oval, measuring no more than fifteen meters at its longest and five meters at its widest. There were couches set up along the perimeter, each with two fancy circular black tables in front of it. There were lights inside the tables, changing to a different bright color every few seconds.

Beyond that was the rest of the club's floor space, elevated a few steps above the sunken inner part. The tables were placed along the walls, each surrounded on three sides by luxurious couches draped in white. Large, fluffy white pillows completed the lounge-like feel. The widest table was centrally located, fenced off by a red velvet rope.

Kiril and Ivanka entered confidently and with the poise characteristic of models on the catwalk. The swagger was exaggerated and emphatic. Stefan and Nikolai followed, guarding the flanks. The foursome temporarily drew the attention of the rest of the patrons, but no one made eye contact. A waitress with tight jeans and a revealing top removed the red rope and invited the group around the table. Kiril nodded and gestured to Ivanka, who shed her coat.

She did it slowly, first revealing her naked shoulders and then allowing the coat to slide down her front and waiting until the very last moment before removing her arms from the sleeves and handing the coat to the obliging waitress. Underneath, Ivanka was wearing a backless red dress that tied simply behind her neck and went halfway down her thighs. Expensive high-heeled Prada shoes sparkled around her bare ankles. Kiril held her hand as she scooted behind the table to the center of the couch. Envious eyes observed silently as the techno blared.

Kiril sat next to her, putting a protective arm around her shoulders and whispering into her ear. Ivanka smiled seductively. Stefan and Nikolai took their positions at the edges of the table, blocking any unwelcome visitors.

The surrounding tables and couches were occupied by exceptionally well-dressed and self-important people, the men ordering and paying with no regard for the amounts changing hands. Most had either suits or crisp white shirts and shiny black leather jackets. The only cigarettes smoked here were Davidoff, sometimes ostentatiously tossed on the tables with the label clearly visible. The unspoken rule in this specific social circle was to be seen as one with deep pockets. Even the bottled spring water cost about ten dollars for a small bottle. No one had ordered it yet. The name of the game was expensive whiskey, at the least. The bottle would be placed in the middle of the table and sometimes stay there untouched the whole night. Champagne served with fireworks was even more decadent, but that typically happened only once a night.

Kiril saw a man in an Armani suit waving at him. He gestured for him to come over; then, he snapped his fingers at Nikolai, a signal that he should get up and let the Armani through.

"Are things going well?" the Armani suit shouted into Kiril's ear.

"*Absolyutno*," Kiril replied plainly. "Everything is under control."

"And the new shipment?" the other asked.

"Should be on schedule," Kiril answered confidently.

The Armani suit stepped back and gave him an approving look, a wide smile spreading on his unshaven face. "I'm glad to be working with you!" he announced loudly and leaned in again. "When they come, you call me and I'll pick up my share. Money is no problem."

Kiril understood. "Where I don't distribute, your boys will." He smiled a beguiling grin. "It's a win-win."

"Of course."

"Trust me," Kiril said, reaching up and firmly patting the man on the cheek.

The Armani suit left, and Nikolai returned to his position as one of the two guardians of the table.

Kiril turned toward Ivanka and kissed her, softly at first and then more passionately. His fingers played across her exposed back. The lighting made the red dress appear purple, except when one of the lasers shone across it. They were at it for a few minutes and then stopped. Kiril was satisfied and readjusted his tie while Ivanka lazily sipped her martini.

On the dance floor were three round stands, elevating the dancers about fifty centimeters above the floor. A plethora of small lights concentrated on the area, providing better lighting than that applied to the rest of the club. The dancers were young women, their long legs raised on impossibly high heels. Their thin, tight white shorts were glowing, as were their skimpy white tops. The three of them gyrated with the suppleness of gymnasts. Their movements were provocative, scandalous, sexual. Everyone was allowed to admire, but only a select few could touch. Time passed quickly.

At one point, a sweaty businessman approached one of the ladies and slid his hand down her leg. She stopped dancing and bent down. The man, who was in his midthirties and had unbuttoned his collar and loosened his blue tie, cupped his hands and spoke into her ear. She nodded, and he lent her a hand as she stepped off the platform.

Meanwhile, the DJ put on a new track and a roar went up from the crowd. Suddenly, gold and silver confetti sprayed down on the crowd, eliciting another, louder roar.

The long-legged dancer gently grabbed the man by the hand, and they walked away, disappearing through a door and a hallway near the bar. Stefan saw this, and his brief sexual arousal made him jealous. Feigning indifference, he looked away.

The dancer returned twenty minutes later and stepped onto her raised island platform.

Kiril tapped Nikolai on the shoulder and motioned for him to get closer.

"Get the car," he instructed. "It's late, and I want to go home."

Nikolai acknowledged and got up. He made for the exit and brushed past the bouncers without a word.

In the old Skoda across the street, Martina rubbed her palms together and shivered. It was around two in the morning, and the car had cooled long ago. There was no activity on the deserted street and its sidewalks, so she immediately noticed when the same two black Mercedes she had seen earlier pulled up in front of the entrance.

She uncapped the camera and took a picture. *Finally!*

Martina felt her adrenaline flowing again and made sure to hide, lowering her body as much as possible while still maintaining a visual of the scene. The driver of the first Mercedes stepped out and left the door open, circling around the vehicle to open the passenger door.

Meanwhile, Ivanka and the reputed mobster emerged from the entrance. Now facing the street, they were readily identifiable, and Martina happily took a few more pictures. She was giddy with excitement at her good luck and the prospect of an original story, complete with pictures. Ivanka was walking quickly and had neglected to close her coat, carelessly exposing her body and the red dress to the hungry lens of the camera.

Martina assumed the second car was for protection, because it contained the two men in black clothes, while the first Mercedes was driven by the mobster, with Ivanka at his side and the third bodyguard in the back. She took a few more pictures and zoomed in, hoping to get a view of the license plates.

The two cars turned away from the disco and toward the street, perpendicular to the flow of traffic. They turned left, their lights shining across the row of parked vehicles.

Shit!

Martina caressed the camera close to her bosom and dived onto the passenger's seat, her head disappearing just before the lights from the Mercedes briefly exposed the inside of the cabin. She breathed heavily, turning her body to look out the window without raising her head. She heard the noise of engines and tires against the asphalt. Then the noise stopped abruptly. *Why have they stopped?*

Martina told herself the light must be red and calmed down. Now on her back, she lay motionless and waited, the seconds seemingly taking forever to pass. She breathed a sigh of relief when she heard the two cars moving again.

She waited a few more seconds and got up. The two Mercedes were moving away, speeding up as they went.

What now?

She glanced at her camera. There were plenty of pictures; the scoop was complete. She was tired, and a part of her wanted to go home and sleep. But her more adventurous side was thinking differently. She was curious to find out where they lived. Up ahead, the two cars were about to make a turn and disappear.

Hand on the ignition, Martina deliberated.

"You only live once," she said to herself. "Why not be brave and make the most of it?"

Against her better judgment, Martina turned the key and started the engine.

Chapter Twenty-Two

September 5, 1997

The two Mercedes turned and disappeared. They were driving comfortably above the speed limit, keeping close to each other as the second car tailgated the first. Kiril gripped the wheel firmly, reclining into the cushioned seat and glancing over at Ivanka. The model looked bored as she stared mindlessly out the window.

"Open the glove compartment," Kiril instructed, nodding his head in the appropriate direction.

Ivanka leaned forward and did as she was told.

"The first disc," he continued.

Ivanka pushed aside an envelope stuffed with papers and grabbed the top disc out of a pile of three. Her expensively manicured nails scratched against the plastic.

Kiril put the disc in and pressed play.

"Vivaldi," he said coolly, announcing his sophisticated taste. "My favorite."

The Four Seasons filled the car.

Martina could feel her heartbeat accelerate. She pressed down on the pedal and skillfully shifted up through the gears, trying to gain speed without drawing undo attention by screeching the wheels of the car. She cleared the first intersection and headed for the next one.

The light turned yellow. Martina stepped on the pedal with more force and hoped for the best. The right turn was unruly and unnecessarily wide, drawing the curious stare of a taxi driver parked nearby. He briefly raised his eyes from the night paper and then continued reading.

Martina breathed a small sigh of relief as the light turned red just as she sped away underneath it. She looked ahead, her eyes searching for the now-familiar black vehicles. She saw them in the distance, about one hundred meters away. The street lamps reflected a yellowish light off the shiny exteriors of the German cars. The Skoda remained in pursuit. It was a long boulevard with two lanes on each side, and there were no other cars except for a yellow taxi responding to the waving hands of a young couple.

Martina eased her foot off the accelerator and stayed focused. The boulevard was coming to an end, so the cars would soon have to turn either left or right.

They turned left. The windows of the first car were tinted, and Martina could not see inside, but the when the second vehicle showed its profile, she saw the silhouettes of the driver and that of a man riding in the backseat.

She slowed down, letting the cars clear the intersection and move temporarily out of view before she again pressed down on the pedal to make up for lost time. The compact car complied, and Martina appreciated its maneuverability. She had always considered the Czechs to be good automotive engineers, especially when compared to the Russians.

Martina made the left turn and saw the two Mercedes in front of her. They were driving almost in the center of the street, violating the integrity of the tram lines. The cars slowed down again and made another right turn. She followed cautiously, staying at a distance. Her camera was on the edge of the passenger's seat, so she let go of the steering wheel with one hand and pushed it back to safety. Her palms were sweaty from the excitement.

They were now leaving the downtown area behind, veering onto a narrower cobblestoned street. Up ahead was a roundabout, which circled a large monument in the form of an obelisk. Referred to as the Russian Monument, it was unveiled in 1882 and commemorated the Russian czar Alexander II. The road got bumpier, and the cars slowed down.

Martina watched as the two Mercedes drove around the side of the monument and continued going straight, heading southwest. They were now on another wide boulevard, speeding away from the city center and toward the side of Vitosha Mountain. To the right was a pedestrian path flanked by bushes and low trees. To the left were two sets of tram tracks.

The road was virtually empty, so Martina deliberately slowed down again, to the point where the two cars were just lights in the distance. She did not want to arouse their suspicion by getting too close. Luckily, there was no need. The Tsar Boris III Boulevard was a couple of kilometers long and almost completely straight, making it possible to follow someone surreptitiously from a distance when there was no traffic.

Martina relaxed and appraised the situation. The clock on the dashboard showed it was 2:11 a.m., and she was getting tired. With the exclusive pictures in the camera, she could call it quits now and all would be well. She took her hat off and shook her liberated hair loose. The boulevard at this point was still wide, and she could easily turn off along one of the many side streets and intersections and disappear. She turned her head left and right, observing that the windows of the residential buildings were dark, except for the displays of some first-floor shops with bright neon lights.

Far ahead, the two Mercedes made a right turn onto a street that led up toward a glitzy residential area in the foothills of the mountain. It was a narrow road with more turns, meaning she would have to get closer if she wanted to continue the pursuit.

Martina hesitated. She could go home. Then again, she had come this far; it would be a shame to turn around.

The Skoda turned and continued the pursuit. Martina's heartbeat again jumped. Her thin arms gripped the steering wheel tightly. This amount of danger was new to her, but she was beginning to enjoy the thrill.

The Mercedes slowed to a speed of forty kilometers per hour as they made their way up the winding roads. A cat darted from one side to the other, the bright reflection from its eyes briefly piercing the night. The houses flanking the streets were getting progressively larger, wide satellite dishes often appearing outside second-floor balconies. The sidewalks were narrow and elevated high above the streets, a diversity of fence designs separating them from the lawns. Circular trash cans were placed outside, each with white numbers painted on it. Most of the streets were unlit, but there was moonlight showing the way. The night was clear and quiet.

Martina turned off the lights of the car. She drove as far behind the two Mercedes as she could, catching just glimpses of the second car. In the approach to every turn, she feared that she would run into the two cars ahead of her, so she prepared herself to slam on the brakes.

Do they carry guns with them?

It was very likely.

Would they shoot me?

Also very likely. Her stomach tightened, and she pushed the thought out of her mind.

The road was too narrow for a U-turn, so she would have to put the blue Skoda in reverse and pray. Martina did her best to stay calm but noticed her hands were beginning to tremble. The moon above was nearly full.

The two cars were no more than fifty meters away, hidden behind a corner. There wasn't much road left, and Martina feared that she could no longer continue the chase. She made the next turn and slowed down, just in time to see the red brake lights of the second Mercedes disappear behind another hill.

She looked for a place to park. She saw a secluded part to the side of the road, underneath the dense crown of a plump tree. The gravel underneath the right tires crunched as Martina parked the car so close to the fence that the shrubs creeping through the mesh scratched the Skoda and enveloped its side.

The car came to a stop, and Martina turned the key. The engine quickly became still.

Silence.

Somewhere in the distance, she heard the muffled barking of a dog. She was in the dark, the branches of the tree casting a thick shadow. Martina reached for the camera and opened the door, making sure to close it as softly as possible.

The crisp mountain air coolly washed over her face, giving her sweaty temples a chill. She hid the key in one of the pockets of her white denim shorts, which she wore over full-length black pantyhose.

Looking down, Martina realized the white she was wearing made her easily visible. It was a somewhat frightening thought. Nevertheless, she scurried briskly up the hill and reached the top in less than a minute. The road then swooped downward and forked into two separate roads that disappeared into the streets. There weren't very many houses left, for up ahead was the mountain.

Suddenly, Martina saw bright lights shining through the trees to her left. The lights were clear and strong, occasionally disrupted by the trees and bushes. The cars must have reached their destination and were now parking. She took advantage of the slope and jogged forward, careful to ensure her footsteps were as quiet as possible.

At the bottom of the slope, just as the road was about to begin climbing up again, Martina noticed that a dirt road veered away from the asphalt. She crossed over the path and into thick grass that reached above her ankles. She was not sure what she was stepping on, but it felt like a mixture of dried mud and twigs.

Something snapped underneath her feet, and Martina froze. She knelt down and looked ahead.

The cars were now thirty meters away, parked in front of a large house hidden behind a high white wall. From where she was positioned, she could see the top half of the second floor.

One of the men opened two wide, black metal doors. The headlights of the cars illuminated the area, and Martina could see that the wall extended along the visible perimeter of the property. The paint looked fresh, and the house appeared to be quite large.

The two Mercedes passed through, and the man grabbed one of the heavy doors and pulled on it until it closed. He walked across and got hold of the handle of the other door, dragging it until it closed shut with a metallic bang. There was a clicking noise from inside and the sound of high heels. Martina heard footsteps across the pavement; a key turned, and a door opened.

There was more shuffling and then silence. Martina stood still and did nothing except swat a night fly away from her face. She was now keenly aware of her warm breath in the night cold.

Moonlight illuminated the road so she approached the house by moving along the bushes and hiding underneath the trees. On the other side of the short, narrow dirt road was the mountain. Martina carefully made her way through the shrubbery until she was standing almost directly in front of the house.

Moonlight spilled over the wall, creating shades of whiteness as the trees cast their long shadows. The wall had a triangular dome of red shingles, the front door located in the middle and complete with an oversized dungeon-like metal ring that was a handle as well as a knocker.

Now what?

She had found out where Ivanka and the mobster lived, but that suddenly seemed the least of her priorities at the moment. Martina looked around in vain. Her back and waist were hurting from all the bending over. She was running out of places to hide, for the terrain here dropped off abruptly into a little crevasse before rising again into the mountain. There was a tree directly in front of the entrance.

Martina moved in that direction, careful not to lose her footing and slip down into the crevasse. *Could I climb the tree for a better view?*

She was about to find out. There were some low branches on the other side of the tree, and Martina reached up and grabbed one, making sure the camera strap was securely around her neck. She placed her feet on the trunk and kicked around with her legs until she found traction. Pulling up with her arms and pushing with her legs, Martina managed to hoist herself up onto the first branch. The hard bark scratched her exposed forearms, and she was sure the pantyhose had picked up a few tears.

Regaining her balance after cautiously getting up on the branch, Martina reached for another and climbed half a meter higher. She brushed some leaves away and climbed higher still as something thorny scratched her neck.

Now just over three meters above the level of the road, Martina had a clear view over the imposing wall surrounding the compound. The house was larger than she had expected, a long terrace extending across most of the second floor. There was a yellow awning over the terrace, obscuring the windows to the bedroom.

The front lawn was meticulously mowed, small lamps placed next to the paved pathways. The two Mercedes were parked in the open, underneath what looked to be a deck with vines growing up the wooden structure. The lights of Sofia were shimmering in the distance. It would have been postcard perfect under different circumstances.

Martina leaned against the hull of the tree and secured her footing. The lights inside the big second-floor bedroom came on, lighting up the terrace. Martina prepared her camera but had no shot. The awning was too long and covered too much.

Come on! She was hoping Ivanka or her criminal boyfriend would come out onto the terrace, making for a great picture. Instead, the light in the master bedroom went out, leaving the second floor in a moonlit darkness.

Martina exhaled in boredom. Fatigue was getting to her, and she was struggling to stay focused. The sound of the crickets was all she could hear. Occasional gusts of wind caused the branches to sway softly and rustle. She began to shiver.

Chapter Twenty-Three

Zhivko turned off the water and let the last few drops drip down onto the tiles. The bathroom was small and L-shaped, the toilet placed in the narrow end. The wider area contained the sink and a towel rack. The shower was equidistant between the toilet and the sink. The water ran across the checkered tiles and pooled around the drain. The oval mirror was foggy, incapable of reflection.

He turned around, grabbed a towel, and ran it forcefully over his head. His short hair offered little resistance. Zhivko dried his chest, abdomen, and back and wrapped the towel around his waist. It went down to his knees, where the edges of the old fabric were fraying. He unlocked the door and stepped out.

The door to the guest room was left slightly ajar, and Zhivko walked in, taking advantage of the corridor lamp shining behind him. He made for the drawers and opened the top one. It contained only blankets and sheets.

Zhivko frowned. He proceeded to open the other drawers and rummaged through their contents, but there was not a single article of men's clothing.

Zhivko made sure the towel was securely around his waist and put his feet into the slippers. He walked out and descended the stairs. The first floor was dark as well, except for the light coming from the kitchen. He assumed Mira was still cleaning up and confidently opened the door and stepped in.

Mira was standing with her back to him, leaning over to put something in the washer. The sound of the door opening startled her, and she abruptly turned around, a look of utter surprise on her face. Zhivko saw that she was topless, her jeans halfway unbuttoned and hanging slack around her hips.

"What are you doing here?" she yelled, hands instinctively rising to cover her breasts. "What are you doing?" she repeated louder, tone even more demanding.

Just as surprised, Zhivko lifted one hand in front of his eyes, making sure the other was on the towel as a precaution.

"I'm sorry," he replied, looking through his fingers. "It was an accident."

"Get out!" Mira ordered, approaching him with hands still covering her chest.

"Okay," he said in a conciliatory voice and took a step back. "I didn't know."

Mira moved forward and reached for the door with one arm. Looking at the commando's chiseled, muscular physique had somewhat tempered her anger.

"Why are you in here?" she asked, voice slightly softer.

Zhivko stammered. "Ah …" he began. "I'm looking for some shorts or underwear that I can sleep in," he explained, looking at Mira's wide brown eyes. They were now less than a meter away from each other. "There weren't any in the drawers in the room."

"Try one of the other bedrooms," Mira said. "There should be a pile of clothes placed inside one of the closets." She looked down and then up again, but not because she planned to. During that same split second, he stole a glance at the area not covered by her arm.

"Thank you," he said, nodding and taking a few steps back. He was relieved the awkward situation had come to an end. Mira watched him and closed the door.

Zhivko returned to the second floor and made his way down the small corridor into the first bedroom. His fingers crawled over the wall in search of the light switch. Unlike the guest room, this room was elaborately furnished. There was a double bed near the window and paintings hanging on the walls. A bookcase was stacked with old books and decorative statues.

The wooden closet doors creaked and protested when he opened them. Zhivko saw a pile of folded athletic shorts and picked up the top pair. He loosened the towel, quickly pulled on the shorts, and placed his feet back into the slippers. It was a surprisingly good fit. The shorts were red polyester and looked like they were part of a soccer outfit.

Zhivko returned to the guest room and closed the door, placing the towel on the back of the chair to dry. He turned the lights off and looked outside through the window. It was dark and peaceful. The sky was cloudy, and the outlines of the trees were barely visible against the gray background. Light from the kitchen directly below illuminated the nearest row of dying plants as crickets chirped softly.

The springs of the mattress recoiled with a groan as he sat down. He was tired, and his legs ached, so he put his palms over his face and closed his eyes.

Two days ago, I was sleeping in my own bed. Two days ago, everything was normal!

The thought angered him. He pursed his lips together, and his jaw clenched. For a moment, his tired eyes were restless.

Downstairs, Mira turned off the kitchen light. Zhivko could hear her footsteps and listened as she climbed the stairs. He heard her pause at the midfloor platform. When she reached the second-floor hallway, Mira turned on the light, and Zhivko raised his head to look through the door's tinted window.

He could see the outlines of Mira's head moving about. Next, he heard the bathroom door open and concluded that she was getting ready for her shower. He hoped the noise would not prevent him from falling asleep.

But Mira did not walk into the bathroom, and he did not hear the sound of running water. Surprised, Zhivko got up. The bed groaned again. The distorted silhouette of her head was still visible through the curved glass. She appeared to be standing still just outside the door.

The corridor lamp was turned off, and now there was total darkness, except for what little natural light came in through the window. Zhivko heard a footstep and saw the door opening cautiously. Mira came in and turned to face him.

She was topless again, but this time, her arms were not in front of her. The brown hair fell symmetrically down both sides of her face, ending at the two collarbones. Her eyes were fixed on his, and her wet lips were just barely apart in anticipation.

Mira needed an experience like this. Her workaholic lifestyle had deprived her of romance and intimacy. There was no time to make a connection with someone or pursue an amorous adventure, but she desperately longed to be wanted, held, and caressed. And yes, she wanted orgasmic sex in compensation for all those lonely nights by herself.

She let go of the door handle and took another step forward. Moonlight danced across her body. She was naked except for the hip-hugger panties. Zhivko stood and watched, his body no longer feeling tired. She raised herself on the tips of her toes and leaned forward into his torso. He placed his arms on her waist, gently running his fingers over her underwear and tugging at the edges. Under normal light, they were a faded red, a kinky purchase made years ago.

Mira was still looking into his eyes, biting on her lower lip. She opened her mouth and cupped his face in her hands, her sensitive skin reacting to the unshaved texture and ruggedly masculine appeal. A lightning bolt ran through his body as the warmth of her hands simultaneously soothed and excited him.

Zhivko pulled her closer, causing her breathing to skip a beat. She responded with a seductive smile. Their noses touched, and they could sense each other's breath. Mira was radiating intense heat and a repressed passion that unlocked the animal in him and made him want more.

His crotch expanded quickly against the loose constraints of his shorts.

Emboldened, Zhivko leaned her against the door and pushed his body into hers. She was soft, except for the hard nipples now tantalizingly touching his chest. He kissed her gently, and she moaned approvingly, held her breath, bit her lip, and asked for more. In her mind, there was no reason to take things slowly.

Chapter Twenty-Four

Zhivko woke up abruptly, his breathing unnecessarily heavy. He felt confined and uneasy. Memories of years past were poisoning his sleep. He was spooning Mira, his right arm over her body. He could feel her chest rise and fall.

He was hot, and a check of his forehead revealed he was sweating profusely. The warm liquid was pooling on his forehead and neck, resulting in the irresistible urge to scratch. Zhivko carefully freed himself of Mira and got up, careful to create as little disturbance as possible. The reporter moved, wrapping herself even more tightly with the blanket and continuing to sleep.

The sky had cleared some, and there was more natural light coming into the large bedroom from outside. Zhivko walked to the mirror and observed his reflection. He looked up to stretch his neck and wiped the sweat away, spreading it over the remainder of his torso.

Virtually everything had changed over the years. His hair was shorter and more organized. The hairline may have receded just a bit, he thought as he slowly ran his hand over his hair. His body was completely different, scrawny and weak no more. Zhivko moved closer, as if to study his face. He was looking directly at himself, into his own eyes.

They used to pound me into the ground! They spat on my face!

They are spitting on my face again!

He had been spat on before, in his earlier school years.

After lunch one day, the children were in the yard. The girls were in groups, either chatting or playing jump rope with a raggedy rope that was missing one of its handles because the orphanage could not afford a new one.

The boys were by the fence, some trying to sneak in a smoke while the others were talking about the girls.

"Some of the girls are maturing," one teenager said with a laugh. "They might be sexually curious soon."

The others snickered. Mitko, one of the bigger boys, produced a lighter from a specially stitched extra compartment in his gray sweatpants and cupped his hands to his face to light a cigarette. The younger kids negotiated with the older ones for smokes. There was a rumor that some of the girls offered a chance to have their breasts squeezed in exchange for a cigarette.

"You want one?" Mitko taunted, provocatively blowing smoke in Zhivko's face.

"No," he replied, waving his hand at the gray smoke. Cigarettes disgusted him, and he didn't really belong in this group, even though he thought it would be a chance to fit in and be seen as one of the guys.

"Come on, just one! Be a man!" Mitko continued, blowing a second cloud at Zhivko.

"No," Zhivko replied firmly, stepping away from the suddenly claustrophobic circle that had formed as the other boys surrounded him.

Mitko extended his hand and pushed Zhivko back. The mop-haired teenager was taller and of heavier build. He knew Zhivko could not offer much resistance.

"Don't walk away from me," he said sternly, enjoying his position of power. A mocking grin spread on his face. "You don't leave until you have a puff."

"Fuck you," Zhivko said, trying to sound tough.

Mitko threw the cigarette down. "What did you say?" His mouth twisted into a sneer.

"Fuck you." The words were articulated slowly for extra impact.

Mitko looked around at the other boys, who were urging him on. A cocky anger swept over his face. "Is that so?" he pushed Zhivko hard, forcing him a few steps back until he crashed into the fence and reclined against the steel mesh.

Zhivko could not take it anymore. He regained his balance and shoved Mitko, but he was too weak and too small to damage the hulking boy.

Mitko laughed. "Idiot!" he exclaimed and grabbed Zhivko by the collar. He spun him around and launched a kick into his backside, sending him flying into the fence. The pain was sharp as a protruding piece of metal sliced into his left shoulder. The young Zhivko screamed and stayed pinned to the fence for a few seconds before stumbling and falling on his back.

"Shit, he is bleeding!" one of the boys yelled. The expanding circle of red was clearly visible against the white long-sleeved shirt. Zhivko's mouth was open wide, a look of anguish on his face.

"I'm out of here!" Mitko announced and broke into a slow run toward the main building. The other boys followed, occasionally turning their heads to take a look at the scene.

Zhivko lay there, hand pressed to his shoulder to numb the pain as the cold air whistled overhead. The ground was wet from the recent rains and cold, overpowering the thin fabric of his clothes. He raised his hand and saw that his fingers were bloody. He kicked violently with his legs and eventually propped himself up. He walked slowly toward the building, the bloody spot on his shoulder now measuring ten centimeters in diameter. All the time he was pressing down on the wound with his palm.

Eventually, he made it back to the building, where the nurse cleansed the cut, stitched him up, and put his arm in an immobilizing brace. Zhivko complained to the ward, who was not sure how to respond. Mitko was punished and forced to help the janitors clean the bathrooms for a week, while Zhivko was moved to another orphanage. He was fourteen. There, the abuse continued, but at least he was never seriously hurt again.

It has always been just me.

In the dark, Zhivko ran his hand across the scar. Even in the daytime, it was now almost invisible, a thin line just below the left collarbone. The emotional scar was much bigger. His brow furrowed as anger and determination wrapped into one.

He looked over at Mira sleeping. She was in the fetal position, one arm on top of the other. The scene was one of complete serenity. Even the crickets outside were quiet, and there was no wind to bother the trees. Zhivko walked toward the bed and knelt down, his face just centimeters from Mira's.

He gently stroked her hair and pushed the strands away from her cheeks. He once again admired how soft and warm and clear her skin was. Her features were so delicate. He touched the tip of her nose and admired its beauty. She was soundly asleep.

The young reporter was either just looking for some good sex or desperately needed to establish an emotional connection with someone. He continued to softly weave his fingers through her hair and hoped for the latter. Mira shifted slightly and purred. Zhivko crossed himself.

Chapter Twenty-Five

It was shortly before sunrise, and Martina, getting a chill, was frantically rubbing her hands together. The unpleasant sensation of blood draining toward her feet from too much standing was becoming unbearable. She looked over the wall one last time.

Nothing. Nothing had happened in or around the expensive house for the last five hours. She cursed herself for spending so much time hidden in the tree hoping for an exclusive photograph. Martina lifted her right foot cautiously and dropped it onto a lower branch, carefully holding onto the tree bark with her hands. Assured of the branch's firmness, she stepped on it with all of her forty-eight kilograms.

The tree's lush crown and thick leaves had shielded her from someone looking out from the criminal's mansion, but the rising sun threatened to blow her cover. Martina looked up as the morning's first rays pierced their way over the clear blue sky. The sight was a beautiful one, even for her tired eyes. She yawned and exhaled painfully. Her eyelids felt heavy, and her forehead was throbbing. She slid down one more branch, the camera bouncing against her chest.

Martina's feet hit the ground with a soft thud. She sank into the dirt and kicked up loose pebbles, sending them bouncing down the slope of the hill. She readjusted her shorts, which had risen up during her descent, and blew loose strands of hair away from her face. Her body cried out for a bed to lie in.

Somewhere behind her, the metal garage doors suddenly opened with a loud noise. Martina froze, gripped by paralysis. She dared not move, fearful of drawing attention. She was trapped with no way out.

The garage doors opened fully, swinging just a few centimeters above the dust. Martina heard numerous footsteps on the dirt road above her and pushed herself up against the tree, minimizing the odds that she would be seen. But if someone walked a few feet down the road and turned around …

Her heart pounded. She held her clenching, shaking fists in front of her mouth and bit her knuckles. She was scared, very scared. The previous feeling of tantalizing excitement had completely left her.

The shuffling of feet continued and then abated briefly. Martina swallowed and stood still. She heard the car engine coming to life with a roar, followed by the soft crunching of dirt as the black Mercedes rolled forward through the garage doors. The car turned right onto the beaten-up road and stopped. Martina leaned her head out beyond the tree to take a look.

She saw the back of a man who had just come out of the car. He left the driver's door open and the engine running, walked in front of the car, and returned to the garage doors. From her position in the ditch, she could not see him as he stood behind the other side of the vehicle.

"Why so early, boss?" Stefan asked in a tired voice, rubbing his eyes. "And why me?"

Nikolai looked at the man with an indignant expression. As a former athlete, he was used to waking up early to train, though after last night's engagements, he definitely would have preferred to sleep a little longer.

"Ahmed is praying," he retorted, as if giving a lecture on religious freedom. "You know it's important for him."

Stefan frowned but said nothing. He considered all religions silly, and the sight of Ahmed kneeling on his little Muslim prayer rug was for him a source of constant amusement. Yet the young man from the middle of nowhere was loyal and committed, qualities that Nikolai appreciated.

"Okay," he replied curtly. "Got it. So what is the plan?"

"First, get the other car out and take it to a gas station," Nikolai instructed while Stefan lit a cigarette. "The reservoir needs to be full."

Stefan nodded, and Nikolai took a whiff, putting the lighter in his pocket.

"But not the gas station nearby," Nikolai warned. "Drive into the city and find a place there."

"Sure," Stefan said. "Then what?"

"The three of us will go to that pesky reporter's apartment, see if she is coming or going. We have to take care of something, remember?"

Stefan blew out a puff of smoke and scratched his face, picking at his beard with his fingers.

"Are we actually gonna kill her?" he asked.

"If she is with the commando and the situation allows, we kill both," Nikolai replied calmly, trying to hide his moral objections. "If she is alone, we'll play it by ear."

Martina could not believe her ears. *Are they talking about Mira? Dear God!*

She swallowed hard and felt the need to escape. Somehow, she would have to get out of this ditch and run as far away as possible. The men she had been following were scaring her more than she had initially imagined. Her hands trembled violently.

Stefan blew out smoke and used his palm to rub his sleepy eyes once more. His head was still throbbing from the inadequate amount of sleep. Nikolai walked past him and through the garage doors.

"Oh, and one more thing," he said, prompting Stefan to turn around. "Buy a map when you're at the station."

"A map?" Stefan asked, puzzled. "I think we have a map in the car, don't we?"

"Buy a map of Plovdiv," Nikolai clarified. "I don't think we have a regional map, and it's important."

Stefan lowered his head in agreement but raised his open palms above his head in a pointed gesture to signify that the command to him seemed random and illogical. Nikolai focused a stern look on the man.

"The boss and I have to go to Plovdiv to take care of the arrival of an important shipment on Saturday," he explained curtly, his lips barely parting. "You two will take the other Mercedes and follow us from a distance, so no one gets suspicious."

Stefan noticed Nikolai's tone, and even though it bothered him, he didn't let on.

"If that is what you want," he replied dismissively. "What about the blonde?"

"We'll leave her in the house and lock up," Nikolai said with a shrug. "The boss does not want her around when he's conducting business."

"How is the big man after last night?" Stefan asked jokingly, hoping to clear the tension. A devilish smile spread on his face, the cigarette momentarily suspended from the corner of his mouth.

Nikolai chuckled. "I bet he's tired," he began. "I could hear them all night."

"Can't blame him," Stefan responded and shook some ash off the cigarette, making an exaggerated arch with his eyebrows.

"Yes," Nikolai replied, looking up to make sure there was no one on the terrace. "Neither can I."

Stefan laughed.

"Listen," Nikolai said, retreating to his usual serious demeanor. "I gotta go to the bathroom. You find Ahmed and tell him the plan."

Stefan made the thumbs-up sign in agreement. Nikolai turned around and disappeared into the house through one of the side entrances. Stefan stood outside for a few more seconds, smoking the cigarette and taking in the crisp mountain air. It energized him, and he liked to believe it neutralized the effects of the tobacco.

The trees were now swaying gently in the breeze. Stefan looked around in admiration before throwing the butt away onto the dirt road and stepping through the garage doors.

Martina breathed a cautious sigh of relief. She was still hugging the tree closely, wanting to escape but fearful she would be seen. She had heard everything and was trying to make sense of it in her head. Making a splash with her exclusive pictures was no longer her primary objective. Her journalistic curiosity had led her to information that she needed to disseminate as quickly as possible.

The sounds of the man's footsteps grew fainter and eventually faded from earshot. Emboldened, Martina peered out from beyond the tree. She had a full view of the stylish black car, its spotless exterior contrasting with the road. She looked underneath the car but could not see legs on the other side. Stepping out from behind the tree, Martina crawled up the ditch on all fours and raised her head, looking up through the windows of the car into the visible front yard of the house.

No one.

Her fingers were getting grimy, dirt piling up beneath her fingernails. Still in the ditch, she crawled parallel to the road for a few more meters, moving her bony limbs as quickly as she could while trying not to make noise.

She looked up again, now staring at the shiny car diagonally from the front. She could not hear any footsteps. Martina thrust herself forward with her legs, sending lines of dirt sliding down as she moved up. She reached the road and knelt. There was no one coming through the garage doors.

If she was going to escape, she needed to make a dash now. Martina nervously licked her lips and prepared herself mentally. Inside her slender ribcage, her heart was pounding. She removed the camera from around her neck and wrapped the strap around her wrist, holding the apparatus tight with one hand.

Martina raised herself to her feet and took one last look at the large house.

She ran as fast as her legs could take her. She kicked up small clouds of rock and dust as she moved, her breathing becoming heavier and more difficult as she descended the road. She was near the improvised intersection when at one point she lost her balance and stumbled forward, inefficiently attempting to break her fall with only one hand while the other protected the camera.

Martina hit the ground hard, skidding across the dirt while her left knee banged against the road. The dry and compacted dirt grated violently against her skin. She wanted to scream in pain but instead bit her lips and stifled the cry, producing instead a pitiful whimper.

She sat up and assessed the damage. Her free palm was skinned and bloodied, brown dust mixing in with the blood to create a filthy-looking wine-colored mess. Martina wiped herself on the white shirt, trying to rub away the dirt. The camera was fine, but the knuckles that had been protecting it were skinned raw.

Her black pantyhose were torn at the knee, a wide area of which was scraped, small droplets of blood appearing on the surface. Her heart was pounding now. She could not stay here, for she would be easily seen should the criminal's men return to the Mercedes. Martina groaned and forced herself to stand up, putting her weight on the good leg. Her white clothes were a dusty yellow.

She hobbled as quickly as she could, reached the intersection, and turned right. Her black pantyhose were brown with dirt and dust. The feeling in her knee was coming back, and she started walking with an awkward limp. Having turned the corner, she was out of view of the house, separated by trees and thick bushes. She wiped her hand, brushed the blood away from her knee, and wiped her hand again. Her shorts were beginning to resemble a pizza.

Martina made her way down the road with quick steps, hoping the routine would blunt the pain. In the morning light, the houses looked different. The walls were a clean white underneath sloping roofs with red tiles. The paths leading toward the entrances were of cobblestone, arranged lovingly with neatly trimmed bushes on the side. Cats lazily slept on the porches and fences.

She stopped, suddenly hearing a car come to life on a nearby street. Was it the black Mercedes following her?

The noise was coming from somewhere else, giving her a measure of solace. The roar of the engine was getting louder, and just as she was expecting it to come upon her, it must have turned along some other street. The noise grew faint and quickly disappeared.

Martina looked around, but there was no one. It was early morning, and she guessed most of the residents of the nice houses were asleep. She saw the little Skoda hidden underneath the large tree. She crossed the street and approached the door, fishing the key out of her pocket.

Pain filled her knee as Martina extended her leg to press the clutch. She threw the camera in the back and turned the ignition key. With a few skillful turns in the limited space, the car was facing the city. She pressed the gas and shifted into second, checking the rearview mirror as she went. The blood on her palm was clotting and drying.

The Skoda snaked its way down the empty road. Martina was tired, and her eyes were a bloated red. Her fear was replaced by renewed fatigue. She needed sleep, but she would not get it soon. First, she would have to swing by the newsroom and warn Mira.

Martina closed her eyes and opened them again. Her eyelids were weighing heavily. She decided it was necessary to stop for water, coffee, and something to clean her scrapes with. After five minutes of aggressive driving and a few risky turns, the car was now cruising along one of the wider roads. Czar Boris III was not far away. Martina managed a weak smile, her parched lips revealing teeth stained by nearly twenty-four hours of neglect. She wiped sweat away from her brow and pulled over into a side street, seeing a mom-and-pop bakery that was open. She killed the engine and got out.

No longer trying to hide her diminishing limp, she hobbled up to the old, four-story building with peeling yellow paint and stepped inside the bakery. It was a confined and narrow space, the baked goods displayed under a glass cover.

"Do you have mineral water and *banitsa*?" Martina asked the middle-aged woman behind the counter. She looked up from the crossword puzzle and got up.

"One moment," she replied and reached for a napkin. She grabbed a slice of the traditional Bulgarian pastry, which was prepared by layering a mixture of whisked eggs and pieces of cheese between filo pastry and then baking it, and placed it on the counter.

"A large or small bottle of water?" the woman asked and saw the injuries and dark-brown stains for the first time.

"Large," Martina quickly answered. She intended to drink a little and use the rest to cleanse her wounds. "And give me some extra napkins, please."

The woman complied and walked over to the refrigerator.

"Do you sell newspapers?" Martina asked before hungrily biting into the banitsa and chewing.

The woman pulled open the fridge door and grabbed a large bottle of mineral water. "On the stand behind you," she said and pointed.

Martina turned around. Her jaw fell as she took a look at the front page.

Chapter Twenty-Six

Ivan Dobrev gripped the steering wheel tightly in a moment of frustration and then let go, having calmed down and realized the gesture was futile. He threw the butt of his cigarette out the window and tore open another pack. He lit a new cigarette and took a drag. He held it in his left hand so he could casually tap off the ashes while resting his arm outside the window.

Despite progressing at an excruciatingly slow pace, the white big rig was near the front of the line of trucks and buses. By the looks of it, Dobrev would be free in thirty to forty-five minutes. He turned off the engine to conserve fuel and leaned back into his cushioned seat, the fabric worn thin and the colors faded from years of use. Both windows were rolled down all the way, but breezes were intermittent and the temperature inside the cab was rising. The asphalt below was hot from the scorching sun above.

Dobrev hated the Turkish-Bulgarian border. The crossing point handled a large percentage of the traffic between Europe and Asia and was always busy—a long wait in line was a guarantee. Worse, the driver in the neighboring lane also had his windows open and was loudly blaring incomprehensible Turkish music. Dobrev frowned and shook his head.

A large concrete gate stood approximately fifty meters away, its simple outline visible from afar. "Republic of Bulgaria" was painted in bold black letters on its white facade. A similar "Republic of Turkey" sign was painted on the other side. The motherland was tantalizingly close.

Suddenly, the truck in front revved its engine, the exhaust pipe spewing a cloud of black smoke into the air. Dobrev grinned, threw his cigarette out the window, and then brushed any errant debris from his shirt. He was a portly man with a well-formed round belly that stretched his clothing. The fifty-one-year-old professional truck driver liked to believe the tight clothing made him look leaner.

Dobrev followed the truck in front of him, which advanced a good thirty meters before coming to a stop. He turned off the engine again and smiled. He was now second in line. But the smile was one of caution, for behind it lay nervousness. Dobrev had received numerous assurances that everything would go according to plan and he need not worry, but he remained a little uneasy. He reached for another cigarette and noticed that his hands were shaking slightly while operating the lighter.

In another twenty minutes, it was his turn. Forcing himself to be calm, Dobrev moved his truck up to the designated line and stopped. He next applied the handbrake and climbed down out of the cabin. The thick soles of his leather shoes protected his feet from the hot asphalt. He kicked both legs straight, one after the other, and pulled on his belt to make sure the jeans were secure and not hanging down. Dobrev then made a quick, involuntary nervous twitch and chided himself for it.

Nearby, two customs agents began walking in his direction. Both were men in their thirties, fair-haired and energetic. Their shift had just begun, and after a quick card game back at the station and a brief read-through of the day's newspapers, they were looking forward to work. One of the agents carried a clipboard with documents and a pen, while the other firmly held the leash of a German shepherd. The purebred dog had its tongue out and was panting heavily.

"You ready?" one asked.

"Da," the other responded. "As always."

"Listen," one of the men began, pulling his colleague aside. "Let me check the truck by myself and you take care of the guy's papers," he looked reassuringly and with a soft smile. "It will be faster that way."

"You sure?" the other asked, confused.

"Why not?" the man replied, sounding confident. "The guy is just carrying oranges, probably grown in Turkey somewhere." The agent pointed to the large healthy orange painted on the white cover of the truck's body, near the rear doors. The picture also featured a straw impaled into the top of the orange, as if to suggest that someone on the roof would be sipping on juice.

The other agent raised his eyebrows in acceptance. "Sure," he said. "I will take care of the paperwork."

"Okay."

Dobrev saw the agents coming and nodded. He was standing in a shady place directly in front of the cabin.

"Good day," Dobrev said, greeting the men. "How are you?"

He realized he was speaking slightly faster than normal and told himself to slow down.

"Good day," the man with the clipboard responded. "May I see your documents?"

"Certainly," Dobrev moved to open the driver's door. "Let me get them for you."

"I'm going to start at the other side," the man with the German shepherd said to his partner, who responded with a nod. Meanwhile, Dobrev opened the glove compartment and retrieved a folder stuffed with papers.

Agent Venkov circled around to the other side of the truck and knelt down to pet the dog. The animal responded by raising its head and briefly exposing its neck. Venkov looked around cautiously to make sure no one was watching him. There was a truck in the adjacent lane, but the driver was nowhere to be seen. Venkov assumed he must be with a group of drivers noisily discussing something a few trucks down the lane, where someone had opened the hood of a truck and revealed an engine steaming from overheating.

Venkov smiled and ran his hand over the dog's head and back. It was panting even louder now, gulping in air as fast as it could. The agent got up and reached inside his jeans pocket, pulling out a slim, small bottle that had once contained rubbing alcohol. He knelt down again and shook it, carefully taking off the top to make sure nothing spilled out.

Predictably, the dog had an immediate reaction of revulsion as soon as the scent of vinegar hit its nostrils. The trained animal energetically swayed its head and moved away, its paws pushing back as it stretched the leash. Venkov looked up to make sure he was safe and then pushed the bottle in front of the dog's muzzle once more. Again, the animal protested.

Satisfied with the result thus far, Venkov vigorously caressed the dog's hide with his hand and then intentionally spilled some vinegar onto its muzzle, just behind the nose. The German shepherd snorted.

Satisfied, Venkov got up and capped the bottle, hiding it in his jeans again.

"Let's go, boy," he said loudly, making sure his partner would hear him. "Get to work."

The dog leaped up and approached the tires of the truck, sniffing at their base and occasionally jumping up to smell underneath the covers, which were tied in loops to the floor of the chassis. The agent observed in silence and walked the dog down the length of the truck. Within a minute, they had reached the end and circled around back, coming up alongside the driver's side. The dog repeated the same meticulous but futile routine.

Meanwhile, Agent Georgiev was looking through the papers Dobrev had given him. It was the standard information, indicating who was importing what, at what price and quantity, and where the merchandise was headed. He looked up when he saw his partner approaching.

"All clear?" Georgiev asked, perspiration starting to slide down his clean-shaven face. The sun was unforgiving, and he wanted to finish quickly.

"So far, yes," Venkov answered, discreetly positioning his legs so that his partner would not see the small bulge created by the bottle of vinegar in his pocket.

Georgiev closed the papers and handed the clipboard to Dobrev.

"Sign here, please," the agent instructed and handed over his pen. Dobrev looked down and quickly signed on the line, eager to get the procedure over with and move on. He returned the pen and looked on with anticipation. The German shepherd licked its leg.

"Thank you," Georgiev said and let the clipboard rest against his hip. He looked over at Venkov. "And now for the final check."

Dobrev did his best to hide his annoyance. The heat was causing him to sweat and uncomfortably wet his tight clothes. He saw the other agent waving at him and started walking.

"Come this way," Venkov instructed and pulled on the dog's leash. "Come with us to the back and open the cargo area."

He did as he was told, sandwiched between the two agents as he walked to the back of the truck. He climbed up to unlock the doors and pulled down on the lever. They swung open with ease. Wooden crates of oranges were stacked on top of each other from the floor to the roof, a thin mesh netting across the top of each crate to keep the oranges from falling out.

"That's a lot of fruit!" Dobrev exclaimed in a childlike manner, hoping the comment would make him look silly and thus incapable of criminality. The two agents said nothing. Venkov raised his foot up to the first railing and reached for the side handle to pull himself up into the belly of the truck. The dog jumped up to join him.

"Come on, boy," Venkov said encouragingly, loosening his grip on the leash. The dog walked around, sniffing at the bottom of the crates and moving from one side to the other. Within a few seconds, he sat down at the agent's feet.

"Clear," Venkov announced and climbed down onto the asphalt. Dobrev immediately reached for the doors and swung them to the closed position, making sure the lever was down and locked. Georgiev handed him some papers and smiled.

"Here you go," he said. "Drive safely and enjoy your trip."

"Thank you," the truck driver replied, satisfied that everything had gone down smoothly the way he had been told it would. "And you have a nice day," he said, looking at both agents and nodding.

The three men walked their separate ways, Dobrev heading for the truck cabin while Georgiev and Venkov were returning to their station. They needed to file the paperwork and sign off before moving on to inspect the next truck. And the German shepherd looked like it needed to drink some water.

Dobrev sat down in the driver's seat and closed the door. He turned the ignition and powered the engine, simultaneously releasing the handbrake. The man was about to step on the gas when he heard one of the agents talking to him.

"Watch the second turn when you get outside the city limits," Venkov said loudly, having first looked back to make sure his partner was nearing the station and thus out of earshot. "It's a sharp turn, so be careful."

Dobrev immediately understood the code and responded with a mischievous closed-lip smile. He raised his hand and waved at the helpful customs agent.

They've gotten to him. I'm benefitting from his intentional dereliction of duty.

On the other side of the border crossing lay the town of Svilengrad, which Dobrev did not like much and considered entirely unimpressive. On some previous occasions, he had nevertheless been seduced by its numerous duty-free shops, but not today. He was on a mission for which he had been promised a lot of money. He shifted into gear and accelerated.

Chapter Twenty-Seven

The National Assembly was a stately Neo-Renaissance building in the heart of Sofia. Constructed in the 1880s as an elegant but simple three-story building, it directly faced the monument of Alexander II, the Czar Liberator. The inside was a combination of white columns, grand chandeliers, and wall-to-wall red carpets. The red carpeting extended to the voting hall, the walls of which were of dark-brown wood. The speaker's podium was slightly elevated, positioned next to box seating for when the ministers were present. The chairman's seat was the highest, perched behind the speaker and overlooking the entire room.

Stoyanov sat reposed at his seat near the speaker's podium and stared absentmindedly at his hands, folded in front of him. The weekly Friday parliamentary control was undoubtedly his least favorite professional duty. He considered it a meaningless opportunity for opposition parliamentarians to grandstand and assault the ruling party with annoying questions and smartass sarcasm. The minister adjusted his stunning yellow tie and thoughtfully raised his hand to his chin.

The prime minister was two seats away, quietly taking notes and occasionally conferring with the finance minister to his right.

"The member from the opposition will now speak," the chairman said over the microphone, interrupting the chatter echoing throughout the chamber. "You may approach, sir."

A middle-aged man in an old gray suit walked up to the podium and adjusted the height of the microphone.

"Thank you, Chairman," Angelov said. He cleared his throat and looked across at the members of parliament seated before him. His colleagues from the opposition party were watching him with anticipation. Members of the ruling party were talking among themselves, paying him no attention.

"Dear deputies," Angelov began, forcing his mind to stay focused on the remarks he had prepared earlier that morning, "there is a matter of pressing urgency that I must bring up today."

The noise level in the chamber was still too loud.

"I kindly ask you to be quiet," Angelov said. "I have something to say, and you will listen."

"Quiet in the hall!" the chairman thundered, raising his hand to bang the gavel. "Quiet!"

Most ruling party members stopped talking, and the chamber quieted down.

"Thank you," said Angelov.

"Proceed," urged the chairman.

"The issue at hand is the current economic crisis and the inappropriate response of the government," he began, turning his head from left to right in a scanning motion. "What concerns the people the most is their salaries or lack thereof!" Angelov said. "All I see from the government is increased state involvement in economic affairs and more and more quasi-Communist attempts to control prices. These efforts are deeply misguided and counterproductive."

A subdued mixture of hollering and hooting rippled across the chamber.

"The days of state economic control are over, my friends!" Angelov said loudly, his voice gaining force. "It's about time you learn the basics of economics."

The opposition burst out in applause while the ruling party jeered and whistled. Angelov raised his palm to enforce silence. His confidence was building.

"Quiet!" the chairman thundered.

"Thank you," Angelov said and continued, this time with vigor. "Your policies are bankrupting the economy and dooming people to poverty and crime. This is the reality." The man raised his finger in the air and waved it dramatically. "Shame on you!"

The roar from the opposition was deafening, mixed with bursts of loud clapping. Some of the deputies got up to applaud. The ruling party whistled and banged their hands against the wood tables.

"I said quiet," the chairman implored, banging his gavel more than once. "Quiet!"

The chamber calmed down.

"And, to make things worse, what is the response of our interior minister?" Angelov turned to face Stoyanov, who paid him no attention and continued to stare away in defiance.

"Even my children know that crime has escalated, yet the government does nothing," the opposition member continued, again raising his finger. "Everyone but you, Stoyanov," Angelov pointed his finger angrily, "knows that there is corruption within the force and that drastic action is needed at all levels."

The farmer's son was on a roll, and there was no stopping him. The escalating noise from his colleagues only pumped his adrenaline.

"What we need are more police officers and more investigation of corruption allegations!" he yelled. "Yet the government is reducing ..." Angelov smirked condescendingly as he paused. "No, *optimizing* the number of police personnel while the crime wave continues. That is unacceptable, and you know it!"

The opposition members were on their feet in loud applause.

Angelov moved away from the podium and walked back to his seat, head held high in triumph. He doubted his speech would do much other than raise the emotional level of the discourse, to the extent that there even was discourse between the ruling party and the opposition. But the verbal assault on that smug son of a bitch felt good.

"Order in the chamber," the chairman said loudly. "Order please."

The ministers looked at each other and said nothing. The prime minister was still writing on his notepad, seemingly oblivious to the commotion around him. The TV cameras in the back of the chamber were rolling and capturing all the drama.

"The interior minister will be allowed time for a response if he so chooses," the chairman announced, looking Stoyanov's way. The minister got up, readjusted his suit, and walked to the podium.

"Dear Chairman and respected colleagues," he began, dispensing quickly with the obligatory courtesies. His arms gripped both sides of the podium in a power hold. "Let me assure you that I share your concerns about the situation in the country. All of us in the government are paying close attention and doing our best."

A few deputies sitting in the front seats laughed mockingly. Stoyanov pretended he didn't hear anything and continued, "Most of the circumstances leading to this mess are beyond our control, so

I would not be so quick to lay blame. Will the opposition ever offer something constructive, as opposed to just mouthing off?"

"Exactly!" yelled a deputy from the ruling coalition and implored his colleagues to do the same.

"Mr. Angelov," Stoyanov added, trying to spot his accuser in the crowd, "you speak of the processes going on within the ministry. I want to tell you, and everyone watching," for he was acutely aware that his appearance would most likely make the evening news, a circumstance that had influenced his choice of necktie, "that the changes are necessary. They would not be so drastic had you guys done *your* job when *you* were in power!"

The chamber was electrified again, and the chairman banged his gavel.

"Order!"

"That is all I have to say," Stoyanov concluded. He adjusted his glasses, which had begun to slide down his nose, and returned to his seat. The finance minister to his right waved him in for a huddle. Stoyanov leaned in to within twenty centimeters of the other man's face. From the other side, the prime minister did the same.

"This grilling is pointless," the premier said with a quiet hiss that revealed his frustration. "As part of procedure, the two of us are going to stay here until the end. As for you," he said and looked up at Stoyanov, "I want you to leave and arrange a meeting to begin as soon as this session is over."

The premier paused, turned his head to glance at the chamber, and then spoke quietly but firmly. Very firmly. "Decisive action is called for," he said to his two subordinates. "The time for talk is over, and now it's time to act." He looked at the men's thoughtful faces. "I intend on doing something."

The interior minister looked at the finance minister, who shook his head in understanding and moved it in the direction of the exit.

"I understand," Stoyanov replied. "I will do it right away." He made eye contact with the prime minister, whose silence needed no interpretation.

The minister pushed his chair back and got up. He briskly walked toward the side wall and the path that cut between it and the seats. There was an exit nearby, and Stoyanov pushed through the door.

Along the way, he brushed past another opposition member headed for the podium.

Stoyanov's shiny shoes glided swiftly and silently along the red carpet in the outside corridor. Reporters, photographers, and parliament staff were talking among themselves and looked up when they saw him come out of the chamber. He walked straight to the back entrance and waved them away, indicating he was in no mood for interviews. Flashes went off anyway as photographers took pictures.

It was raining, a persistent drizzle beating down on the pavement and forming puddles. Straight ahead was the Alexander Nevsky Cathedral, its golden cupolas shining despite the overcast sky. Portable metal fences cordoned off a makeshift parking area where a number of government vehicles idled. Stoyanov walked over to his car and tapped on the window.

The startled driver dropped the newspaper and looked over. He recognized him and immediately unlocked the doors.

"Sorry, sir," the man said cheerfully as Stoyanov climbed in the back. "I was not expecting you this early."

"No worries," the minister said. "Something urgent came up, and I have to see the general secretary."

The driver turned the ignition and started the engine, his eyes checking the mirrors. The wheels splashed water as the vehicle gained speed.

Chapter Twenty-Eight

It was a short drive to the Ministry of Interior, and Stoyanov spent the time gazing out the window and trying to organize his thoughts. Though he did not want to admit it, he knew the government's position was a difficult one. He suspected the prime minister thought so as well and would probably soon act. Animals fought ferociously when they had their backs to the wall.

The driver pulled the car to a soft stop in front of the main entrance and turned around.

"Here you go, sir," the man said with a quick smile on his handsome face.

"Thank you," Stoyanov replied and opened the door. The raindrops beat against his head and shoulders as he hurried across the sidewalk and through the entrance. The two security guards recognized him and waved him through. The minister nodded in appreciation and walked to the reception area. The woman behind the somewhat clouded windowpane looked up and scrambled to push the open newspaper out of view.

"Hello …" she began, unsure of herself and surprised at the unannounced visit of a leading administration official. "Can I help you?"

Stoyanov looked down at the brunette and pretended he did not suspect her of doing the crossword puzzle, despite the fact that the uncapped pen was still in her right hand.

"I need to see Mitov," he said quickly. "Do you know where he is?"

The woman scratched her chin and looked helpless for a moment.

"The general secretary should be in his office," she answered, feeling a little rushed. "Do you want me to call him?"

"Yes," Stoyanov replied and began giving instructions. "Tell him I want to see him."

"Right away," the woman responded and picked up the phone. Stoyanov walked away toward the elevators.

"Thank you," the minister said with a fleeting glance.

There were two elevators, each with narrow, sliding doors and bright-red displays on top. Stoyanov pressed the button and waited just a few seconds before a subdued beep ushered him through. The cabin was tight, barely accommodating three people pressed shoulder to shoulder. Unlike the creaky elevators in most Communist buildings, these were remarkably quiet, their vertical movements soft and nearly imperceptible.

Mitov was standing outside when the doors slid open. Stoyanov eyed him curiously and walked out to greet him.

"What brings you here?" Mitov asked, extending his hand.

"We need to discuss something urgently," Stoyanov said, looking up and down the long corridor and noticing that an aide was standing a few meters away. "Will you join me in the conference room?" he invited, extending his arm warmly. "The prime minister will be coming shortly."

Mitov looked confused, a state of mind reflected in the moving lines of his forehead. He stared into Stoyanov's small, steely eyes and decided that the venue was not appropriate for a more thorough discussion.

"Get the two deputy secretaries," Mitov said, turning around to face the aide and speaking firmly. "Tell them to join us as soon as they can."

The young man nodded, turned around, and began walking away down the deserted corridor. His footsteps echoed against the cold mosaic.

"Let's go," Mitov said with a forced smile and joined the minister. The two men walked side by side for another twenty meters before reaching a set of thick wooden doors. Each man grabbed one of the handles and pulled a door open. The old black carpet on the other side was visibly depressed near the entrance. The lighting was poor and the walls barren.

The room was windowless and rectangular, a long table with a maximum capacity of twenty people running down the middle. In tune with the predominant style inside the building, the chairs were of thick oak with a padded back and seat. Similar to opening the doors, moving the chairs was a bit of a workout.

Mitov and Stoyanov took positions opposite each other. The minister passed his hand over his thick black hair, collecting rainwater. He reached inside his suit pocket and produced a handkerchief to dry his hand. Mitov observed in silence. His own graying hair was thinning, a development he'd hoped his buzz cut would somewhat obscure.

"What's on your mind?" Mitov asked dryly. "What's going on?"

Stoyanov put his handkerchief away and rubbed his hands together, readjusting his wedding ring.

"I was just in parliament," he began. "Taking part in the parliamentary control." He focused his eyes directly at Mitov. "Seems you and Angelov have been talking."

The tone was not to Mitov's liking. He clenched his jaw and assumed a sterner look.

"He asked to speak to me earlier this week," he clarified, refusing to lower his eyes. "I think it's my duty to speak openly to members of parliament."

"Of course," Stoyanov said diplomatically, trying to hide his sarcasm. "But your position contradicts the stated plans of this ministry and the government as a whole."

Mitov flinched for a second and then leaned forward, calmly placing both hands on the table. "I don't view myself as a politician," he answered. "You know that."

"Da," Stoyanov replied. "I know."

"Then what's the problem?"

"Angelov spoke in parliament earlier today," Stoyanov explained, traces of anger in his voice. "Needless to say, he does not approve of our plans. He says you told him they are foolish and ill-conceived."

"They are," he said with a tone that bordered on condescension. "That is what I told Angelov, and that's what I think."

Stoyanov rubbed his palms together and then thoughtfully scratched his chin.

"You're walking on thin ice here," he began, trying to soften his tone so the words would not sound like a threat. "I assume that the prime minister will tell you as much when he comes."

Mitov cocked his head back and smiled. If this table were not too wide, he would reach across and …

"So be it," he replied coolly, his pale face unmoved as he pretended the thinly veiled attack on his competency did not bother him. "I have been here for a long time, and I know what is going on." *Unlike you.*

"Your principled stance is admirable," Stoyanov said. "But we're going to continue with our plans regardless."

"What does that mean?" Mitov asked, stabbing the question at his opponent. He feared he knew the answer, and it was making him upset.

"We have to let go of another four hundred police personnel by the end of the year," Stoyanov explained. "The reduction will be factored into the budget when we start discussing it this fall."

Mitov leaned back and shook his head, making sure to look Stoyanov directly in the eyes when making the exaggerated motion. He clasped his hands in front of his face for a moment and then returned them to the table.

"That's a mistake," he began, raising his voice and breathing heavily. "It's a mistake," he repeated, making sure Stoyanov saw his flushed cheeks and fiery eyes.

"We have to continue," the minister replied, brushing him off without a hint of hesitation. "Those are our intentions."

"Why?" Mitov asked, his head moving around in search of a solution.

It was time for Stoyanov to show his annoyance.

"Come on!" he said loudly and theatrically. "We can barely pay the ones we have. There is no money in the budget. Have you asked your mother what her pension is?"

"Is that what you are worried about?" Mitov retorted. "You are concerned about politics?" The man clenched his fist in frustration. "Listen to me ..." He leaned forward and pointed to the table. "What do you think happens when you let go of these guys, ah? People with their skills and connections—especially when you're talking about customs agents or officers of a higher rank—aren't just going to go out and apply for a job at the local supermarket."

Stoyanov looked unsure and weak for the first time.

"It's a risk; I know," he replied sheepishly.

"It's more than a risk; we're talking about people's lives here," Mitov said in a righteous tone. "The security of the country is at stake."

One of the doors opened, and the aide walked in, carrying coasters and small bottles of mineral water in his arms. In the heat of the discussion, the men paid him no attention as he began to place the bottles on the nearest edge of the table.

"What do *you* propose?" Stoyanov asked pointedly.

"Don't fire any more people," Mitov replied and leaned in, drawing on the table's surface with one hand. "Particularly those above the level of a parking enforcement officer. Keep them here. Let's remind them of their patriotic duty if we have to."

The minister shook his head. "I'm sorry, but I can't do that," he said.

Mitov slammed his fist on the table, causing a tremendous sound and creating a shock wave that rippled across the wood. The aide fumbled one of the bottles in his hands and dropped it on the table. He pressed his body forward against the edge so that the bottle rolled into his thighs and did not fall to the floor.

Stunned, Stoyanov pushed himself back, raising his hands to calm the general secretary.

"Goddamn!" Mitov yelled and snorted, his breathing heavy. "Listen to me! We've got serious problems, and you're only making things worse." His deep roar reverberated across the room. He chewed on his knuckle and strained to come up with an example. Stoyanov watched with trepidation.

"You know all the companies the state established during communism, to facilitate arms smuggling, steal technology, et cetera?"

The minister nodded. The exploits of the former state security apparatus were legendary, albeit obscured by the thick fog of secrecy.

"Okay," Mitov replied, calming down. "Well, all those channels are being rebuilt. Except this time, they are in private hands. No government, no control, nothing. Organized crime is using the networks we set up. Worse still, our own people, former officers, are pulling the strings."

The minister looked confused.

"How do you know?" he asked.

The ignorance shocked Mitov. *These political appointees, they have no idea what they are doing. Who the fuck made a slick politician head of the interior ministry?*

He paused, forced himself to take a few deep breaths, and continued, "Some of our men are being lured by the criminals." He was encouraged to see Stoyanov paying close attention as he enlightened him. "One of the guys the commandos killed during a drug bust last spring was a former lieutenant from one of the regional police departments. He had also been recruited by the former state security in 1980."

Stoyanov stared back incredulously. He had read the report of the incident, but there had been no mention of that.

"That information was classified," Mitov explained. "The point is," he continued, barely catching his breath, "we are screwed if we let this process continue. If we keep our people in-house, we can control them better. Keep tabs on them. Let the criminals come to us. If we fire a bunch of our staff, we might as well be sending new recruits to the smugglers."

The doors burst open with a thunderous bang. The prime minister walked in, his powerful stride contrasting with the more demure demeanors of the two police deputy secretaries—Mitov's immediate subordinates. Special Forces Commander Veselin Iliev walked in last. The aide closed the doors from the outside.

Stoyanov and Mitov got up.

"Everyone take a seat," the prime minister said tersely, shifting the position of the folder and notepad he held in his hand. "We have some important issues to discuss, and I don't have much time."

Chapter Twenty-Nine

Heavy chairs were noisily pushed back and then forced forward. The men took their seats around the table and waited. The prime minister put his folder and stack of papers on the table and removed a stylish blue pen from his vest pocket. Playing with something was a nervous tick for him, an annoying habit that had only accelerated a few years ago when he finally quit smoking.

"I don't like being here, gentleman," the man announced, leaning forward and looking left, right, and across the table. "Unfortunately, there are some urgent matters that need to be discussed."

Mitov shifted his gaze from Stoyanov to the prime minister to Iliev. The three of them were sitting in that order across the table. Iliev was dressed in dark-green camouflage overalls, indicating he had been rushed over from his unit's training facility with little preparation. He was leaning back smugly, head held up high.

The balance of power was clearly lopsided. The prime minister was decisive and incompetent, a combination of characteristics Mitov did not appreciate. Nonetheless, a decision would soon be made. The three men on the other side did not look like they were there to negotiate. The air felt heavy.

Someone cleared his throat.

"There is a security situation that has been drawing a lot of attention," the premier explained and looked around with heavy eyes. "And that has become a concern to me."

"What exactly do you mean?" Mitov asked.

"We have a rogue commando who has gone berserk," the man said, his pen levitating between his middle and index fingers. "The situation has escalated, and I want it resolved immediately."

"The police are already after the man," Mitov replied, speaking quickly to make sure he was not cut off. "Isn't that the case?"

His eyes studied each of the three men before him in succession.

"There has been a complication," the prime minister replied and reached into the stack of papers, pulling out some cutout and folded newspaper pages. He placed them on the table, twisted them 180 degrees, and slid them in Mitov's direction. He read the headline immediately.

"Commando Kidnaps Star Investigative Reporter," screamed the *Trud* daily. The bold letters were above the fold on the first page, followed by some brief paragraphs that then led to two full pages inside the paper. It was rare for a story to get this much ink.

Mitov took a few seconds to read the first few sentences. There was also a picture of Mira Lyubenova, the kidnapped reporter. She looked familiar; he was pretty sure he had seen her at press conferences.

"You can read the rest of the article later," the prime minister snapped, forcing Mitov to look up.

"It appears this guy has been collaborating with the bad guys and giving them inside information, thus compromising the missions of the special forces and making the interior ministry, and by extension the entire government, look like fools. All of us," he added angrily and pointed at the article with his finger. "Because of one man."

No one said anything. Mitov scratched his chin and looked down at the newspaper.

"How does this reporter fit in?" He looked up again, puzzled. *How do the dots connect?*

"She has been writing these kinds of stories for a long time," Stoyanov answered, looking over to the prime minister to make sure he had permission to speak. "We think she knows something, perhaps something that makes things worse for this guy. He apparently decided to shut her up."

Mitov thought for a few seconds but was not convinced.

"That's one explanation," he said casually.

"Do you have another one?" Iliev asked abruptly, more than a hint of condescension in his voice. He appeared very confident for someone who was not important enough to regularly attend such meetings.

Mitov clenched his jaw and swallowed his pride. Iliev was below him in the chain of command. He would certainly know his place if it were not for the prime minister's protection.

"No," Mitov replied. "I don't."

"We don't have time for this," the prime minister said, flicking his wrist to take a look at his watch. "We have to catch this man as soon as possible." He looked around and raised his finger threateningly. "I can't emphasize this point enough."

There was a moment of silence during which no one dared to speak.

"We are working on it," Stoyanov offered cautiously. "I have alerted all the police departments across the country."

"Has he left the city?"

"We don't know," Stoyanov admitted and immediately realized that comment made him look bad. He decided to continue talking. "He stole a cab and escaped with the reporter. We later found the cab parked in front of the train station."

"So he could be anywhere," the prime minister said, coldly eyeing the minister. "Is that what you are saying?"

"*Da*."

The prime minister exhaled and frowned. Lines wrinkled his worried forehead.

"Okay," he said. "Tell me more about this guy. Who are we dealing with?" He looked around impatiently. "Who has his file?"

"I do," Iliev said and opened the folder he had placed on the table before him. "I thought you might ask so I picked this up before rushing over here."

The captain of the special forces unit licked his fingers and ruffled through the papers, eventually pulling out a single sheet. An old picture of Zhivko was in the top right corner. Iliev cleared his throat and began to read.

"Zhivko Mladenov was born on September 6, 1965, in the town of Shipka. His mother died a few months afterward. The birth documents say his father is unknown, but we believe he was a local alcoholic who died a few years later. Anyway, he ended up in an orphanage."

Iliev paused and then continued, "He was apparently transferred to another orphanage due to abuse. Things were apparently no better at the second orphanage, because the file indicates he had disciplinary troubles. At eighteen, he was released into the real world and began his mandatory two-year service. He was trained as a sniper and excelled at hand-to-hand combat. He applied for the special forces as soon as his military engagement ended."

"Did he have difficulty getting in?"

The captain emphatically shook his head. "No."

The authority of the answer piqued the premier's curiosity.

"Was he good?" he asked.

"Among the best," Iliev replied, taking a second to think.

"The best!" Mitov clarified forcefully. All eyes immediately shifted toward him, and an awkward, tense silence followed. He repeated the assertion once more. The prime minister stopped playing with his pen and put it down.

"How do you know?" Stoyanov asked.

"I trained him." The jaw tightened into a confident pose, the lips barely moving to enunciate the words. "I made him into what he is today."

"You were his instructor?" the prime minister asked.

"I was with the special forces until the eighties when I briefly became an instructor and handled the new recruits," Mitov explained. "After that, I had various desk jobs in the ministry."

Stoyanov readjusted his glasses.

"Does that mean you have a personal connection to Mladenov?" It was more an accusation of bias than a question.

"That was years ago," Mitov snapped with a frosty glance.

The prime minister had put his hands together in a dome shape and listened with interest. A chair creaked as someone shifted his weight.

"Any known relatives?" he asked.

"None that we know of," Iliev answered, putting the paper down.

"So he could be anywhere …" the prime minister said. "Our best guy is loose, we don't know what he is up to, and there is no one we can contact."

He took his glasses off and placed them on the stack of papers and folders. The others watched in silence as the prime minister rubbed his hands over his eyes and yawned loudly and slowly.

"I won't tolerate this situation," he said, placing his hands down on the table and nervously bouncing his fist. "As of now, apprehending this man is our first priority."

He looked around the table at the faces of the other men.

"Do you understand?" he asked. "I want him caught, and I want him caught immediately. I don't even want to think what can happen if this circus continues any longer or—God forbid—something should happen to the reporter."

The prime minister looked around the table, ascertaining each man's reaction.

"Do you all understand?"

Everyone but Mitov nodded.

"We will not sit with our hands crossed while one man makes a mockery of the ministry and the entire government."

The finger was raised threateningly again. "Release his picture to the public," he instructed, looking at Stoyanov. "We will spare no resource in bringing this man to justice."

"That will hardly solve the problems of the ministry of interior," Mitov boldly interrupted. All eyeballs turned to him.

"Excuse me?" the prime minister asked, indignant but not surprised.

"The problems facing us are profound," Mitov reiterated, holding the prime minister's eyes and scooting forward on his chair. "They don't begin and don't end with Mladenov. That I know for sure."

He paused and contemplated whether to continue. He was a veteran who had nothing to lose. Now was his opportunity to shine, and he wasn't going to miss it.

"I also know your policies are making things worse."

"I have been told you don't approve," the prime minister said, eyes fixed on Mitov. "You even said so …" He shook his head to one side. "… to the opposition."

"I was asked for my opinion and gave it," Mitov explained calmly.

"You are part of this government, no?" the prime minister asked with an ominous tone. Mitov could see he had become more jaded than he had been when he took office, likely the result of being increasingly unpopular and frequently hounded by the media. His restless fingers clicked the pen on and off with lightning speed.

"I was appointed by the previous one," Mitov clarified. "But I view myself more as a professional, not a political figure." He knowingly looked at Stoyanov.

"That's honorable," the premier said. "It really is. That's how I viewed you as well, until recently." The tension was palpable.

"Everyone in this room knows what my priorities are," Mitov explained. "They have always been the same."

"But right now they are not aligned with ours," the prime minister retorted. "And that's a problem."

"Only for you, sir," Mitov pointed out, refusing to retreat.

"For you as well, General Secretary," the prime minister replied icily. "I don't want you leading this operation."

The words were spoken softly and with clarity. The head of the government was looking directly at him without blinking. "I feel that Iliev and your two deputies are more than capable of taking care of this matter."

"Iliev reports to me, sir."

"Not on this mission."

Mitov did not flinch, unwilling to give ground and look weak in the face of his public humiliation. Iliev raised his chin and did nothing except to nod his head gently.

"Why have you made this decision?"

"Because of your recent behavior," the prime minister replied. "I will take other measures if you continue to oppose the government's policies."

"With all due respect, sir," Mitov said, "but you don't have the authority."

"I do," Stoyanov said, looking at Mitov with a quick glance at the prime minister. "Formally, the decision is mine."

Mitov cracked an ugly smile. "Stoyanov," he began mockingly, "why am I not surprised?"

The minister of the interior wanted to say something, but the prime minister cut him off.

"The decision has been made," he said. "I trust you will abide by it."

The anger inside Mitov was building and about to reach a boiling point. Perhaps for the first time in his life, he was outmaneuvered and humiliated, thrown to the wolves and left without options.

The unexpected slamming of the hand caused a loud bang that reverberated down the wooden table and jolted the water bottles, stirring the liquid inside. Mitov heaved like an enraged bull and thrust back forcefully, nearly losing his footing in the process and causing the heavy chair to fall to the ground with a thud. The general secretary stormed out of the room, his receding footsteps echoing loudly across the tiles of the long hallway outside.

Chapter Thirty

The toaster threw the two slices of bread up with a ding while nearby the teakettle whistled. Zhivko turned off the electric stove and picked up the kettle, filling two cups with the near boiling water. He added linden blossoms for flavor. Mira put the two pieces of toast on the table and reached inside the small refrigerator for butter and feta cheese.

Zhivko sat down and crossed his arms in front of him, gently blowing the steam away from the cup of tea. Mira sat down opposite him and smiled.

"You still look a little sleepy," she remarked.

Zhivko laughed and rubbed his eyes. "Maybe."

"Did you sleep well?"

"For the most part," he answered. "And you?"

"Mmmm," the woman responded with a telling grin. "Very."

Zhivko caught her eye and offered a charming closed-mouth smile. Mira's hair, still a little wet from the morning shower, fell loosely over her shoulders, moistening the top of her plain shirt. He spread butter across the bread and let it rest for a few seconds to ensure it would melt before adding a thin slice of cheese and taking a bite. The mixture crunched deliciously in his mouth. He swallowed and washed it down with a sip of tea.

"What are we going to do today?" he asked, looking up at Mira.

She put down her cup of tea. "At some point, I have to call the office and tell them that I'm safe," she responded. "I'm sure they're getting worried."

Zhivko took another bite and chewed, using the time to think.

"Don't tell them anything more," he said with a serious look. "It could be dangerous."

"Why?" Mira asked, puzzled.

"Those men are still out there, following us," Zhivko explained. "Following you. There could very well be someone on the inside tipping them off, passing them information about you."

Mira looked thoughtful as she used her finger to free a piece of food from between her teeth.

"You really think so?"

"It's possible."

Mira took another bite and said nothing. She reached inside the plastic bag and picked up two more virgin pieces of bread and popped them in the toaster. The spring compressed with a screech.

The old, handmade wooden clock on the wall showed a quarter past ten. Despite its age, it was very accurate when wound. She looked up and took notice.

"I want to hear the news," Mira said. She walked over to the refrigerator and reached for the cupboard directly above it. She had to stretch in order to fling the door open, careful not to let it bang against the wall. The small, black transistor radio was in front of some random boxes and plastic bags. Mira picked it up and closed the cupboard.

The transistor radio was soon plugged in and emitting an annoying buzzing sound. Mira played with the dial and classical music replaced the static.

"Please turn it up," Zhivko requested. Mira found the appropriate knob and twisted. Then she looked up at the clock again. The distinctive triple beep, beep, beep came on about half a minute later.

"Good morning again, dear listeners," began the authoritative voice. "We're glad that you're with us again." Zhivko poured himself some more tea and stirred. Mira waved with her hand to indicate that she was full.

"We come to you now from the halls of parliament, where our correspondent Boris Ivanov is standing by," the voice said, the background music trailing off. "Boris, what news do you have for us?"

"Good morning," said an energetic, youthful voice. "I am standing here in parliament, where just a few minutes ago, members of the opposition attacked the government for its inability to reign in organized crime and improve the economy."

The reportage transitioned to an audio clip of Opposition Member Angelov's speech.

"Similar fiery rhetoric was heard numerous times today on the floor of parliament," Boris explained.

"The opposition has certainly grown some teeth then, hasn't it?" the voice from the studio commented. "And now, Boris, is there any news on how the government is reacting to the mounting criticism?"

That caught their attention; they looked at each other in silence.

"The government is indeed reacting, and I have some breaking news to report," Boris explained. "Literally a few minutes ago, sources from the Ministry of Interior told us that the police are intensifying their search for a rogue commando who is believed to have been passing along sensitive information to drug traffickers."

Zhivko winced.

"He evaded arrest two days ago, and yesterday, as you heard during our early morning broadcast, he kidnapped a reporter working for one of the major newspapers."

Mira raised her eyebrows. Zhivko was listening with a stern and expressionless face.

"Do the police know where the suspect and the victim are at the moment?" the man from the studio asked.

"They do not," Boris responded. Muffled voices and the shuffling of feet could be heard behind him. "But I can tell you that his picture has just now been released to the public. Officials speaking on the condition of anonymity tell us that his arrest is now of the highest priority, as the government is worried about its plunging poll numbers and perceptions of internal corruption."

"Thank you, Boris," the studio voice said. "We'll check back with you later."

"My pleasure. I'm Boris Ivanov, reporting from parliament."

Zhivko looked down and bit into his knuckles.

"For those of you listeners who don't remember all the details," the man in the studio said, "two days ago in Sofia, the police attempted to arrest a member of an elite special forces unit suspected of working as a mole for smugglers. Large amounts of US dollars and two bags of drugs were found in his apartment. According to the official police statement released yesterday, the drug has been identified as cocaine."

The voice paused, and a jingle began. "Okay, and now let's move to the world of sports."

Zhivko sat with a stunned expression on his face. His breathing was suddenly heavy.

"What's wrong?" Mira asked with concern as she shut off the radio and sat down.

Zhivko hid his face by looking down at his empty plate. The words of the radio announcer grabbed his attention, and a terrifying memory entered his head.

"Because they found cocaine in your apartment?"

He closed his eyes and attempted to push the thought out, but it had already taken root in his conscience.

"Did you know that it was cocaine that they found in my apartment?" he asked with a voice of urgency, looking up and Mira with raised eyebrows and a sense of dread.

"What?" Mira asked, unprepared for the question and the sudden outburst.

"When you were writing the article about me, did you know that it was cocaine they found in my apartment?" He demanded an answer but did not want to hear it.

"Ahhh." Mira scratched her head and forced herself to think. "No," she replied, brushing hair from her eyes. "That information was not released until yesterday. The lab conducted an analysis early in the morning."

Zhivko looked away and shook his head.

Could it be? Could it really be?

"He set me up," Zhivko said slowly, looking at the wall.

Mira looked confused, failing to comprehend what was going on.

"What are you talking about?" she asked. "Who set you up?"

He pensively leaned back in the chair, eyes still unfocused. Zhivko's left hand was on the table while his right was rubbing his lips.

"Hey," Mira said, speaking up. "What are you trying to say?" She reached out to touch his hand, now clenched in a tight fist. Mira watched in amazement, eyes wide. Zhivko's face was flushed and his neck veins enlarged. No one said anything.

"Tell me," Mira implored. "Help me understand."

"My best friend," Zhivko began, grabbing hold of the chair and returning it to its position. "I talked to him the night they tried to arrest me."

"So?"

"He told me ..." Zhivko said excitedly and then forced himself to calm down. "Vassil told me they found cocaine in my apartment."

Mira opened her mouth and nodded. The realization was beginning to come to her.

"If that information was only released the day after," Zhivko explained. "Then how did he know it was cocaine and not some other drug?" He stared at Mira and raised his hands helplessly.

"I can't believe it," he said softly, almost mumbling. "I can't believe it."

The reporter let him come to terms with his emotions before speaking.

"I take it he's a fellow commando; you know him well?"

"We signed up the same year," Zhivko replied and sat down. "We've been close ever since."

"I'm sorry," Mira said, apparently seeing the pain in his eyes.

"That certainly explains a lot," he said finally. "How the drugs and money were hidden inside my apartment without my knowledge."

"I knew there was more to this story," Mira said with relief and a measure of joy.

Suddenly, there was a sound coming from outside that caused both Zhivko and Mira to freeze in their positions. Somewhere not far away, an automobile was moving, tires making the familiar noise as they rode over the asphalt. The sounds got closer.

Zhivko put his finger over his lips, gesturing to Mira to stay quiet. He got up and moved away from the window. There was nothing outside, just the usual view with the driveway and the neglected front lawn.

The sound of tires and an automobile engine were getting louder and nearer.

"Get down," he instructed and pulled Mira off her chair. "Keep your head down so they can't see you from outside."

They were kneeling down next to each other, their shoulders on par with the table.

"And what are you going to do?" Mira asked nervously, looking into Zhivko's eyes. She could see his training was kicking in, his professional instincts taking over.

"I'm going upstairs to get my gun," he responded and made for the door, opening it just wide enough to squeeze his torso through. She heard his swift feet against the rug as he rushed up the stairs. Left alone, Mira was once again scared.

Chapter Thirty-One

Zhivko was in the guest room on the second floor, cautiously peering out from behind the curtains. The gun was firmly in his hand, ready to fire if necessary. A small blue Skoda was pulling up in front of the entrance. Zhivko strained to see who the driver was, but his vantage point did not allow him that type of view. The person was obviously looking for this house specifically because the car veered into the dirt beside the road, brushed up against the shrubs, and stopped.

The driver's door opened a crack. Zhivko heard the sounds of rushed footsteps from the first floor as Mira apparently swung open the kitchen door and proceeded to unlock the front door of the house, the bolts turning with a series of clicks.

"Martina!" Mira yelled, waving and looking around for her shoes, unwilling to step out in her slippers. "What are you doing here?"

A young woman opened the car door cautiously and got out. A slight breeze tossed her curly hair as she looked around and yawned, slapping her face with her palms as the cool morning air gave her a much-needed boost of energy. She walked around the car and approached the entrance. Zhivko put the gun away and descended the stairs.

"Hold on," Mira instructed. By this time, she had put on her sneakers, shoelaces untied, and walked across the pavement. She reached the gate and slid the bolt open.

"I'm glad to see you!" Mira gushed and gave the groggy woman a hug while Zhivko watched from the foyer. Martina barely reciprocated, her eyelids struggling to stay up.

"Aha," she mumbled, relieved. "Good to see you too."

Mira stepped back and took a good look at the young woman. She noticed the ripped pantyhose and the numerous splotches of dried mud, and the injury to Martina's wrist, and her face expressed a look of concern.

"It's a long story," Martina replied, her eyes red and bloated. "Let me come in and I will tell you." She took a few steps forward and looked inside the foyer, seeing Zhivko for the first time as he stood by the door. Martina stopped and turned to Mira, mouth agape.

"Oh my!" she said, slowly turning her head back and forth. "Is that him?"

"Come inside and I will explain," Mira assured her.

"And hurry up," Zhivko said sternly, turning left and right to look up and down the road. "There is no need for unnecessary risks."

"Ouch!" Martina complained after stepping uncomfortably on a small rock. She looked down at her feet in surprise. "Why is there gravel all over the place?" she asked bewildered, kicking some of the rocks aside.

Zhivko frowned and stepped aside to let Martina come in. She walked in and stopped just beyond the doorstep, her eyes directly on Zhivko. She looked him up and down, head to foot, and nodded hello. They stared at each other for a second, and Zhivko noticed her thin eyebrows and slim nose, the eyes slightly almond-shaped. She had two large pimples, one on her forehead and the other on the cheek. The eyes betrayed fatigue and a serious lack of sleep.

He watched as Martina sat down and untied her shoes, kicking them off and then extending her legs and stretching her toes. Pieces of dirt broke off and scattered across the clean floor.

"Come into the living room," Mira invited. "Zhivko will get you a glass of water." She glanced at him and turned away. He took one last quick look out the door and closed it, making sure to lock it. In the kitchen, he grabbed a large plastic cup from one of the cupboards and filled it with mineral water.

"Thanks," Martina said as she took it from his hand and raised it to her pale-pink lips, progressively lifting the cup until she had swallowed almost everything.

"Ahh," she exclaimed and put the cup down on the table. "Now, that's more like it."

Mira sat down on the adjacent couch while Zhivko preferred a seat opposite the newcomer.

"Are you the special forces guy with the drugs in your apartment?" Martina asked, looking across the table at Zhivko. His emotionless face was fresh and cleanly shaven.

"Yes," he replied. "That's me."

Martina weaved her hand through her hair and said nothing, forcing herself to stay awake as her head briefly slumped to one side. She raised her finger and pointed it back and forth.

"They say you were kidnapped," Martina said, looking at her colleague. "Though I would say the situation looks a little different." A tired half-smile played on her face.

"Who says that?" Zhivko asked.

"It's in the newspaper," Martina replied.

"Which paper?" Mira asked.

"Our paper," Martina replied, a little annoyed to be saying the obvious. "It's in the car. I picked it up this morning."

Zhivko and Mira looked at each other knowingly.

"That's not exactly true," she said and glanced at him. "It's a little more complicated."

"Apparently," Martina responded with a giggle.

"How did you find us here?" Mira asked. "I've never given you the exact address, and it's not easy to find this house."

Martina yawned and spoke up.

"You've told me your parents have a villa in the small village of Grivitsa, where your grandfather was born," she began explaining. "I know you came here with your fiancé—" Martina immediately corrected herself. "*Ex fiancé*, when you wanted to escape from the city. House number twenty-one, not far from the only school? I remember."

She picked up the cup and drank the remainder of the mineral water.

"Anyway, I spent half an hour driving around these little streets here."

Martina reclined into the soft sofa seat and closed her eyes, acutely aware her head was throbbing painfully. She forced herself to focus.

"I read the newspaper a few hours ago," she continued. "Something struck me as odd when I read it," she said and scratched her nose. "It just did not make sense that someone would kidnap you in the middle of the city. I figured something must have happened that forced you to hide, or at least escape. The article says you are not answering your home phone, so I decided I might as well look for you here."

Zhivko and Mira were listening intently.

"I've been driving since sunrise," Martina explained. "There is something urgent that I have to tell you."

Martina proceeded to tell them everything in great detail, from the time last night when she stopped across from the disco to her arrival in the village just outside Pleven. She spoke uninterrupted for almost ten minutes, answering their questions as best she could despite being exhausted.

"You heard them talking?" Zhivko asked impatiently as Martina neared the end of her tale. "What did they say?"

The young reporter looked at them and spoke up, careful to enunciate.

"They want to kill you," she told them matter-of-factly. "Both of you."

The backyard was beautiful in a wild nature sort of way. The square concrete tiles leading toward a table positioned underneath a large linden tree were overgrown with weeds and grass, their outlines barely visible. The linden tree was massive, its heavy branches filtering most of the incoming sunlight. The table was in the shade below, its surface overrun with leaves, twigs, linden, and a splatter of bird feces. Sparrows flew about, their sharp movements contrasting against the placid background.

Zhivko's hands gripped the railing of the second-floor balcony as he observed the scene, deep in thought. He didn't react when he heard Mira coming up behind him. She appeared next to him and slid her hand across his back.

She moved to his shoulder and then to his upper arm, feeling the flexed muscle. He turned around to look at her and said nothing. A bird chirped somewhere in the yard. Martina had just fallen asleep in the guest room, the fluffy smooth sheets like a soothing balm on her exhausted body.

Mira gripped Zhivko's arm and moved in closer to rest her head on his shoulder.

"I believe you," she said softly, looking up into his eyes. "I know you didn't do it."

His facial features relaxed. She looked so pretty he wanted to hug her.

"How do we get out of this mess?" she asked him. "How can we prove that you are innocent?"

Zhivko took a moment to think.

"I have a plan," he said finally, catching Mira's hopeful eyes. "We can't go on running and hiding like this. I have to turn around and face the people responsible. We also have to get the information Martina has to Mitov; he's the only person I can trust."

He paused to study Mira's face.

"Can I count on you to help me?"

"Of course," Mira said. "We're in this together."

Chapter Thirty-Two

Dobrev was breathing easier now, relaxed and confident. Svilengrad was already behind him, its low-level buildings no longer visible in his rearview mirror. The E 80 Trans-European Motorway cut through the Thracian Valley, the flat southeastern part of the country where Bulgaria met Turkey and Greece. The road was narrow, two lanes each way with a thin metal divider between them. To the left and right, the landscape was flat, a mixture of yellow and green fields that extended as far as the eye could see. On the southwestern horizon were the Rhodope Mountains, their outline rising sharply into the sky.

The sky itself was partly overcast, a patchwork of gray clouds against the traditional blue and white. Dobrev reasoned it must be raining somewhere up ahead as he took yet another puff from his cheap cigarettes. The warm air outside whistled past the partially opened window, the breeze blowing against the side of his face. He checked his wristwatch. It was a quarter after one in the afternoon.

Just on time. Right on schedule.

He congratulated himself and smiled. Forewarned about the police checkpoint upon entering into Svilengrad, the truck had preemptively slowed down to avoid unnecessary attention. Nothing to worry about now. He was driving just below the speed limit in the right lane, letting the faster drivers pass him while he gently kept his hands on the steering wheel. He reached over and began playing with the radio, turning the knob until it finally landed on a Bulgarian station blasting pop folk music. Dobrev turned it up and cracked open the window on the other side, creating a powerful draft.

Twenty minutes later, traffic slowed down. Dobrev looked ahead concerned and saw the red brake lights flashing. He cursed silently and shifted to a lower gear. The left lane was merging into the right lane, which was being diverted onto a side road. Signs placed along the motorway indicated there was construction and directed drivers to take a detour. There was a traffic police car at the intersection, one officer waving the column of vehicles through single-file while the other had a radar gun trained on them for good measure.

Dobrev slowed down and followed the instructions, veering off onto a small road that ran parallel to the motorway. The asphalt here was older and rougher, the harsh unevenness causing a louder sound as the tires crunched over it. Two lanes, one each way, trees lining both sides.

The vehicles were moving at fifty kilometers per hour now, an uncomfortably slow speed that unnerved many of the drivers. Some broke the traffic laws and attempted to pass the person in front by accelerating into the opposite lane and returning seconds before the onrushing traffic. It was a risky maneuver, which made the drivers heading in the opposite direction pump their horns in anger.

Dobrev was tempted but knew better. He accepted the inconvenience and proceeded.

Ten kilometers down the road, a new Opel was speeding at ninety kilometers an hour.

"Yeah!" the driver yelled, his hands shaking the steering wheel as his foot pressed down on the accelerator. He had shiny new sunglasses and gel in his hair, a silly juvenile attempt to look cool.

"Whoo!" the teenager screamed again in exhilaration, looking to his girlfriend for approval. The girl smiled and brushed her auburn-brown hair away from her face. The window on her side was down all the way, the air swooshing in violently. The Opel was a gift from the boy's father. He could not be more thrilled.

It had been smooth cruising until then, the car occasionally flying at more than one hundred kilometers an hour and deftly hugging every turn. The new Opel approached the vehicle in front, a vastly inferior former Eastern Bloc car traveling at just above the speed limit. Milen pressed on the pedal and moved closer, tailgating the car while tapping on the horn.

"Come on!" he yelled, the adrenaline pulsing through his veins. "Come on!"

The headlights flashed on and off but to no effect. The driver in front was not interested in scooting to the right so the Opel could zip around him with ease. Instead, the man casually observed the nuisance in the rearview mirror and shook his head.

This angered him even more. Not only was the car in front an old-school sedan, which probably belonged to some rural farmer, a class of people he and his family did not like much, but he was being uncooperative as well. The oncoming traffic was unusually busy for this quiet road, the distance between the vehicles rarely large enough for him to attempt a complete passing maneuver. To do so would be too risky.

He honked once more, but the farmer's car did not react.

"Idiot!" the girlfriend said with mocking laughter, her full lips expressing displeasure. "We're going really slow!"

Milen intended to rectify the complaint. He licked his lips and anxiously looked ahead to his left, hoping to find a gap in the stream of vehicles. He moved the car slightly to the left but was forced to retreat each time, blocked by opposing traffic. His hands grew itchy and sweaty.

They approached a small hill and slowed down, the farmer's car in front struggling to make the climb. It was weighed down by a trunk full of potatoes that caused the back tires to sag unnaturally while the small engine struggled.

That was too much for Milen. He put on the left turn signal and started desperately searching for an opening. They were nearing the trough of the hill when one finally presented itself. He slammed his foot down on the gas and veered left with a jerk of the wheel, overtaking the farmer with ease. The Opel's powerful engine roared as the car gained speed. The mixture of speed and freedom was intoxicating.

They were near the top of the hill when the girlfriend saw the oncoming truck.

"Watch out!" she yelled, face suddenly pale. Her terrified voice rose above the roaring engine and the sound of the wind. Her eyes grew wide with fear as the large truck approached.

Milen froze, unable to react to the unexpected turn of events. He had not seen the truck approaching from the other side of the hill, and now his stomach was sinking and his heart racing relentlessly. He felt nothing but absolute fear.

The girlfriend screamed in horror as the foreboding grill of the truck loomed large and descended upon them. In the final split second before collision, Milen veered sharply to the right.

Dobrev threw his cigarette out the window and burped loudly. His truck was beginning to climb a small hill, and he hoped the detour would be over soon and he would be back on the motorway. He pressed down on the pedal to maintain a consistent speed. The truck was at the top and about to begin its descent when a red car suddenly appeared in its way.

That provoked Dobrev to immediate alertness. His trained eyes analyzed the situation and realized the danger. His foot hovered just above the brake as his right hand slammed into the horn.

There was not enough time. The driver of the red car had space to return to his lane but didn't. Dobrev had a sickening feeling as he hit the brakes hard and turned the steering wheel to the right; the truck ran off the road. The tires skidded, tearing up the gravel and dirt and throwing debris in the air.

The truck lurched violently as part of only the second serious accident Dobrev had experienced in his long career. His cabin was high above the red car, and he had a good view as he watched the driver overcorrect in his attempt to return to his lane. The Opel fishtailed, its rear slamming into the front left of the truck. The sound of crunching metal was awful.

The red car bounced up and twisted in midair, landing on its wheels with a loud thud and the sound of breaking glass. The tires screeched madly and left deep marks on the asphalt. Dobrev brought his truck to a stop and stood still, shocked by what had happened. His hands were still shaking when he breathed a sigh of relief, kissed his fingers, and raised them to touch the Orthodox icon tacked onto the wall near the sun visor.

Milen and his girlfriend screamed at the top of their voices as their car hit the truck, the affected metal crumpling on impact with a loud, tearing bang. They were weightless as the vehicle went airborne, throwing them up into the roof and then slamming them down again. Their bodies whiplashed violently, thrown in different directions like dolls without strings. Glass cracked and shards cut through the air. Their vision blurred; they had lost all sense of time and place. Just as abruptly as it began, the nightmare was over. The car was perpendicular to the road, traffic stopped both ways. A few meters away, the farmer was staring in disbelief.

His heartbeat still elevated, Dobrev opened the cabin door and climbed down. He looked in both directions and saw that the other cars were still, some cautiously approaching the scene. The left side of the grill was smashed, the damage extending to the side. There were deep scratch marks in the area not directly affected by the collision. Dobrev shook his head and did not know what to think.

He walked across to the red Opel, sidestepping the broken glass. One of the rearview mirrors had been tossed aside and was resting underneath the truck. The Opel was crushed from the back door to the trunk. The door had nearly folded in half, the window broken. He feared for the passengers. He worried also that the accident had thrown a wrench in his plans, and there were important people counting on him—people who did not like to be disappointed.

"Are you okay?" he asked, approaching the car and leaning in to look through the window. The teenager in the driver's seat was sitting up, his head reclining on the headrest. He had bitten through his lower lip as a result of hitting his head against the roof and was bleeding, the blood running down his chin and spilling onto his shirt. He looked at his girlfriend and sat motionless, letting the numbing pain subside.

The girl was moaning and holding her right arm. The jerking had burned the seatbelt into the soft skin of her neck and one leg hurt from hitting the dashboard. Shocked and in apparent pain, she looked up at Dobrev.

He was relieved to find out they were not seriously injured. Still, the police would certainly have to be called, then an ambulance, and then a tow truck.

Fuck!

Dobrev looked down at his feet and noticed that gasoline was dripping from the fuel tank and pooling in the cracks of the asphalt.

"Turn off the engine," he called out to the driver. The boy heard the voice, but it did not register. "The engine," Dobrev repeated and worryingly glanced at the widening puddle of gasoline. "Turn it off!"

This time, the teenager heard the command properly and responded. He groaned as he raised himself forward and reached for the key. The humming of the engine stopped.

"How are they?" asked an unfamiliar voice. "Is anyone seriously injured? I'm a doctor."

Dobrev turned around and saw the "farmer." A man of moderate height in his early sixties, he was dressed casually in a cheap jumpsuit and a plain shirt with a ripped right sleeve. The pieces of glass broke as he stepped on them.

"Not too bad," Dobrev responded, surprised at the man's presence. "Thank God."

"Indeed," the other man said and got closer. The girlfriend was still moaning, holding her arm and convulsing in pain. The doctor swung around the car and attempted to open the passenger door.

Dobrev saw an opportunity and took it.

"I'll go call the police," he announced, looking up at the other man, who opened the door and was leaning over the girl.

"Sure," the man replied and turned to the girl. "Shh," he said and pushed her hair back, revealing a cut just above the temple. "Let me see."

Dobrev walked away and climbed into the truck. He brought his trembling hands to his mouth and forced his rattled brain to think. He could not stay here. It was the wrong thing to do, but he had to. The tires kicked up more dirt and gravel as Dobrev brought the truck back on the road and sped away.

Chapter Thirty-Three

Light drizzle fell from the overcast sky and slid down the windows of the car, leading Zhivko to turn on the windshield wipers. It was the type of casual summer rain carefree souls enjoyed. The gentle beating against the glass was soothing. Freshness was in the air.

He closed the window and focused. Driving Martina's car was an adequate disguise, an opportunity to slip back into Sofia unnoticed. The car itself was very clean, the cabin empty and virtually spotless. Before driving off, he had popped the hood to take a look at the engine, finding it in very good condition, with all the liquids in sufficient quantity. The gas tank was nearly two-thirds empty, however, and he intended to stop at a quiet gas station along the way and fill up.

As an extra precaution, Mira had given him an old baseball hat to wear. It was currently messing up his hair. He lifted it up, scratched his scalp, and adjusted it again. Perhaps surprisingly, the ski masks worn by the commandos during operations were more comfortable. Or maybe he was more used to them.

He wondered what his colleagues were doing. Was it business as usual, or were they consumed by the scandal that now threatened to destroy his life? Did they believe the official story? Did they have their own explanations?

Zhivko knew his colleagues well, but he could not come up with definitive answers to these vexing questions. They trained together. They laughed together. In theory, they were supposed to cry together as well, but (knock on wood) thus far, nothing too bad had ever happened. Once they had had the unusual task of helping to protect a soccer derby at which one of the guys had gotten hit by a rock and had to have seven stitches to his lower face. The man was proud of it.

Everyone took their professional duties very seriously. They were a cohesive unit, bonds forged over the years as the men took care of each other and entrusted their lives to their comrades. Even though the commandos were masked and wore identical gear, Zhivko could immediately ascertain the identity of his teammates through subtle telltale signs, such as posture and movement.

That was why being stabbed in the back hurt so much. It was shocking to think that one of his colleagues could do such a thing. Zhivko shook his head in disbelief. He was driving with the radio off, preferring to be alone with his thoughts. It was: 4:09 p.m.

Not just a colleague, but a friend.

Not just a friend, but his best friend.

My best friend!

He could sense the anger rising in him, his nerves fraying and the determination building. After all these years, he was again alone and abandoned.

Well, maybe not entirely. There was Mira. He didn't yet know quite what to make of her. At this moment, she was a godsend, someone who could help him clear his name and restore his reputation. But was she more than that?

Zhivko scratched his chin.

Did he want her to be?

Hmmm.

Perhaps. He had opened up to her and she to him. As sudden and dramatic as their introduction was, they had established a level of trust, and that was a good start. As for last night ...

He smiled.

That was a good time.

A car whizzed by and raised his alertness level. He was driving at just below the speed limit, making sure not to draw attention. The Skoda's headlights were turned on.

But back to Vassil.

What exactly does he know? Why does he know it?

Zhivko searched his brain but could not come up with a suitable answer. Whatever it was, he had legitimate reasons for concern and anger. His best friend had been evasive over the phone. He had refused to help him in his time of need. Zhivko had been there at his wedding; he had visited the hospital the day after their child was born.

As a show of gratitude and loyalty, Vassil had decided to plant drugs in his apartment? Or maybe not? Zhivko did not want to rush to conclusions based on incomplete information.

Still, his best friend was obviously complicit in one way or another, and he had to find out the details. The car was slightly cool, so he zipped up the dark waterproof windbreaker Mira had given him and stared ahead. The narrow regional roads had taken him to the highway, where the driving was faster and more relaxed. There were police patrols here as well, so he would not let down his guard. The loaded gun was on the seat next to him, placed inside a small bag with other essential items.

The drizzle continued to fall softly.

Chapter Thirty-Four

The lunch felt heavy in his stomach as Bogdan walked back to his office. He feared that within an hour, he would have to rush off to the bathroom. The damned cook had made the fries too crispy and the meat too raw. He stopped abruptly and held his hand to his bloated stomach. He let out a cautious burp, breathed a heavy sigh of relief, and moved on.

The lab was actually a number of small rooms strung together, each with a central table for two or three people. Microscopes, test tubes, burners, and other devices were all over the place. Only two of the rooms were actual medical-evidence-examination facilities, the remaining three were for general work, storage, and paperwork. Bogdan walked in and took off his blazer, placing it over a coat hanger in one of the closets.

"Good lunch?" asked Doctor Filipova, a heavyset fifty-something-year-old biologist who acted as the lab's supervisor. She was sitting at her desk, reading through a medical report.

"Not today," Bogdan responded with a frown, pretending not to notice that the sandals were squeezing the woman's feet tightly and causing ugly lines across her flesh. "It was actually kind of gross."

Filipova chuckled. "It happens," she said and added philosophically, "You're young; you'll get over it."

Bogdan smiled dryly and then self-consciously ran his tongue over his teeth, searching for morsels stuck between them.

"I'm going back to work," he announced and headed for the next room.

Bogdan walked through the door and closed it behind him. The next room contained two more desks and another small closet. The third room was mostly a storage facility for the lab's expensive and outdated equipment. It also contained the gear necessary to handle evidence without contaminating it. Bogdan went in and closed the door. He walked over to a large closet and pulled open the doors, revealing three bodysuits. The rusty hinges objected with a nasty and prolonged scratching sound.

Ten minutes later, he was covered from head to foot and ready to work. As a safety precaution, the final two rooms had no windows and were separated from the rest by a heavy door. Bogdan walked in and flipped on the fluorescent lights, which slowly flickered to life. Every surface was painted white and was kept as clean as possible. The forensic scientist stretched his arms, cracked his fingers, and pulled up a stool.

The evidence was in two plastic bags. One contained the stained underwear from an allegedly raped woman, the other her fingernails. She had scratched her assailant, and investigators had cut off her nails as evidence.

The examination, testing of hypothesis, and subsequent analysis was up to him.

Bogdan used his palm to push the small glasses up his bony nose and got to work. When there was no one around, he preferred to violate policy and keep his visor raised; otherwise, his breath sometimes fogged the screen. Filipova would surely yell at him if she found out.

The door suddenly opened with an unexpected click. A startled Bogdan quickly pushed down his face mask and turned around, hoping his indiscretion had not been noticed.

"Da?" he asked, trying to look calm while ascertaining whether the supervisor would ask about the face mask.

"Someone is calling for you," Filipova said with more than a trace of annoyance in her voice. "It's a woman, and she says it's urgent."

Bogdan looked confused. He was not expecting anyone, and his girlfriend always gave her name when calling the lab. "It's urgent?" he asked baffled.

"Apparently," Filipova puffed. "I first told her to go away and hung up on her, but she called again."

A part of him wanted to smile, but he suppressed the impulse.

"Okay," he replied and got up. "I'll see what's going on."

Filipova watched as Bogdan left the lab and took off his gloves and headgear. They walked into the outside room, and she closed the door to the lab.

"Take it from here," she instructed, pointing to a phone on the wall. "You don't have time to take off the suit and come to my office. I'm certainly not going to hold the line open for that long, because I'm expecting a phone call from a detective."

The biologist cleared her throat and eyed him suspiciously.

"Do you understand?"

"Yes," Bogdan answered.

"That's good," Filipova said and flicked off a loose piece of cloth from her sweater. "I will be at my desk waiting for the report." With that, she walked away, her sandals squeaking across the tiles on the floor.

Bogdan listened for the sound of her footsteps to disappear and picked up the phone.

"Hello?" he said shyly, not knowing what to expect.

"Is this Bobo?" a voice belonging to a young woman asked.

"Yes," he answered cautiously. His mind was working furiously to make sense of the situation but still drawing a blank.

"Pay attention," the pleasant feminine voice continued. "This is important."

"Who's calling?" Bogdan interrupted.

"Pay attention!" The mysterious woman was unforgiving. "There is a large shipment of drugs coming in on Saturday," she said. "It's headed for Plovdiv. Look for a black Mercedes."

Bogdan stood silently, holding the phone pressed to his ear as his eyes aimlessly searched throughout the room.

"Okay …"

"Give the information to Mitov."

"What?" The information was coming too quickly, outpacing his ability to comprehend.

"Tell the general secretary," the female voice repeated. "Do you understand?"

"Yes," Bogdan replied, still bemused.

"There is one more thing," the woman continued.

"What?"

There was a brief pause at the other end.

"Zhivko Mladenov is innocent," the soothing voice said curtly. "He was setup by someone on the inside."

The mention of his friend's name piqued Bogdan's curiosity and paused his breathing.

"Hey, wait," he said loudly, readjusting his position to push the phone closer to his mouth. "What do you know about him?" He had barely caught his breath when he fired again. "Where are you calling from?"

Silence.

"*Alo?*"

The woman hung up, and the line went dead. Bogdan stood in disbelief, trying to make sense of the situation. Afraid to forget anything, he reached for a notepad. Something caught his attention as he was writing. He stopped and scratched his neck.

Bobo?

Chapter Thirty-Five

Mitov was sitting behind the large mahogany desk, trying to busy himself with paperwork in a futile attempt to focus his mind elsewhere. He had effectively been sidelined from participating in one of the year's biggest police cases, a humiliating blow to his authority. In his more than thirty years of service, he had never experienced such an outrage, so publicly and in front of so many people.

He unbuttoned the top button of his white shirt and freed his neck. He then loosened his tie, enjoying the newfound freedom. Mitov did not like suits and preferred not to wear them, feeling more comfortable in athletic attire. But he took care of himself and liked to think that at fifty-four he still looked good dressed formally, for his figure and posture had barely degraded since his glory days.

Mitov's back, however, was another matter. He casually rubbed his hand over his lower back, softly massaging the area. *You're getting old, my friend.* The mirror check he conducted each morning was uncompromising: the lines under his eyes were becoming more pronounced, and the gray hairs on his scalp multiplying.

At least I still have hair. He somehow looked younger than he was, despite his stressful lifestyle. He liked to remind his wife she married well.

Mitov leaned back and unbuttoned once more. Things at the ministry were spinning out of control, and the selfish politicians had pushed him away. He was their most experienced and smartest asset!

He grunted, shook his head, and continued writing.

The loud banging on the door startled him, the noise echoing throughout the large office. A thin young man with a pointy nose pushed the door open and stuck his head through the crack. Mitov stared back. The man opened the door wider and stepped in, his black leather shoes carrying water onto the parquet.

The clicking sound of high heels followed and got progressively louder as a woman hurried to the door. She was moving as quickly as her long, tight dress would allow.

"I'm very sorry, sir!" the woman said as soon as she appeared at the door frame. "I told him you were busy, but he insisted and I could not stop him." The dark-haired criminal justice student looked at Mitov with helpless eyes, hoping for leniency.

The young man looked back at her and took an additional two steps into the room.

"I need to talk to you," he said loudly, his voice quivering somewhat. "It's very important."

Mitov put his pen down and got up.

"What's going on?" he asked firmly. "Who are you?"

"I have to tell you something very important," the man repeated. His breathing was elevated, hands jittery as he was unsure whether to keep them down or gesture. "Please don't throw me out."

"Do you want me to call security?" the exasperated secretary asked, her lip gloss noticeable from across the room.

"They let me in," the man explained. "I am with the forensics unit." He reached into his pocket and pulled out his ID. "I have a right to be in the ministry."

He looked defiantly at the woman, who put down the phone in defeat just as she was about to start dialing. He had taken a taxi from the military hospital to the ministry, risking the wrath of his superior, and now this broad was about to make irrelevant his sacrifice.

"You have a right to be in the building but not in my office," Mitov clarified a bit too harshly. "What do you want?"

"It's about Mladenov," the man blurted out, looking directly at Mitov. "I have information you need to know."

The general secretary's ears perked as soon as he heard the name. The nervous young man had just closed his mouth and swallowed hard; he was now anxiously rubbing his fingers together. The secretary was looking back and forth between the two of them.

"You know something about Mladenov?" Mitov asked.

"*Da*," Bogdan replied and then added confidently, "I know a lot."

Mitov came out from around his desk and approached the door.

"It's okay," he said to his secretary. "Let me talk to him. No need to call security."

The woman gave the two of them a confused look and stepped away.

"Sure," she replied awkwardly. "As you wish." She moved back toward her desk.

Mitov closed the door and looked at the intruder. The young man was taller than he was and considerably thinner. His brown hair was heavy in the middle but receding at the temples. The detail was noticed immediately by Mitov, who had unfortunately developed an interest in men's hair.

"Sit down," he said with a forced warm smile, gesturing toward two chairs placed facing each other on a rug island. "Please."

The man complied with the request. Drops of rainwater slid down his head and onto his lap as he bent over. Mitov sat down opposite him and crossed his legs. He leaned back in his chair and eyed him curiously.

"Why don't you begin by telling me who you are," he invited.

"My name is Bogdan Borisov and I'm a forensic scientist at one of the police labs," he said, clearing his throat and gripping the armchair for support. "I'm also a friend of Zhivko's."

Mitov was studying him, putting to work his behavioral training skills. The man before him seemed honest enough.

"Zhivko came to the hospital to see me on Thursday," Bogdan began. "He said he was innocent and that someone had set him up."

The general secretary was listening, his fingers thoughtfully scratching his chin. He had neglected to shave that morning.

"Have you seen him since?" he asked.

"No," Bogdan replied. "But there's more."

Mitov changed his posture.

"What?"

"Someone called me half an hour ago at the lab," he said. "It was a woman." He stopped to think, careful to retell everything accurately.

"She said a shipment of drugs will arrive at Plovdiv on Saturday," he continued. "She wanted me to tell you. Also mentioned something about a black Mercedes."

Mitov's mind was racing. "Did she tell you her name?"

Bogdan shook his head. "No, she didn't. Before she hung up she also told me that Mladenov is innocent and has been set up from the inside."

Mitov looked down, took a deep breath, and looked up. "From the inside?" he asked.

"Yes."

Mitov leaned forward and cupped his hands over his face in a prayer-like fashion. His necktie swayed freely in the air.

Bogdan felt awkward and shifted in his seat. He looked around the room, noticing that the window looked out into a small park; he watched a squirrel deftly balancing on the nearest tree branch. A large map of the country was nailed onto the wall next to the armchairs. Pictures and awards decorated the walls. A large flag stood proudly in the corner.

"Did this woman identify herself?" Mitov asked after a period of deep thought.

"No," Bogdan replied.

Mitov looked down again.

"But I'm pretty sure that Zhivko made her call me."

A puzzled Mitov looked up.

"Why do you think that?"

"She called me *Bobo*," he answered with a blush of embarrassment. "It's my nickname."

"So?"

Bogdan looked straight into his eyes.

"Zhivko is the only one who calls me that," he said unequivocally, his voice firm. "Him and no one else."

Mitov knew immediately what the man was saying. A smile was beginning to form at the corners of his mouth.

"He is trying to send us a message."

Chapter Thirty-Six

The white truck cautiously made its way through traffic, Dobrev consciously staying true to one lane even though he could have moved to the adjacent one and saved time. He decided to play it extra safe and minimize the chances of another accident. The damage to the truck was minimal, and he doubted it would attract the attention of traffic police, but he did not want to take an unnecessary risk. Besides, it was possible he had been reported as fleeing the scene of an accident. If so, the police would probably catch up with him sooner or later.

Fuck!

He angrily gripped the steering wheel and forced himself to calm down and stay focused. He was almost there, just a little more to go. As long as he safely delivered his special cargo and got paid, all would be well. Even if the police did catch up with him afterward, he would pay a fine and that would be it. His driving record was nearly spotless, and he had no prior convictions. He was confident he could find a way to explain the mishap because after all, it was the stupid kid's fault anyway.

Dobrev drew from the cigarette and exhaled a thick cloud of smoke.

Just make sure you don't get caught before tomorrow morning.

He looked around and checked all the mirrors for the thousandth time. The game he was playing was dangerous, he knew that, but the reward was sizeable—particularly if he gained the trust of some important people and they called on him again.

Dobrev stopped at a light. His sweatshirt was getting sweaty around the arms and neck. It must be nervous sweat. The drizzle outside was accelerating; the tires and sides of the truck were sprinkled with dirty water from the passing vehicles. Dobrev turned the knob and closed the window almost all the way up, for errant rainwater was starting to sprinkle onto the side of his head.

The antique Roman theater stood proudly in the center of the city, its white columns rising above the hills and against the dark-blue sky. Dobrev admired it every time he saw it. He had even enjoyed a concert there a few years ago. It was a beautiful facility, remarkably preserved over more than two millennia.

The line of cars inched forward as the light turned green. Dobrev maneuvered cautiously through the busy streets, always staying below the speed limit and careful to change lanes only when absolutely necessary. The cabin filled up with smoke from the cigarette. It would take him another twenty minutes to get to his destination.

The paid garage was on the outskirts of the city, near the highway linking it with Sofia. The garage catered to drivers of trucks and buses who needed a place to park their vehicles when on the road. It also served as a makeshift depot, companies keeping their fleet there during down times and drivers leaving their personal vehicles for safe storage.

Dobrev drove up the embankment and proceeded toward the front gate. The security guard's booth was on the right, meaning the man would not be able to see the dent on the left side of the truck. That was for the better. Dobrev stopped and rolled down the window.

The man on the other side was thin and in his thirties. He was standing outside the booth, which looked like a small shack with a mushroom-shaped roof. The man wore gray overalls and a sweater.

"How much for the night?" Dobrev yelled through the open window. "I will leave tomorrow around noon."

The guard took a quick look at the size of the truck.

"Twenty," he shouted back. "Payment is up front."

"Okay." Dobrev killed the engine and climbed down. In the meantime, the guard went inside the booth. The room was small and full of rolled-up newspapers. A large beat-up notebook served as the entry log. A small safe was under the desk.

Dobrev walked around the truck and approached the window. He took out the money and folded it in his palm. The guard raised a finger, indicating he should wait. He flipped open the notebook to the appropriate page and began writing.

"Move aside, please," the man instructed.

Dobrev did as told. The guard raised himself off the seat and looked at the truck, memorizing its license plate. He jotted it down in the notebook.

"Sign here," he said and turned the notebook around, sliding it through the slit in the glass window.

Dobrev picked up the pen and squeezed his signature into the small area next to his entry. He pushed the notebook and pen back and handed over the cash.

"Thank you," the guard said with a polite smile. He would follow procedure and put the money in the safe. "I think there should be space in the far corner," he added. "Have a nice stay."

Dobrev nodded. He had been assured that a different guy would be on the shift the next morning. That man had been told to look the other way so that someone important with a really nice car could get in without any problems.

Dobrev walked back to the truck and climbed into the cabin. The barrier was raised, and he drove through into the large rectangular yard. To one side, he saw two mechanics looking into the opened engine of a bus, lines of concern etched on their faces. Dobrev drove toward the far corner and found a nice spot conveniently located between two long rigs. Both were parked with their fronts facing the inside of the yard.

He made sure to pull in with the front first, hiding from view the damage done to the truck during the crash. Dobrev brought the vehicle to a stop as close to the perimeter fence as he could. Beyond it were grassy hills and some trees.

Dobrev temporarily sat motionless, enjoying the silence. His mission was nearly over. Tomorrow morning he would hand over the goods and receive payment for his brave work. He was tempted to smile but didn't. That could wait until he was counting the money. Would payment be in dollars or Deutsche marks? He pondered the relevance of the question and the relative merits of the two currencies.

Dobrev made sure both windows were closed and the passenger door locked. He opened his door and got out, locking it and checking twice to make sure. The space between his truck and the next one was narrow, just wide enough for a man's shoulders to come through without brushing against either side.

Because his truck was shorter than the adjacent two vehicles, the rear was not on the same level but almost a meter deeper in. That was even better. Dobrev was beginning to think he was quite fortunate. He planned to get a bite to eat at the restaurant, take a shower, and then return to his truck cabin for some relaxation and later—sleep.

Chapter Thirty-Seven

Mitov stood in front of the window and looked out, hands deep into his pockets and his worried mind preoccupied by recent developments. It had stopped raining now; the wet green leaves of the trees shone brightly. It was a beautiful sight and a shame he could not appreciate it fully.

He scratched his brow and continued thinking. Zhivko was obviously trying to send him a message through the forensic scientist. *But why? Who was the woman that called?*

The newspaper claimed Zhivko had kidnapped the investigative reporter and then stolen a cab as his getaway vehicle. The two of them had not been seen since. Mitov surveyed the scenery out the window and thought some more.

That does not make sense.

If Zhivko wanted to kidnap her, he certainly would not do it in the center of the city, in such a crude fashion. *Could something or someone have forced his hand?*

That seemed more likely. *But who?* There were no real answers, and these dead ends were troublesome. He thrust his hands into his pockets and gazed out the window thoughtfully.

Mitov stood still as his mind moved on. The door to his office was closed, and he had instructed the secretary to send away all visitors and hold all but the exceptionally important phone calls. The cancer of corruption had apparently spread throughout the ministry, and he did not know whom to trust. He was trying to figure this out on his own.

Bogdan said it was a woman who had called, and she had information that only someone who had talked to Zhivko would have. If she was calling on his behalf, she must trust him. She must be on his side. It had to have been that investigative reporter who had gone missing.

Mitov mustered a smile. The knot was beginning to come loose. The woman had confirmed his suspicion that something was amiss with the sudden charge that Zhivko was colluding with drug smugglers. It just didn't make sense.

My boy would not do that.

But who was responsible? *Someone from the inside.* That much was already obvious, but finding the guilty party in a short period of time would be difficult. Mitov could not take the information to his superior—the minister of interior—because the evidence was inconclusive and the source unconvincing. Besides, Mitov had been pushed aside and the political situation was not in his favor.

He could appeal to Iliev and tell him that Zhivko was reaching out. He shook his head. *That won't help either.* The course of action had been charted by the prime minister, and everyone was following orders and trying to execute his tasks. Right now, his opinion did not matter at all.

Mitov cringed and tightened his jaw.

A shipment of smuggled goods would arrive tomorrow in Plovdiv. That was an actionable piece of information. *Who was behind it? Was it the same person who had set up Zhivko? And who on the inside was assisting?*

So many questions, so little time. Not only would he have to conduct the investigation all by himself, but he would have to do it without drawing attention. No one could be trusted. But he was still the general secretary, at least for the time being. There were things he could do that did not involve the political leadership.

Mitov walked away from his window and sat behind the desk, flopping down with a heavy thud that strained the legs of the chair. He pulled open one of the drawers, retrieved the directory, and flipped rapidly through its pages.

The phone rang twice before the other side picked up.

"*Alo?*"

"This is general secretary Mitov calling," he announced in a businesslike tone. "I need to speak with the chief of the border crossing point."

There was a pause at the other end.

"Ah, one second, sir," the man replied. "Let me get him."

Mitov drummed his fingers on the desk in anticipation.

"This is Pavlov speaking," said an older man's voice. "How can I help you?"

"This is Mitov calling," he said. "I need to speak with you about a certain truck that has passed through the border."

Pavlov chuckled.

"Sir ..." he began. "Kapitan Andreevo is one of the busiest border crossings in Europe," the lieutenant continued. "We always have a steady stream of trucks coming in from Turkey. You are going to have to be more specific."

Mitov chided himself for losing sight of the obvious.

"That's true," he said. "You're absolutely right." He pulled out a notepad and a pen.

"Tell me," the general secretary inquired, clicking on the pen. "Has anything suspicious happened in the past twenty-four hours?"

"Define suspicious, sir."

Mitov scratched his chin.

"Has anyone been detained, acted nervously, been uncooperative?"

"Not recently, no." Pavlov answered.

"Has anyone done anything to arouse suspicion?"

"Not to my knowledge, sir," replied Pavlov. "It's been basically business as usual."

There was a pause, during which the lieutenant became emboldened.

"Why, sir?" he asked. "What's going on?"

Mitov did not answer right away.

"I'm trying to find out something," he began explaining. "It's very important and very hush-hush. Do you understand?"

"Da."

"Good," Mitov acknowledged. "Should anything out of the ordinary happen, I want you to call me right away. I'll give you my direct mobile number."

The ministry had recently purchased mobile phones for its high-level officials, a new technology Mitov was not too familiar with and preferred not to use. Besides, with mobile phone penetration still quite low, there weren't many people to call. He reached inside the top drawer and picked up his mobile phone. To facilitate memorization, he had stored his own phone number in the notebook.

"You ready?"

"Yes."

Mitov dictated the number to Pavlov, who diligently wrote it down.

"Thank you, sir. I got it." He said. "I will keep you posted."

"Please do."

Mitov put the phone down and hung up. He pressed both hands together and leaned back, deep in thought. He desperately needed to locate the truck and intercept the illicit shipment. That was the string he needed to pull in order to untie the knot.

He got up and walked over to the wall with the large map of Bulgaria. It was approximately three meters long and two meters wide, allowing for a profound level of detail. Mitov ran his finger along the line indicating the border between Turkey and Bulgaria. His hand stopped at Svilengrad.

Mitov found the main road and slowly began tracing the truck's probable path as it made its way to Plovdiv, in the southern part of the country. The journey would take it through three of the internal ministry's regional directorates—offices headquartered in the cities of Kurdzhali, Haskovo, and Plovdiv. Those were the police departments he would have to call to find out more information. Surely, somewhere someone from the traffic police saw something.

He returned to his desk feeling invigorated and again reached for the directory. He wrote down the names and phone numbers of each regional director and armed himself with patience.

Mitov pressed the phone to his ear and dialed the first number on the list.

"Regional directorate Kurdzhali," said a friendly female voice. "How can I help you?"

"This is Andrei Mitov calling," he introduced himself. "I urgently need to speak to the director."

"Okay," the woman replied. "Right away."

She put him on hold while annoying music played in the background.

"Alo?" began a rough male voice. "What can I do for you, General Secretary?"

"I need your cooperation, and I need to ask you some questions," Mitov explained.

"Okay," the man said, his voice trailing off to reveal confusion. "Go ahead."

"Have the traffic police reported anything suspicious in the past twenty-four hours?"

"What exactly do you mean?"

"Have your officers reported anything, such as stopping a trucker who is uncooperative or a hit-and-run accident or something else out of the ordinary?"

The man on the other end did not answer right away.

"Well, I don't think so," the regional director said. "I have not heard of anything like that, no. But the day is young and most of the traffic police officers are out in the field, so only a few reports have come in."

"Do you read the reports yourself?" Mitov asked pointedly.

"Not unless I have to," the man responded.

"Well, now you have to," Mitov instructed sternly. "This is very important, and I'm asking you to work overtime. Something big has either happened or is about to happen between now and Saturday. I want you to read all the traffic reports and instruct your men to report directly to you should there be anything suspicious."

Mitov did not want to wait for a response.

"Is that understood?" he asked.

"Yes," the regional director grudgingly replied.

"Thank you," Mitov responded. "I will give you my mobile number and expect to be called immediately should there be any news."

"Of course."

"Good."

Mitov put a checkmark by the regional director's name and moved down the list. Twenty minutes later, the necessary phone calls were made and the regional directors alerted. Now he would wait. In the meantime, he would call his wife and tell her she would be eating dinner by herself.

Again.

The demands of the job were a strain on his marriage, despite his best efforts to be a loving husband. Sometimes, he wondered why his wife had put up with him for so long. Without her love and support, his public service would have permanently crippled him.

He got up and walked over to the window. Afternoon rays of sunlight were breaking through the trees while pigeons were lazily perched outside some of the building's windows. A child's laughter could be heard, probably from the nearby playground.

Mitov remembered vividly the first time he had met the young man from Shipka. He was polite but distant, unwilling to trust and get close. His answers were frequently either evasive or very general. A self-defense mechanism, perhaps. A rough exterior protecting something fragile.

"So, you want to join?" Mitov asked with deliberate informality, trying to set a casual tone.

The young man wiped his runny nose with an exaggerated swipe of his hand, pulled back to look at the shiny trail of residue, and dried it against his uniform.

He nodded.

"Why?"

The young man looked down, began opening his mouth as if to say something, and then closed it. Repeat. His eyes moved around the room.

"It is what I want to do," he said finally, looking into Mitov's eyes. "I'll try hard, and I think I can make a difference."

Mitov unlocked his briefcase and placed some papers on the desk. He reached for a bottle of water and twisted the cap.

"Want a drink?" he asked. The room was small and cramped, forcing the young man to sit so close Mitov literally could have reached across the desk and given him the bottle.

He shook his head no.

Mitov took a gulp.

"What makes you think you'll be good at this?"

"You've seen my results," the man replied coolly, barely moving his lips and immediately returning to the previous expressionless face.

"Indeed," Mitov said with a brisk laugh as he flipped through some papers. "Impressive." He looked up at the recruit. "I have not seen a sniper this good in years. Apparently, you fight well too."

The young man nodded.

"Why don't you want to be a sniper in the military?" he asked teasingly. "The pay is not bad, good benefits."

This time, there was no hesitation.

"I don't want to shoot targets all day, sir," the young man said. "I want a life where I matter."

The eyes showed a determination that came from deep inside. The face looked mean and tense, the crew cut giving it an air of intimidation. Mitov studied him for a few seconds before speaking.

"That's good," he replied and raised his eyebrows. "That's good." Mitov closed the folder and took another swallow of water.

"It is not going to be easy," he warned. "Do you think you can handle the training?"

He could. First in and last out, every single day. Over time, Mitov molded his aggression into discipline, his passion into focus and poise. The troubled kid grew up into a man under his watch.

Mitov exhaled heavily and looked out the window. Zhivko was somewhere out there, fighting for his innocence.

Chapter Thirty-Eight

Zhivko parked the Skoda in a sleepy residential neighborhood and unbuckled his seat belt. He looked around, surveying the landscape. He was surrounded by high-rise concrete residential buildings, all recently built and similar in style. The trees planted in the areas between them were still young, their trunks thin and branches soft. The area was quiet, other than an old man throwing away the trash in a large receptacle.

He unlocked the door and got out. He made his way through the neighborhood with quick steps, avoiding the streets and sticking to the narrow paths between buildings. He kept his head down and eyes focused. There was a teenage girl walking her dog and a woman returning home with groceries in both arms, but neither paid him any attention.

Most of southeast Sofia had been constructed in the late 1980s, so it still looked somewhat deserted and underdeveloped. Zhivko continued walking south, zigzagging across the neighborhood and eventually leaving behind the residential buildings. Immediately in front of him, about half a kilometer away, was the training academy for police officers and firemen. It was a large complex, secluded in the woods and protected by a black fence along the perimeter. A two-lane road led to a gate at the front entrance and beyond it, branched off at the various buildings.

To one side was one large, unfinished building, its skeletal outline rising at least ten stories. Random construction materials lay at its base, steel beams, wooden planks and nails littered across the ground. Construction of the ghostly building had been abandoned years ago as funding dried up. The area surrounding it was now overgrown with weeds, shrubs, and wild vegetation.

A sudden gust of wind hit Zhivko, sending dust across his lower legs. He was walking up the road now, sticking to the farther edge of the sidewalk. The gate was about two hundred meters away. He approached cautiously and slowed down.

It was 7:15 p.m., and the summer sun was low in the colorful sky, outlining the western edge of the mountain. Zhivko expected his best friend would soon finish his workout and go home. From where he was standing near a roadside tree, he could see his car. It was a used Hyundai, repainted to look shiny and new. Vassil was a bit of a car buff and used to spend hours a day in the garage before he met his wife.

Zhivko looked up and down the street, assuring himself that no cars were coming. He was confident Vassil would appear soon. He wanted to confront him, to look in his eyes and ask why he had framed him.

My best friend.

He swallowed the pain and stayed alert. Within a few minutes, Vassil walked out through the gate. He had a large duffel bag in one hand and walked confidently with quick strides. His outfit consisted of worn-out jeans and a light-colored short-sleeved shirt, a thin silver bracelet shining on the right wrist. Vassil walked over to his car, which was on the edge of the small parking lot, and put down the duffel bag.

Zhivko left his position and approached his friend, head intentionally kept down. Vassil put his key in the trunk and popped it open to throw the bag inside. Movement suddenly caught his eye, and he turned around.

Zhivko was standing no more than a meter away from his friend, an intense look in his eyes.

"Dear God!" Vassil said, taken aback. "I did not expect to see you."

"You've had the same routine for months," Zhivko responded coolly, studying the mixture of reactions displayed on his friend's face. "It's not difficult to find you." He looked around nervously, but there was no one. The raised trunk of the car shielded them from the guard station near the checkpoint at the entrance.

"Are you okay?" Vassil asked with genuine concern.

"So far," Zhivko answered. "I've been on the run for two days." He saw his friend look down in embarrassment and decided to press his point. "How could you do it?" Zhivko asked, raising his voice as the words escaped through his teeth with a hiss. "How could you!"

A brief gust of wind tossed Vassil's moppy brown hair, which was still moist from the shower he had taken after working out. The man looked at him uncomfortably and frowned, again choosing to avoid his direct stare.

"I'm very sorry," he said in a soft voice. "Really. It has been very difficult for me these past couple of months."

"So?" Zhivko retorted.

"Listen, man," Vassil said, picking up confidence. "You're by yourself, but I have a wife and baby. Okay?" He looked angry now, head shaking and eyebrows narrowed. "We both know salaries are shit while inflation is rising."

"Is that why you stabbed me in the back?" Zhivko asked loudly, his cheeks now flushed with anger.

Vassil didn't answer right away, instead looking over Zhivko's shoulders and then turning his head in all directions, scouting for danger.

"Don't yell," he warned. "I had no choice, okay? It was either you or my family!"

"Bullshit!"

"I can hardly afford to buy my son baby food," Vassil said almost pathetically with a desperate voice. "We don't have adequate clothes for him; I'm behind with the water bill."

Vassil shook his head in anger and looked down, biting his lower lip.

"Yulia is constantly angry; we're barely talking," he said and swallowed. "She's bitter and tells me I'm not good enough for her." The words were obviously painful for him to say. He looked to the side and contemplated his next comment. "It has been about three months since she last let me touch her."

Zhivko silently listened as his *former* best friend vented his frustrations. He knew him well and could sense his anguish.

"I still don't understand why you set me up."

"It's not that simple," Vassil responded and repeated. "It's not that simple at all."

"Why? What happened?"

"People started approaching me, telling me they could solve all my problems."

Zhivko was confused. "What people?" he asked.

"On a few occasions, when walking home or jogging in the park by myself, men would come up to me and tell me that they know who I am and that they can get me a lot of money if I help them."

"Do you know who it was?"

Vassil shook his head. "It was dark, and I could not see their faces well. They were young and muscular though, probably bodyguards or something. Anyway, I did not pay attention at first. But they were persistent, even hanging out near my home."

"Seriously?"

"It freaked me out," Vassil admitted. His blue eyes were lost as he tried to recall his memories. "They knew where I lived; they knew my routine, my family, my whole life!"

He looked up at Zhivko.

"They said, 'Help us out and all your problems will go away.' I had my back to the wall; it seemed like a way out."

"So you decided to screw me," Zhivko summarized. "And now the entire country is after me and I could go to jail."

"Shh!" Vassil said through his closed mouth and raised a finger to his lips. "I told you not to raise your voice."

"Thanks for your concern, *friend*," Zhivko began, "but it's a little too late."

"Listen to me," Vassil pleaded, leaning on the still-open trunk of the car. "There is more to it. I decided to help them to protect my family and get money. They paid me well." He said that with a cautious chuckle and then realized the sense of humor was inappropriate and continued, "One day, when you weren't looking, I reached inside your bag and stole your house key. I had a copy made and returned the original before you realized what had happened. That must be how they got in your apartment."

Zhivko could hardly contain himself. He tugged on his windbreaker until it almost ripped and then clenched his fists.

"Fuck you!" he screamed, saliva escaping his mouth.

"Don't judge me!" Vassil yelled back, disregarding his own instructions. "I had no choice! All I wanted was a normal life for my family."

"At my expense!"

"If it was not me, it would have been someone else," Vassil replied. "Apparently, they got me first."

"What?"

"My address is classified information," Vassil explained. "As is yours. How did they know where I live? How did they know to follow me around?"

"What are you trying to say?"

"Someone above us has to be leaking information," Vassil explained, staring into his eyes for signs of comprehension. "This is not about you or me. We're just pawns in a much bigger game."

There was a sharp noise coming from the distance, the sound of something crashing through the bushes. Zhivko turned to look. The abandoned building was behind the checkpoint and to the right, obscured by the wild vegetation. He saw nothing.

"Why should I believe you?"

Vassil raised his hands in frustration.

"Look at the facts," he said. "The bad guys know my address and my family. When I saw them to get my money, one of them told me to take care of my pregnant wife."

Zhivko failed to pick up on the significance of that statement. Vassil leaned forward to force a response but received only a blank stare.

"How the hell do they know Yulia is pregnant?" he asked, wetting his lips. "I've told only a handful of people."

Zhivko paused to think and then spoke up. "You're saying that someone else in the squad is working with the criminals?"

"No," Vassil responded and waved his finger. "The guys are confused and don't know what is going on. I'm confident someone above has to be involved."

"Who?"

Vassil shook his head. "Don't know," he said. "But I have little to gain and too much to lose by trying to find out."

"So basically," Zhivko began, eyes fixated on his colleague, "you stabbed me in the back and now you're leaving me out to dry."

Vassil frowned and looked sheepishly at his friend.

"I'm sorry," he mumbled, eyes full of compassion. "I really am." He closed the trunk of the car.

The gunshot came from the direction of the abandoned building. The bang was crisp and loud, piercing the late-afternoon quiet and scaring birds out of the nearby trees. The sound travelled easily across the plains. Everything was happening too quickly for comprehension.

Zhivko watched in stunned silence as his friend collapsed, first stepping backward and then leaning forward and grabbing the trunk for support. His face convulsed in pain as he reached up to clutch his right collarbone, where a dark stain was forming.

Zhivko looked around wildly, trying to ascertain where the shooter was hiding. He could see nothing. Blood was now beginning to pour through Vassil's fingers and cover most of his hand. He let out a tortured gasp and made a sickening choking noise. Zhivko leaned forward and grabbed hold of his friend.

Vassil's weight became a challenge for Zhivko's outstretched arms. The wounded man made another grotesque gargling sound and trickles of blood escaped from his mouth and slid down his chin. Lips quivered in an attempt to speak, but no words came out, just short, tortured coughs.

Zhivko realized that it was pointless, and probably dangerous, to get him to stand up and instead helped him sit down. Vassil's back was against the car's bumper, one arm at his lap while the other still pushed down on the open wound. His breathing was heavy, and his eyes were unfocused and scared.

Meanwhile, Zhivko's heart was racing. The severity of the injury did not allow him to administer first aid, and he pressed his mind for an alternative solution. He needed to get an ambulance there as quickly as possible. Vassil rested his head against the back of the car and looked up.

"Doesn't look good, my friend," he gasped, looking at his bloody palm and then up at Zhivko. His tone was reserved and somber. "I don't think I'm going to make it."

Zhivko pretended not to hear the last remark, which was so chilling that it made him tremble.

"Nonsense," he replied, kneeling down and trying to sound calm. "You'll be fine. Just press down on the wound to slow the bleeding."

Zhivko ran his fingers over Vassil shoulders, trying to determine if there was an exit wound. There was. He retracted his fingers and saw blood. Vassil violently coughed once more, this time spitting out more blood and spraying it over his shirt and legs and the surrounding pavement. He wiped his mouth and looked up at Zhivko, an eerily relaxed expression on his face. He seemingly knew his fate and accepted it. His moving lips revealed teeth red with blood.

"I love Yulia," he said. His breathing was raspy, and his eyes began to moisten and glaze over. "I love her very much!" Vassil gasped once more and leaned to the other side, his arm dropping and the bracelet scratching against the pavement.

"No!" Zhivko screamed, his mind losing it. "No!" He grabbed his friend's shoulders and shook them violently, forcing the man's head to bob back and forth.

Nothing.

Zhivko moved his mouth but could not find any words. Tears were welling in his eyes and obscuring his vision. He shook his friend once more but could not get him to show signs of life. He was sobbing now, his hands trembling. He brushed the tears away from his eyes.

The killer was still somewhere out there, hiding most likely in the wild bushes that surrounded the abandoned building. *Is he preparing for a second shot?* Zhivko reached for his belt and pulled out the gun. He scooted over to the edge of the car and looked at the building. The killer could be hiding behind the fence, the thick vegetation making him invisible and providing the perfect vantage point.

Zhivko raised the gun and fired. The bullet whizzed across the parking lot and ripped a path through the bushes. He blindly fired two more shots, pressing down on the trigger so forcefully his finger began to hurt.

The first bullet made a popping sound as it hit a brick wall on the first floor. The second bullet must have hit one of the thin, short trees behind the fence, for the sound was entirely different, and Zhivko could see something shaking in the shrubs. What followed next was the sound of movement and footsteps as some invisible body made its escape.

Zhivko fired again, trying to judge where the noise was coming from. There was more movement, and the leaves rustled for a few seconds before everything stopped. He exhaled and slowly removed his finger from the trigger. Vassil had completely fallen to his right, his body sprawled across the pavement. Zhivko got up and looked around.

"Hey!" yelled the guard, who had left his checkpoint and was now standing in the middle of the parking lot. "What's going on?"

Zhivko looked at him in surprise and said nothing, contemplating his next move. The guard saw the gun in his hand. Glancing over at the car, he saw the top of Vassil's body protruding from behind the vehicle. He immediately put two and two together.

The man reached for his holster and pulled out his gun.

"Don't move!" he ordered. "I'm armed."

The gun was pointed straight at Zhivko's torso. From that distance, it was unlikely the guard would miss. Zhivko looked straight at the man without blinking.

I can't afford to be caught.

The man took two steps forward, the firearm securely in his grip.

"Drop the gun, and lie on the ground!" he ordered. "Now!"

Zhivko looked down and dove behind the car, using his free arm to partially break his fall. The pavement stung his palm and caused minor abrasions. The guard watched this and contemplated firing, but Zhivko's speed did not allow for a sure shot. He was now a few meters from the car and dared not get closer.

The guard cautiously moved one hand off the gun and reached for his radio.

"A man resembling Mladenov has just shot someone in the parking lot!" he said loudly. "I request immediate backup!"

Within seconds, the place would be swarming with cops. Zhivko needed to do something and quickly. He twisted his body so that he was lying on his back and looked underneath the car. He could see the guard's feet in the distance, between the wheels of the Hyundai. The commando extended his arm underneath the car, closed one eye for better scope, and pulled the trigger.

The bullet hit the sole of the man's left shoe, tearing through the rubber and ripping through the soft skin of the underfoot. It was a harmless but painful flesh wound.

"Agh!" the guard screamed in surprise and lost his balance, tripped over, and fell backward. Zhivko quickly rolled away and got up, careful to come around the car so that the injured guard could not easily shoot him from a horizontal position. He ran toward the man at full speed.

The guard heard the rapidly approaching footsteps and watched in horror as Zhivko stood over him and pointed the gun at his face.

"Don't move!" he ordered sternly, not raising his voice above the necessary. "Don't move." The guard shook his head. Zhivko looked at the gate, expecting cops to come running any moment.

"Let go of the gun," he instructed.

The guard let go and retracted his arm. Zhivko put away his own gun and picked up the guard's. It was the same model, standard police issue. The guard watched in frightened puzzlement as Zhivko swiftly and skillfully disassembled the gun and removed the magazine, placing it in one of the windbreaker's pockets and closing the zipper.

Zhivko's gun had only a few bullets remaining, and he wanted to get additional ones. Just in case. He now again pointed the gun squarely at the guard.

The guard swallowed hard and became ever more frightened. There was another bullet in the chamber, and Zhivko's eyes were fierce and determined.

"*Dai radioto*," Zhivko commanded, ordering the man to give him the radio.

The guard let go of the walkie-talkie, which was still in his other hand. Zhivko slammed his foot down on the equipment, breaking it instantly and sending bits of plastic flying in all directions. The guard flinched as some of the shards hit his face.

Zhivko looked around, but there were still no cops coming. He had a few more precious seconds. He studied the man at his feet. The guard was wearing the standard uniform, which consisted of dark-blue pants and a light-blue shirt. Zhivko saw that the man had a mobile phone holder clipped to his belt. He reached down and opened it, lifting the phone while the guard watched bewildered.

Mladenov stepped away and put the phone in his other pocket.

"Don't even think about moving," he threatened. The guard shook his head no and raised both hands innocently.

Zhivko moved away and returned to the car. There was now a pool of blood around Vassil's torso. He knelt by his friend's lifeless body and patted his jeans. He grabbed the car key as soon as his finger ran over it and forced it out of the pocket. The guard was still lying on the ground, his head raised to observe what was going on.

Mladenov stepped over his dead friend and opened the car door. He jumped in the driver's seat and started the engine, glancing quickly at all the mirrors. The car quietly came to life, the mechanics obviously more sophisticated than those of Martina's Skoda. Zhivko slammed his foot on the accelerator and drove away, going through first and second gear within seconds.

In the rearview mirror, he saw the guard getting up. Vassil's dead heap was barely distinguishable as it receded in the distance.

I will have my revenge.

Chapter Thirty-Nine

The hours passed slowly for Mitov, who spent his time either anxiously walking around, unable to find his place, or standing and studying the map hung on the wall. A man of action used to seizing the moment, he didn't like feeling helpless and relying on other people. The sun had already set, and the sky was slowly darkening. There was still some light coming in through the windows, and Mitov decided not to turn on the lights. The secretary in the room outside was long gone, confident he was staying behind to finish some overdue paperwork. She was a good girl, hardworking without being nosy, gullible but not stupid.

The ringing of the mobile phone shattered the silence and echoed throughout the room. Mitov had intentionally set the volume to its highest level, a decibel so forceful it would make a deaf person uncomfortable. He practically lunged for the phone, which was placed on the desk, and picked it up.

"Hello?" he inquired with urgency.

"General Secretary Mitov?" a male voice on the other end asked.

"This is he," Mitov responded. "I'm listening."

"This is the director of the Haskovo region," the man said. "We spoke on the phone earlier."

"Of course," Mitov replied. "I remember. Please go ahead."

"As I promised," the man began, hoping his diligence would be duly noted, "I have been reading the traffic reports filed by my men. There is something interesting I want to share."

Mitov reached for his notepad and grabbed a pen.

"Go ahead," he encouraged. "I'm listening."

The regional director was holding a file in his hand, flipping the two pages inside to make sure he wasn't missing anything.

"Earlier today, a patrol car responded to an accident involving a truck and compact car driven by a teenager," the man began. "Witnesses confirm the young man was speeding and driving erratically, crossing into opposing lanes to overtake slower cars."

Mitov shook his head. *Stupid kids.*

"Go on," he said.

"During a passing maneuver he was not able to get back into his lane and crashed into a truck," the regional director continued. "Luckily, it was not a head-on collision. Nevertheless, the car was badly damaged and thrown nearly off the road."

"Was anyone injured?"

"The driver had some cuts to his face and head, as well as a concussion," the regional director flipped over one of the pages. "His girlfriend suffered a broken arm. Both were taken to the hospital at Haskovo."

"What about the driver of the truck?"

"That's the funny thing," the other man answered. "The driver left the scene."

"A hit-and-run?"

"Exactly," the director answered. "That's what makes this so strange."

Mitov tapped his pen on the notepad and took a moment to think.

"Why is that strange?" he asked.

"The accident was obviously the fault of the young man behind the wheel," the director explained. "He even admitted it to the officer who wrote the report. The eyewitnesses also claim the same thing. The truck driver was not at fault at all."

Mitov closed his eyes and scratched his forehead.

"Is there a reason for a truck driver to leave the scene of an accident like this?"

The reply was firm and convincing. "Not at all," the regional director said. "That's the funny thing. In fact, they are eager not to be blamed for causing an accident, because if they are at fault, the company punishes them. Any normal truck driver in a similar situation would have looked forward to the police report because it clears his name. Not to mention the fact that the young man had insurance. Now the trucker will have to pay for the damage out of his own pocket."

Mitov exhaled audibly and said nothing.

"Did anyone catch the license plate of the truck?" he asked.

"No," the regional director replied disappointed. "Unfortunately."

"So he drove off?" Mitov repeated, as if to reassure himself of the facts. "Just like that?"

"Da," the other man said. "That's why this doesn't make sense."

It made sense, all right. He just did not have enough actionable information.

"Is that all the report says?"

"Yes," the regional director said, looking through the papers once more. "That's it."

"I understand," Mitov responded with disappointment. "Thank you."

"No problem; hope it was helpful."

"It was."

"Glad to hear it," the regional director said. "If that's all, I'll be—"

"One more thing," Mitov interrupted, his mind alive with a new idea. "Do you know the officer who submitted the report?"

"Ah," the man was caught off guard by the question. "I know him, yes. He's good at what he does."

"Can you contact him?" Mitov asked. "Either him or his partner."

"Well …" the regional director was taken aback by the unexpected request. "Their shift has ended, and they've gone home, sir. I won't have access to them until tomorrow morning."

The situation was frustrating. "Can't you call them at home?" Mitov asked. "You must have their numbers."

"I don't have that information readily available," the man admitted coyly and then realized he needed to sound more professional. "But I can find their files and ask some of the other men."

"Please do," Mitov instructed with relief. "It's very important."

The regional director frowned, annoyed by the sudden change in plans. He had been looking forward to some homemade food.

"Okay," he said reluctantly, an edge creeping into his tone. "What kind of information are you looking for?"

"Any description of the truck and the driver," Mitov explained. "Any description at all, even if it's something minor. I want to know more about the truck and the man driving it."

"I understand," the regional director said and grimaced in anger and annoyance. "I will try to reach the two officers."

"Thank you."

"I want to warn you though, it will take some time."

"How long?"

The man helplessly shook his head and looked at his wristwatch.

"I don't know."

Mitov did not like unspecific answers.

"Take a guess," he prodded. "Give me an estimate."

"Maybe three hours," the regional director answered, exasperated and at first unsure of himself. "Three hours sounds right."

"Listen," Mitov instructed with a firm voice and moved the mobile phone closer to his mouth. "If you want me to recommend you for promotion, you will call me back in two."

It was now dark outside, and Mitov had no choice but to turn on the lights in his office. The occupants in the other rooms had long ago left for the weekend. Save for a handful of guards positioned at strategic locations within the building, the ministry was empty. Mitov was sitting in one of the armchairs around the table and nervously playing with his pen.

The mobile phone was in his hand this time, assuring a nearly instantaneous reaction when it rang.

"Yes?" he asked loudly. "This is Mitov."

"It's me again, sir," the regional director from Haskovo said. "I've got news for you."

"Please proceed," Mitov instructed. "Have you been able to track down the police officer who prepared the report?"

"I have," the director answered with pride. "I just spent more than twenty minutes talking to him."

Mitov reached for his notepad. "What did he say?"

"He gave a detailed description," began the director. "According to an eyewitness that apparently had a brief conversation with the truck driver, the man appeared to be in his late forties or early fifties. He's also fat."

The general secretary pressed the pen deep into the notepad and wrote with big letters.

"Is that it?" he asked.

"As far as a description of the driver, yes."

"Any clues on why he left the scene?"

"No," answered the regional director. "According to the same eyewitness, who saw the entire accident happen before his eyes, the driver got out to check the condition of the people in the car. Once he was assured they were not seriously injured, he announced that he was going to the truck to radio for police and sped off."

Mitov snorted. *He must really be hiding something.*

"Anything on the truck?" he asked.

"Just your standard cargo truck," the man answered. "Nothing special. The impact apparently dented the front left of the vehicle, as well as some surface damage on the side."

"Is that the extent of it?"

"Appears so," the regional director replied. "There was plenty of debris on the road, but the officer says it most likely all belongs to the car."

"I understand," said Mitov. "Is that all?"

"Almost," answered the regional director. "There is one minor thing."

"What?"

"The eyewitness remembered that there was an orange painted on the side of the truck. The officer did not include it in the report because he felt it was irrelevant."

"A fruit?" Mitov asked, the curious detail grabbing his attention.

"Yeah," replied the regional director, stifling a yawn. "A grapefruit, or an orange maybe. Possibly even an apple. Something round, in any case."

Mitov wrote down the detail with bold letters and circled it.

"Thank you," he said with relief. "The information is very helpful. I appreciate your hard work. It won't go unnoticed."

The regional director smiled to himself.

"Thank you," he replied with fake modesty. "Do you mind telling me what this is for?"

"I'm afraid I can't do that," Mitov told him curtly. "But it's very much a secret, so please keep this conversation to yourself."

"Okay."

"I wish you good night."

"Good night."

Mitov hung up and put down the mobile phone. Relieved to finally have actionable information and filled with a renewed sense of mission, he walked over to the little bathroom in the corner and flipped the light switch. The small room lit up with a yellowish tint. A hanger suspended from the curtain bar of the tiny shower held his suit and necktie. Mitov quickly stripped off his pants and shirt and placed them on the hanger as well.

The cold water provided a welcome energy boost as Mitov cupped his hands underneath the faucet and refreshingly splashed his face, neck, and shoulders. He stood over the sink for a few minutes, gathering his thoughts and watching the water escape down the drain. The general secretary then wiped himself off and slipped into the infinitely more comfortable jeans, T-shirt, and dark sweater.

Mitov gathered his most necessary belongings and left. The car was waiting for him at its usual location. No one noticed as he slipped out of the building and onto the sidewalk. He looked at his wristwatch and accelerated his stride.

Time was of the essence.

Chapter Forty

Zhivko walked through the revolving door of Hotel Princess and stepped onto the shiny marble tiles of the lobby. A bellhop wearing a burgundy uniform smiled at him and pointed in the direction of the reception. He continued walking, his shoes gently squeaking with each step.

Hotel Princess was a large, multistory hotel near the train station. Known mostly as an inexpensive location for travelers who wanted to spend the night without venturing into the city, the hotel had a rather mediocre reputation. Its casino never closed, and the staff provided an agreeable mixture of comfort and anonymity. Zhivko would have preferred something smaller and more discreet, but the circumstances had forced his hand.

"I need a place to spend the night," Zhivko said to the woman behind the reception desk.

"Just one person?" the young woman asked with a forced smile.

"Yes," replied Zhivko.

The receptionist typed something into her computer and punctuated her efforts with a forceful pressing of the enter key. "We have plenty of rooms available," she said and looked up. "Will one on the eighth floor suit you?"

"Yes, ma'am," he replied plainly and took out his wallet. "That will be fine."

The woman smiled again, the strong lipstick staining one of her teeth with an ugly smudge.

"Let me give you the card to your room," she told him and retrieved a piece of paper coming out of the printer. "Please sign your name here and here," the receptionist added, pointing to the desired spots with her pen. She handed it to Zhivko, who quickly made up a name and forged a signature. His suspicion that the hotel was not too serious about checking identification documents had mercifully proven to be true.

"Thank you," he said with a brief look at the receptionist and slid the card off the counter.

"You're welcome," responded the woman. "Enjoy your stay. Breakfast starts tomorrow at eight in the morning."

Zhivko nodded. He walked past a row of low tables and fluffy couches, some occupied by tourists smoking and loudly discussing something in a language he could not understand. Perhaps it was Arabic, or maybe Turkish. An older woman in slippers and a full-body bathrobe walked into a spa intentionally obscured by a dark glass door. She turned around to give him a quick glance and continued on her way.

Confident her work was complete, the receptionist put the signed form in the designated box and congratulated herself on a job well done. She liked to think she had a special touch with clients, making them feel welcome while expediting their requests—a skill not blunted despite the monotony and the long shifts.

Her colleague had observed the interaction with silence, standing quietly in the corner and sorting through the guests' mail. The man did not strike her as a tourist and had behaved oddly. Guests usually asked the hours of the cafeteria or how to find the gym or the casino. This one just picked up his card and left.

Strange.

The eighth floor was quiet, a sign on the wall indicating the locations of the different rooms. The hallways were narrow and long, a brown rug running along the middle from end to end. The walls were painted in soft beige that looked darker because of the poor lighting. His room was not far from the elevators. The door was of a thick and sturdy wood, the peephole inadequately small.

Zhivko put the card in and pushed down on the knob. The room was unimpressive but functional, with a small closet near the door and a cramped bathroom that featured all the bare amenities. The room had a standard-sized double bed, a nightstand with a lamp and an old television set the size of a briefcase. He closed the door behind him and took off his shoes.

The view was of the boulevard that led to the train station. Rush hour had passed, and traffic was easier now, but the tourist buses kept coming and going while the trams rumbled along the tracks, their drivers periodically ringing their bells at the impolite cabs that got in the way. The sun was gone but the street lights and neon signs provided the room with an appropriate amount of light.

Zhivko drew the thick curtains closed and stepped away. He reached for the nightstand and turned on the lamp. He took off his windbreaker, emptied all its pockets, and then reached down for his jeans and did the same. He unfolded a little piece of paper and picked up the phone, which was on the nightstand near the lamp.

Mira picked up after the third ring.

"Hello?"

"It's me," he said, sounding tired.

"Thank God!" Mira replied with relief, bringing her hand up to her chest. "I was worried."

"I'm fine," Zhivko said soothingly. "At least for now. I'm in Hotel Princess."

"Everyone is looking for you," Mira warned. "I've spent the entire day flipping through the channels and radio stations."

"What are they saying about me?"

"You're being blamed for the murder at the police academy." Mira sounded worried and spoke quickly. "The guard says he clearly saw you escape and leave the other man dead."

Zhivko's thoughts clouded, and his eyes became misty. His hands shook.

"Alo?"

"I'm here," Zhivko regained his composure. "I'm here."

"What happened?"

"I was there," he began. "I talked to Vassil, but I did not kill him. Someone fired through the woods and got him. There was nothing … nothing …"

Zhivko's voice broke. He gulped in air to regain his composure while the scene of his friend clutching his open wound played before his eyes.

"There was nothing I could do."

"My dear God!" Mira exclaimed. "I'm so sorry"—she was shaking her head and trying to make sense of the situation—"I can only imagine how you must feel right now."

Zhivko said nothing and brushed tears away from his eyes. *No, you can't.*

"Vassil said someone higher up is involved," he offered in a weak voice. "They just used him to further their aims."

"Who?"

"I don't know." His voice firmed. "He did not say."

"Try to stay safe," Mira said hopefully. "Martina and I will be traveling to Sofia tonight. I want to speak to my editor about writing an article about all this. The public deserves the truth."

"Thank you."

Mira smiled. Martina, who was in the room with her, had not seen that particular smile in months. It carried a certain tenderness and warmth that Martina had not witnessed recently in her friend. It conveyed not just happiness but caring as well.

"Of course," she said. "We called your friend and told him to alert Mitov. Let's hope there is someone who can stop this madness."

Zhivko forced a chuckle.

"There is nothing I can do right now," he said plainly, seemingly accepting his helpless position. "I will try to find Mitov tomorrow. I have a feeling he may be on my side. At the very least, he'll be willing to talk."

"Sure," Mira responded slowly, unsure of what to say and slightly annoyed by Martina's presence in the room with her. "Call me when you have the time. You know my office number," she added with a nervous laugh.

"I do," Zhivko replied. "And I will."

Silence.

Mira turned her back to Martina and pushed the phone to her lips.

"If they arrest you," she began, emotion nearly overwhelming her trembling voice, "I will wait."

More silence.

"That makes me happy," he replied. He needed to hear her voice, to feel her support.

"Good-bye."

"Good-bye," Zhivko said.

Mira pressed the phone to her mouth and spoke softly, careful to enunciate the words.

"I miss you."

Zhivko had already hung up. Mira let the phone dangle in her hand and put it down. Martina looked at her with a knowing grin.

Chapter Forty-One

The highway occasionally dipped and curved as it made its way through the countryside. Traffic was light, white and red lights periodically flashing by and disappearing. The beautiful hills along both sides were quiet, their trees motionless.

Mitov was tense, firmly clenching the steering wheel with both hands and driving a few kilometers above the speed limit. He did not know exactly where he was going, or what—if anything—he would find there. At times like these, hunches and professional guesswork were all he had left.

The mysterious truck driver most likely did not work for either a major transportation company or a major food company with its own truck fleet. Those guys usually parked their vehicles at company warehouses and distribution facilities, which were off limits to outsiders and subject to internal controls. No, he would have to be a small timer, a freelancer carrying whatever load he was paid to carry without asking too many questions. Such drivers typically arrived at a depot, picked up a load, and received payment upon delivery.

Mitov looked at his watch and kept his foot on the accelerator.

It was even possible the company that had commissioned the freight, as well as the company awaiting its delivery were simply front companies used by criminals. The bastards were smart and resourceful.

The question was: Where in the Plovdiv area should he look for a parked truck with a fruit painted on it? Excluding the facilities run by large companies for the use of their own fleets, there were two depots used by random truck drivers. The larger one was not far ahead. He yawned and stayed focused.

The depot was located near the highway, about a kilometer's drive along an auxiliary road. Mitov saw the ramp and slowed down, intentionally passing it and moving into the highway's shoulder lane. He turned on the emergency lights and brought the car to a stop. A sedan whizzed by at top speed. Mitov stepped out, the cool night air a refreshing relief from the stuffy interior of the car.

He popped the trunk and reached for a fluorescent triangle and then walked away and placed it on the pavement, about fifteen meters behind the car. He went back to the trunk, took out his binoculars and a red handkerchief, and closed it. At the front of the car, Mitov raised one of the windshield wipers and used it to pin down the red handkerchief. The illusion that the car had broken down and the driver ran off to find help was complete.

Binoculars hanging around his neck and bouncing against the sweater, Mitov took off down the auxiliary road toward the depot. He walked with stealth, stepping on the dust and gravel at the edge of the road. The clear sky and large moon provided the necessary visibility. He could hear crickets and occasionally saw flashes of black as birds silently flew by.

The depot was visible in the distance, floodlights shining on the entrance and the guard post nearby. There were lights in the middle of the parking yard as well, illuminating the café and rest station. Mitov stepped off the road and into the grass, his feet sinking somewhat in the soft terrain. He cautiously walked up the hill and toward a wooded area. He did not want to be seen by the guard, or anyone else for that matter. He walked into the woods, hiding behind the first row of pine trees. The smell of bark and amber filled the air. Mitov raised the binoculars to his eyes and surveyed the terrain beneath him.

It took a few seconds to adjust the settings to be able to see clearly through the lenses. The depot below him was a large square, a thin wire fence running along the perimeter. The white lines on the asphalt were fading and turning gray, while small puddles of water and car oil were all over the place. There was a fuel pump in one corner, adjacent to an air pump and a pile of old tires precariously stacked on top of each other. He also saw a tractor and some earth-moving equipment.

Mitov surveyed everything closely, his trained eyes spotting every detail. There weren't any video cameras on the fence, and the guard only occasionally left his post to walk around near the entrance. There appeared to be some people in the café, probably drinking and playing cards. Their muffled conversations were the only noise he could hear.

From his vantage point, Mitov could see the tops of the trucks but had a limited view of their sides and could not determine whether the mysterious truck was there or not. He put the protective cover over the lenses of the binoculars and emerged from hiding. The gust of clean mountain air was refreshing. He then jogged down the hill, careful to step silently and not trip. He skipped across the grass and reached the fence, grabbing it with both hands. It was sturdy, the pillars planted securely in the ground and the mesh stretched tightly. The trucks were a meter or two away. There was no sign of movement and no noise, save for the occasional rowdy chatter from the café.

Mitov wrapped his fingers around the mesh and hoisted himself up, pushing away with his feet for leverage. The wires dug into the sensitive flesh of his hands, causing flashes of acute, concentrated pain. He climbed up cautiously and threw one foot over the fence, shifting position with his hands while the top of the fence precariously scratched against his crotch. After swinging his other leg over the fence, he climbed down a bit and then let gravity do the rest.

He landed with a barely audible thud, bending his ankles and knees in an attempt to cushion himself. *I'm getting too old for this.*

Mitov wiped his hands and looked around. Nothing.

He then began carefully checking each truck's bumpers and fenders, looking for a fruit painted on the side.

It didn't take long to find something. The cabin of the truck was entirely white, as was the single freight compartment attached behind it. There was no marking or insignia that identified it as belonging to a specific company. Mitov felt his hunch was about to be proven true. He quietly walked around the front of the truck, examining the bumper. There were cracks and dents on the left, the paint peeled off to reveal the shiny metal underneath. The damage continued on the side, where the protective rim around the tire was scratched.

Excited, Mitov walked down the narrow alley formed between the truck and the one parked next to it. He glanced up and saw what he was looking for. A large orange was painted on the side of the truck. If one were facing the side of the truck, the succulent fruit was positioned in the top right corner, the image nearly three meters in diameter. It was perfectly round and painted a bold orange, two bright green leaves sprouting from its top.

Mitov smiled and felt reinvigorated by the discovery. He returned to the front and took out a small notepad from his pocket to write down the license plate of the truck and some other identifiable details. He then moved down the row of trucks, looking for a secure place to hide. He found a spot near the corner, from which he could easily see and hear anyone approaching. Mitov slowly climbed the stairs of one truck cabin and peered inside. It was empty and the curtain to the sleeping compartment was open. There was no one. A look inside the opposing truck's cabin revealed the same.

Perfect.

Mitov sat down and rested his back against the truck's tire. He exhaled and looked up at the starry sky.

Chapter Forty-Two

September 6, 1997

Rays of sunshine spilled across the light-blue sky. Being driven by someone else was a luxury you didn't get accustomed to right away. Kiril sat quietly and observed as Nikolai skillfully controlled the car. The former wrestler's bracelets jingled slightly when his arms made wider movements in turning the steering wheel. Kiril straightened his shirt and adjusted the brand-new tie. It was very important to look wealthy and powerful. The different social statuses of the two men was apparent.

"Slow down," he instructed, noticing the Mercedes picking up speed as the highway sloped downward. "I don't want any problems."

"Of course, boss," Nikolai said and looked in the rearview mirror, briefly catching his sharp glance. "Sorry." He eased his foot off the accelerator and tapped on the brakes. The sun had just peered out from under the horizon, and its bright rays pierced the sky, sending light streaking across the plains.

Kiril put his hands together in front of his face and admired the manicured nails and the shiny cufflinks that sparkled at his wrist. *Everything is going according to plan.* All the pieces were coming together to form a perfect picture. He was tempted to think ahead and make plans for spending all the money he would soon have but cautioned himself against hubris.

As a child, his parents taught him to get his work done first and enjoy the rewards later. "Do your homework, and I will let you go outside and play soccer with the other boys," his mother used to tell him. She was a wise woman, practical in her advice and disciplined, but in a loving way. He missed her intensely.

It was his mother who taught him the virtues of being patient and methodical, thinking through everything twice before taking action. She was the polar opposite of his father, who was impulsive and reckless, drinking away the family's money and forcing him to leave the university before finishing his degree.

Then again, perhaps it worked out for the better. He put his ample skills and talents to work elsewhere, much more profitably.

They reached a straight stretch of the highway, and Nikolai gently pressed on the pedal. The German car responded with a smooth and quiet acceleration as its sleek frame, headed toward the sunrise. Up ahead in the east, the sun was rising above the horizon. Nikolai put down the sun guard to shield his eyes. The day promised to be sunny and hot, the air slightly moist from the recent rains.

Behind them in the distance the second Mercedes appeared, barely visible in the rearview mirror. Stefan and Ahmed were good at following instructions. The dance between the two cars was carefully choreographed so that they were always within view but never too close to each other. In his mind, Kiril had taken care of all the details.

He leaned to one side and lazily observed the scenery. The endless roaming hills unfolded before his eyes, the interchanging green and yellow fields capturing his imagination. It was beautiful, save for the occasional roadside billboards. Kiril looked at his watch and became thoughtful.

As for Nikolai, who was now cruising at a constant speed, he was a reliable if somewhat naïve man. He asked for a surprisingly small share of the money, given that as distributor, he bore most of the legal and physical risks. Kiril liked him as much as he looked down on him. Nikolai simply did not have the leadership qualities and could be replaced if necessary. He was a reliable workhorse without the means or ambition to climb to a higher rung on the ladder.

The master plan was broken down into small pieces and spread out across a number of actors. Everything was compartmentalized, and no one knew the entire picture—no one but him, that is. Only he could put together all the pieces. Kiril was elated.

Everything would be blamed on the hapless commando, who would soon be caught. With the other man dead, critical information was forever buried. Not even Iliev knew the full extent of what was going on. He was just being paid to leak strategic information and be their man on the inside, assisting when asked to.

The plan was flawless.

Chapter Forty-Three

Mitov was tired and bored, his head resting in his hands. His forehead was warm, and he could sense a headache coming on. It was possible he had dozed off a couple of times during the night, each time for a few minutes. But he was not sure. It was light now, a beautiful day in the making.

A glance at his watch revealed that it was 7:38 a.m.

Suddenly, there was noise. The door of one of the truck cabins opened, and there were clanging sounds as someone awkwardly climbed down. Mitov got up and walked to the truck in front of him, prostrating himself against its side and cautiously extending his head to peer down the line of trucks. He watched as Dobrev stumbled out of his truck and approached the fence. He repeatedly ran his hands over his bearded face and then arched his back, his naked belly spilling out as the small shirt he was wearing climbed up his torso.

"Agh!" the man exclaimed, apparently still sleepy. His shoes were untied, and he was not wearing a belt. Dobrev quickly looked around and, apparently confident no one was watching him, stepped closer to the fence and partially pulled down his pants. A rich stream of urine streaked through the mesh and soaked the earth on the other side. The truck driver spent nearly a minute relieving himself, punctuating the act with occasional verbal outbursts. When he was finally finished, Dobrev pulled his pants up and rubbed his hands against his thighs.

Mitov watched in disgust from a distance. Dobrev returned to his truck and came out a few minutes later. He locked the door and walked away, heading for the café. Mitov was tempted to follow but decided against it for fear that someone might recognize him or possibly strike up a conversation and jeopardize his cover.

Dobrev pushed through the glass door and stepped into the small café. Along the windows were four separated tables, three of them empty. A young mechanic casually eating a cheese sandwich looked up when the truck driver walked in and then turned his attention back to the sports section of the newspaper. Crumbs had fallen on its open pages.

"Black coffee," Dobrev said to the pencil-thin young woman behind the counter. "And get me a croissant as well."

The woman said nothing and reached for a pot on the stove, simultaneously retrieving a small cup and placing the pot on the counter. The coffee steamed as she poured it. Dobrev picked up the cup and reached for a plastic spoon and a pack of sugar.

"What kind of croissant?" the woman asked, bored.

"Chocolate," Dobrev replied and took note of the clock hanging on the wall. There was not much time left. The woman placed the sweet treat on the counter and took the money. Dobrev woofed down the croissant and finished off the coffee in three quick gulps. He wiped his mouth with a napkin and left.

Mitov watched with renewed interest as the truck driver reappeared and headed toward his truck. He looked intense, stride purposeful and previously sleepy eyes now more alert. The gruff face was expressionless, concentration signified by a tightly clenched jaw. The driver disappeared from eyesight, forcing Mitov to search for a new position.

Dobrev reached the back of the truck and stopped. He lit a cigarette and began smoking, standing just in front of the closed doors of the truck's freight compartment. He puffed nervously, taking short, quick drags. He was looking at the entrance to the depot.

He's waiting for someone.

Mitov moved to a different location and resumed his observation. He was crouching behind a stack of construction equipment placed near the fence. The stance was causing him acute knee pain. He could see Dobrev and, in the distance, the entrance and the guard post. He had no choice but to put up with the discomfort in his legs.

A black Mercedes pulled up in front of the barrier and stopped. The guard stepped out of the building and looked at the car, bending over to see its occupants. He acknowledged them with a nod and returned to his post. The barrier was raised.

Yet the car did not move forward.

Mitov's training and professional skills were on full alert as he watched the situation unfold. Dobrev threw away his cigarette and rubbed sweaty palms together, rocking his body back and forth. The Mercedes did not move.

A second black car appeared on the road and pulled up just behind the first. Together, the two vehicles moved forward and entered the depot. The barrier behind them came down. The shiny cars made their way to Dobrev's truck, the second one unexpectedly speeding up and abruptly stopping immediately next to the truck. The other car stopped farther behind, and its rear right door opened.

The general secretary crouched down even more so that only his head from the eyes up was visible. The strain on his knees increased, and he reached behind him to grab hold of the fence with one arm to ease the escalating pain.

A tall man with a youthful face stepped out of the Mercedes. He was impeccably dressed in an expensive tailor-made black suit that looked striking even from a distance. The white shirt underneath was made of silk, giving it a smooth feel and a slightly shiny look. A bold blue necktie completed the image.

The driver of the Mercedes also stepped out, mindful to leave the door open. He wore sunglasses, a black shirt, and dark-blue jeans. Mitov was not surprised. A man wearing a similar "uniform" stepped out from the second car and scanned the depot before turning to face the exit and act as a lookout. The tall man in the suit casually buttoned one of the buttons on his vest and spread his thin lips into a smile.

He glanced from side to side, the turning of his head timed and meticulous, almost like a model striking a pose. He was clean shaven, his cheeks featuring a hint of boyish rosiness. The nose was slender and long, the eyebrows thin and straight. The flowing dark hair was oiled back, a trace of gray around the temples. The man adjusted his suit and walked toward the truck driver, extending his hand and flashing a smile that spoke of expensive dentistry.

A meeting of high-level business partners, if it were not for the circumstances.

Mitov watched as the two men exchanged some words and the driver pointed to the back of his truck. Unfortunately, the other occupant of the Mercedes moved closer and shielded Mitov's view. All he saw was the tall man extending his hand and waving over the other car with a snap of his fingers. Another man dressed in black jumped out and circled behind to open the trunk. Simultaneously, the man acting as a lookout turned around and approached the truck.

Mitov did not need to see any more. He stepped out from behind the pile of construction materials and darted away from view behind a nearby truck. The five men fifteen meters away were oblivious to his movements.

Mitov grabbed the mesh and pulled himself up, scrambling to get his legs over the fence. His knees responded to the sudden quick movements with a burst of tingles extending up and down his legs. He landed on the other side and retrieved the mobile phone from his pocket. He punched in the numbers and glanced over his shoulder.

"Hello?"

"This is General Secretary Mitov," he managed in between gulps of fresh air as he jogged up the hill toward the woods. "Put me through to the regional director immediately!"

"Right away, sir." He was placed on hold. The numbness in his legs was quickly disappearing. Mitov had reached the woods and taken cover behind a tree when he again heard a voice on the other end.

"Good morning, Mr. Mitov," the regional director said. "Can I help you with anything?"

Mitov caught his breath and wiped sweat from his brow.

"Listen closely," he said hurriedly. "I'm outside a truck depot off the Trakia Highway …" He stopped to take another breath. "I want you to mobilize a couple of units and get over here immediately!"

Chapter Forty-Four

Zhivko woke up and lay motionless. Sunlight came in from the edges of the curtains. He sat up and rubbed his eyes forcefully, yawning and shaking his head. He pulled the sheets back and got up. He walked to the window and gently parted the curtains so he could look out. It took his eyes a few seconds to adjust to the brightness. Pedestrians were on the sidewalk and the usual traffic on the boulevard. Nothing out of the ordinary.

He walked over to the bathroom, stopping along the way to take a look in the mirror. He had lost some weight, probably no more than two kilograms. And the six-pack looked a little flabby. He slowly ran his fingers over his abdomen, feeling the outlines of the muscles. He yawned again and scratched his head, hoping to shake loose the cobwebs formed during a night of deep sleep.

The icy water poured out of the faucet at nearly full blast. Zhivko plunged both hands underneath the current and splashed his face and neck, sending lightning bolts through his body. He repeated the process until his face was uncomfortably cold.

Zhivko looked through the peephole and cautiously opened the door. All was quiet. He looked up and down the long, narrow hallway. There were a couple of wrinkles in the brown rug, but other than that, it appeared that nothing had changed since the previous night.

He closed the door and returned to the bathroom, opening the transparent plastic door to the shower cabin. The water gushed out with surprising force, first too hot then too cool as he extended his arm and adjusted the dial. Fifteen seconds later, it was just right, and Zhivko stepped in and closed the door.

Water rained down as steam fogged up the booth. Showering was one of Zhivko's guilty pleasures, particularly in the morning. He enjoyed the water and the heat and was not quick to reach for the soap. When he eventually did, he really took his time and painstakingly made sure to reach every point on his body.

He felt sublime, but there was a persistent worry in the back of his mind. Like an itch he wanted to neglect but could not get rid of. He finished with the soap and put it back.

It's a large hotel. Yet when I opened the door, all was quiet.

The warm water poured over him, the heat filling his lungs. He savored the moment.

There should be some noise, shouldn't there?

The soap was washing away and forming bubbles near the drain. He dispersed them with a kick and leaned against the side of the cabin. He turned the dial slightly to raise the temperature.

Where are the maids? They should be out cleaning the rooms.

The questions gained prominence in his mind.

Chapter Forty-Five

"Now," the police officer said, unfolding a printed page and laying it on the counter. "I just want to double-check; you are absolutely sure that you saw this man come in here and book a room last night?"

The thirty-something-year-old man looked up at the woman, who frowned with displeasure and took a quick look at the printout.

"Yes," she replied. "I'm absolutely sure. I told you guys over the phone already. I saw his picture on the news." She had a particularly annoying way of chewing gum, smacking her lips with each jaw movement.

The cop smiled at his partner and retrieved the picture.

"Okay, ma'am," he told her with a polite smile. "I understand. Thank you for your help."

The two officers stepped aside when they saw their lieutenant appear at the main hotel entrance. The man, wearing the standard dark-blue police uniform, had just put away his mobile phone and was striding across the lobby. His badge hung on a chain around his neck.

"Is this everyone?" he asked, standing in front of the reception. Three receptionists, nine maids, four bellhops, and a small army of other personnel were gathered in the lobby near the reception.

"Yes," replied the hotel manager, a mild-mannered man in his late forties. He was of average build and had a receding hairline. "I assembled everyone, just like you asked."

The men and women were looking at the lieutenant and quietly talking among themselves.

"Do we get a reward?" one of the men asked with a mocking smile. "We're helping you catch a fugitive."

Muffled laughter rippled through the crowd. The lieutenant did not appreciate it.

"No," he said calmly, looking sternly at the young joker. "No reward has been offered for the capture of the suspect."

"Too bad!" The bellhop snickered. "I could use the cash."

"Me too!" His friend laughed and started another wave of subdued hilarity.

"Okay, folks," the lieutenant insisted. "Thank you for your cooperation. I'm now asking you to leave the building and gather underneath the large awning in front of the entrance. Please stay underneath the structure at all times, because we don't want the suspect to see you through one of the windows. That would tip him off and complicate the operation."

The crowd of about fifty people slowly shuffled across the lobby, forming a bottleneck at the revolving door. The lieutenant followed them out and pulled the hotel manager by the arm.

"Did you call all the guests?" he asked.

"Yes," the man replied. "Just like you asked me. We told them not to leave their rooms for an hour because we're doing emergency repairs to the elevators."

The lieutenant smiled. "Excellent, thank you."

The line behind the revolving door was thinning. There were three police cars outside and a total of seven cops of various ranks. One tipped his hat at the lieutenant when he emerged.

"Are the special forces here?" he asked.

One of the cops pointed to a military truck making a turn off the boulevard and heading for the hotel. Its thick, rugged all-terrain tires appeared misplaced on the civilian road. It was painted a mixture of dark green and black, a spotted camouflage canvas stretched over its back to protect its occupants. The crowd moved back in awe and minor trepidation as it approached and groaned to a halt directly in front of the main entrance.

Ten commandos duly jumped out from the back, one after the other in rapid succession. Ski masks down and rifles ready, they were an imposing sight. Veselin Iliev, wearing military trousers with large pockets on each side and a long-sleeve green vest, emerged from the passenger's side and climbed down.

The team assembled in front of the revolving door, where they were greeted by the hotel manager and the lieutenant.

Iliev raised his hand in a salute, forcing the lieutenant to quickly mirror the gesture.

"Is everything prepared?" the commando captain asked, his tone precise and demanding.

"Yes," the lieutenant assured him. "I have seven people here with me," he said, looking around and waving his finger. "I will dispatch two to the casino exit on the side and two more to guard the ramp to the underground parking. The remaining three will stay here."

"Are there any other exits?"

"There is a cargo exit in back, but it has been locked from the inside and the key put away."

Iliev looked at the hotel manager, who nodded in confirmation.

"That's good," he said. "And the guests?"

"They have been told to stay in their rooms," the lieutenant answered. "As for your suspect, he is in room 816 and probably has no idea what's going on."

Iliev spread his moustache into a smile and raised his hand.

"Let's walk inside and discuss specifics," he offered and gestured for the commandos to follow him. The group of ten men walked into the lobby and made for the reception, their heavy boots creating a sound akin to marching.

"Here's a basic layout of the hotel," the manager said, taking the papers out of his pocket and unfolding the map on the reception counter. "We're here," he announced and jabbed his finger at the appropriate spot. "That's the entrance over there." He pointed behind him. "And here are the two stairwells."

Iliev and the commandos were bunched around the map, paying close attention.

"Just two stairwells?" the commander asked.

"Da," the manager replied.

"And the elevators?"

"We've blocked them," he explained with pride, even though the idea was not his. "If you walk that way and to your left, you will see them all on the lobby floor, their doors open."

Iliev looked at the lieutenant and smiled again.

"I like this guy!" he said with a laugh, patting the hotel manager on the back. "Looks like you have thought of everything."

"I hope so," the lieutenant replied, his face lighting up. He was hoping for a transfer to another department, and a successful operation would certainly bolster his chances. Iliev studied the map and then picked it up, passing it along to Pavel. The commandos immediately reassembled and huddled around their squad leader. Their commander turned to the hotel manager and the lieutenant.

"Thank you," he said, looking them both in the eyes. "Great work. Now I want to ask that you step outside and wait." He turned his head to the lieutenant. "Have your remaining men make sure no new tourists or guests come in. If at all possible, push any visitors back and tell them to wait a block away."

"Okay," the lieutenant said.

Iliev turned to the hotel manager.

"And you, sir," he began. "Stay outside with your employees and don't come in until I tell you it's safe." Iliev smiled reassuringly. "Hopefully this won't take too long."

The lieutenant and the hotel manager walked away. Iliev watched them pass through the revolving door and turned to his men.

"Okay, fellas," he said and rubbed his hands together. He could differentiate between the commandos despite the face masks. "Let's treat this like any other mission. Catch him alive unless he offers resistance and begins firing."

The men looked at each other and acknowledged the command.

"I want you to separate into two teams and make your way up to the eighth floor, while maintaining radio contact with each other. When you get there, I want you to converge on his room from both sides, do you understand?"

The men moved their heads.

"Good," Iliev said. "Let's do this and get it over with. I will stay here behind the reception desk and coordinate the activities. I want you to update me on what's going on as frequently as possible."

The squad separated into two groups, each heading for a stairwell.

"Seventh floor, clear!" one of the men spoke loudly in his radio. They were making their way up the staircase with stealth and silence, rifles pointed in all directions in anticipation of possible danger. They sometimes used a peeling technique, rotating the first man to the back and bringing the last one to the front. They communicated silently with quick hand motions and head nods. Despite their training, the tension rose with the floor count.

"Seven clear as well," a commando from the other group said, voice crackling over the radio.

"Proceed to the eighth," Iliev instructed. The men resumed their climb.

The eighth floor was predictably quiet. The two groups saw each other as they emerged from their respective staircases and exchanged hand gestures, quickly fanning out to check the situation up and down the long, narrow corridors. A light bulb was missing in one of the corridors, creating a spooky area of darkness. The obligatory check lasted only seconds, and now it was time for the real thing.

Pavel and Simeon were on opposite teams, converging on room 816 from two different sides. Ten men tiptoed quickly, each aware of his position in relation to the other nine. As they got closer, they became aware of a muffled sound coming through the wooden door. Zhivko was taking a shower, the splashing of the water clearly discernible.

They were standing in front of the door now, rifles raised and pointed.

"Police!" Pavel yelled, smashing his fist into the door with a loud bang. "Police!" he yelled again, the door shaking under the force of his blows. No signs of movement inside. The shower continued uninterrupted.

Simeon and Pavel looked at each other impatiently.

"Come on, Zhivko," Simeon said loudly and hit the door with his palm. "Don't make this difficult."

There was no sound of walking inside the room or someone picking up his things. The showering droned on.

Pavel opened one of his pockets and produced the master card, the one maids used to gain access to all the rooms. He slid it in place and twisted the doorknob. He half expected his former colleague to have barricaded himself by sliding the chain, but the door opened easily when he pushed it.

The men trained the rifles on the widening space as the door swung open. The sound of the showering became louder now, for they were standing right next to the bathroom. The thick curtains were drawn, and the room was dark. The bed was unmade and the sheets tossed. Most of the room could be seen from the door, and it was empty.

Simeon and another man rushed in anyway, pointing their weapons behind the bed while someone else checked the closet.

He had to be in the shower.

The door was closed almost all the way, leaving just a narrow slit.

"We're in the room," one of the commandos in the corridor spoke over the radio to Iliev. "It looks like he's in the shower."

Pavel and Simeon were standing in front of the bathroom door, a tad nervous but focused. In seconds, this would be over. Simeon nodded at his squad leader, who burst through the door.

"Don't move!" he screamed, his finger on the trigger. "Don't move!"

The shower cabin was empty. The sides were fogged up, but it was obvious there was no one inside. The water was coming down in droves, the dial turned to its maximum setting.

Chapter Forty-Six

"What do you mean he is not there?" Iliev barked into the radio. "Where is he?"

"We don't know," Pavel responded, looking around at his colleagues, who shrugged their shoulders in confusion. "He's not in the room."

"Damn it!" Iliev roared and pounded his fist into the reception desk. "I can't believe this." The commandos heard the angry voice and exchanged heavy looks.

"He apparently knew we were coming," Pavel said. "He intentionally left the shower on." The man looked at his arm, which was wet from having to reach in and turn off the water.

Iliev struck a power pose and took a moment to think.

"The question is," he began, raising the radio to his mouth. "How did he get out, and where is he now?"

Pavel shook his head. "We don't know." He looked over and saw that Simeon was getting antsy, energetically pacing back and forth.

"You sure he did not get past you while you were in the stairs?" Iliev asked.

"Of course not," Pavel replied.

"You absolutely sure?" Iliev repeated. "Simeon as well?"

The insult was too much for the large commando. He stepped toward Pavel and lunged for the radio in his hand.

"What the hell is Iliev trying to say, ah?" he yelled. In response, Pavel lifted his finger from the button to turn off the transmission and pulled his hand away to retain his hold on the radio. "Is he trying to accuse me of something?" Simeon continued, his angry eyes boring a hole in Pavel's head.

The squad leader raised his arm to calm Simeon and keep him at bay.

"Hello?" Iliev's voice again crackled over the radio. "Hello?"

"We're here," Pavel replied in a soothing voice, looking over at Simeon, who was still seething with anger, his large chest heaving. "All of us are sure that there is no way Zhivko could have gotten past us."

"Okay," Iliev said. He scratched his chin thoughtfully and looked around.

"Stay put for now," he ordered. The commander had an idea. He stepped away from behind the reception desk and walked over to the elevator lobby. The four elevators stood still with their doors open. The white marble gave the area an airy and open feeling.

Iliev walked toward the nearest elevator and stepped inside with one foot. He looked up through the crack between the elevator and the shaft. It was too dark to see anything. No sounds interrupted the silence.

Except for one.

"If you move, I'll kill you."

The commander abruptly whipped his head around. Zhivko was standing four meters away, both arms holding a gun pointed straight at his head. Iliev looked at him with a mixture of fear and confusion.

"Well done," the commander said with irony as a lump formed in his throat.

Zhivko's jaw was clenched tight and face expressionless, eyes intense. His breathing was rhythmical and paced.

"You must have pried open the elevator doors," Iliev continued, noticing that Zhivko's hands were stained with grease. "Smart decision." A mocking, closed-lipped half smile appeared on the commander's face. Zhivko gritted his teeth and suppressed the urge for violence.

"Tell them to maintain their positions," he commanded. Iliev hesitated, so he took a small step forward and readjusted his grip on the gun.

"Do it now!" Zhivko hissed, gnashing his teeth. "I won't ask you again."

Iliev slowly raised the radio and pushed the button.

"Maintain your positions, men," he ordered. "Wait for my command." All the time, he never took his eyes off Zhivko. He turned his body around to face the commando head-on.

"What do you think you're doing?" he asked. "We've got you surrounded on all sides."

Zhivko kept his eyes trained on Iliev. At this range, the bullet would tear through the man's body like a hot knife through butter. It was a tempting thought. His hands were beginning to sweat.

"It was you all along, wasn't it?" he asked. "You're behind all of this."

Iliev didn't say anything.

"Answer!" Zhivko screamed, scaring even himself with the unexpected loudness of his voice. The veins of his neck popped out, and his arms shook. "Answer me, or I swear, I'll kill you right now!" The gun trembled in his hand as he struggled to maintain his posture.

Iliev was taken aback but quickly regained his composure.

"You have no idea what's going on," he replied, his voice confident and arrogant. "And you are certainly in no position to stop it."

"Perhaps," Zhivko responded, pointing the gun squarely at the commander's moustache. "But I can stop you."

For the first time in their surprise encounter, Iliev feared that Zhivko might really shoot him. Fear filled his mind, and his hands began to shake.

"What do you want?"

"Why did you kill Vassil?" asked Zhivko. "It could not have been anyone else; it had to be you."

"It had to be done," Iliev replied dispassionately, his small eyes showing no emotion. "He was a loose end I had to get rid of."

Zhivko could sense his heart beating faster. Tunnel vision was taking over, blurring everything but his primary focus. Thoughts of vengeance and revenge swirled in his mind.

"Then what was I?" he asked.

"A lamb that had to be sacrificed," Iliev told him calmly. "I knew it would be easy and that no one would stick up for you ..." He paused and then added with menace, lips twisting in a repulsive grin, "Not even your best friend."

Kill him! Kill him, now!

A thousand voices in his mind were screaming for him to do it. He felt his hand acting on its own to carry out his dark fantasy. His breathing was heavy and nostrils flared while he nearly closed his eyes in anticipation of the thunderous bang. Zhivko's finger pushed down on the trigger, but he decided against completing the movement and eased back.

He took one hand off the gun and reached for his pocket. The dull click of a button pressed was unmistakable.

Iliev was stunned and speechless. He tried to vocalize, but no words came out, his jaw dropped and mouth moved mutely in a helpless expression of utter shock. He looked at Zhivko, glancing down toward his leg. The commando's windbreaker was unzipped, and there was a slight bulge over one hip.

Zhivko brought down one hand to push aside the clothing, revealing Mira's recorder sticking out of the pocket. She had given it to him before he left the house. It had been in the small bag with the other items.

"It's all recorded!" he said matter-of-factly, now somewhat relieved and trying to regain a sense of calm.

The color drained away from Iliev's face. He stumbled back and grabbed the side of the walls for support. Zhivko reached for the recorder and put it in his pocket, taking care to zip it all the way. Iliev's eyes were wide in horror and incomprehensible surprise.

The lieutenant had come in through the revolving door and was standing at the opposite end of the lobby, from where he could see Zhivko but not Iliev.

"Hey!" he shouted and paced forward, voice echoing through the lobby. "You! Don't move!"

Zhivko turned around and saw a stranger with a badge around his neck. The man was coming closer and reaching for his gun. Meanwhile, Iliev returned to his senses and took advantage of the distraction to lunge forward.

Seeing the movement out of the corner of his eye, Zhivko brought his gun down and squeezed the trigger.

Chapter Forty-Seven

"Something strange is going on," Simeon announced and took off his face mask. He ran his hand through his short hair and looked at his colleagues.

"What do you mean?" one asked, also taking off his mask and rubbing his shoulder across the side of his face to wipe off the sweat.

"Why is Iliev telling us to stay put?" Simeon asked incredulously. "It makes no sense."

"I'm sure there's a reason," offered Pavel, standing by the door and looking at the nine men assembled around him. "I'm sure of it."

Simeon grunted and laughed.

"I'm not surprised." He snickered.

The tone and accompanying facial expressions were more than Pavel could take. "What is that supposed to mean?" he asked.

"It means ..." Simeon began, staring down his squad leader. "That there is something rotten, and you are the only one who can't see it."

"This is not the time," Pavel scolded, raising his voice. "We're in the middle of a mission."

"No," Simeon corrected and moved closer. "Now is *exactly* the time to be talking about this." He illustrated his comment with a midair tap of his index finger. "What exactly are we doing here anyway?"

He looked around among the group for support.

"We're doing our job," Pavel explained strictly. "That's what you should be doing as well."

Simeon turned to look at the squad leader and gave him a condescending smile.

"Are you thinking with your head?" he asked mockingly. "Or your ass?"

The large man chuckled and continued.

"How do we even know he's guilty, ah?" he asked, raising his hands and looking around. "You mean to tell me he gets involved with drug smugglers and then stashes the stuff in his own apartment?" Simeon exhaled and shook his head. "After which he kills his best friend?" he asked with a skeptical tone.

"Do you have a better explanation?" Pavel asked, taunting him with his eyes.

"No," Simeon retorted. "I don't. But this one stinks and I don't believe it. And you know what else?"

"What?"

"The way you and Iliev have readily turned against Zhivko is a little unsettling. Don't you think so?" the big man was asking for a response, his wide face tense.

"I agree," said one of the other commandos. "There are a lot of things that don't make sense." Some of the other men also bobbed their heads in solidarity. Pavel did not appreciate the breakdown of discipline and the undermining of his authority.

"Listen," he began. "We're professionals. We follow orders. That means listening to Iliev."

Simeon shook his head and rolled his eyes.

"You have that man's cock so far down your throat you're about to choke."

His pride wounded, Pavel landed both hands on Simeon's massive chest and shoved him back as best he could.

"You listen to me!" he hissed, stepping forward so that their faces were just centimeters apart and grabbing hold of Simeon's vest. "You're out of line, and I'm not going to warn you again!"

Simeon easily broke Pavel's hold and pushed him away, sending the squad leader into the doorframe behind with a crash.

"What are you going to do?" he mocked. "Ha? You're going to ask that they remove me from the unit?"

"Maybe I will," Pavel angrily replied, pretending his back did not hurt.

"Maybe you should," Simeon responded and took a threatening step forward, casting a shadow on his superior. "I can go and become a bouncer or something. Beats dealing with you!"

"All right," one of the other men interrupted and stepped between them. "That's enough!" The other commandos joined in and pulled the two men apart, ending the scuffle. Simeon stepped away, still discontent and breathing more heavily.

The radio crackled to life with a sudden burst of static.

"This is Lieutenant Ganchev speaking," the man said with a rapid voice. "Iliev has just been shot by the suspect!"

The commandos exchanged shocked looks and huddled in a circle around the radio held by Pavel.

"The suspect just fled up the stairs of the far stairwell."

"You heard him," Pavel spoke up. "Let's go!"

Chapter Forty-Eight

Zhivko was running up the stairs three at a time, periodically gripping the railing for support. His feet pounded against the concrete as he asked his legs for more power. Eight floors above him, ten men streamed through the narrow doorframe and began their rapid descent. Pavel was leading the group, followed by Simeon and the remaining members of the squad.

When he reached the second floor, Zhivko became aware of the cacophony coming from above him. He heard the thumping of heavy footsteps getting closer, like an ominous wave of noise coming his way. They were on to him. Filled with a renewed sense of urgency, he took four stairs with each stride.

Looking down, the commandos could see their target's hand every time he reached for the railing. Separately, they each asked themselves the same question: *Why is he running up?* The inevitable confrontation was just seconds away.

Zhivko reached the third floor and flung the door open. It was the pool, spa, fitness, and relaxation area. He saw unoccupied lounge chairs and a big sign pointing to the sauna. The dark-blue water of the swimming pool was undisturbed. The air was moist and with a faint scent of chlorine. The glass doors leading to the facilities were locked.

Wrong floor.

He turned around and continued climbing the stairs. The thumping of his former colleagues' footsteps was closer now. Zhivko reached the platform on the fourth floor. He was sweating, and his heart was beating fast.

"Stop!" Pavel yelled. He was standing on the platform between the fourth floor and the fifth floor, his rifle pointed directly at Zhivko's back. "Stop!"

Zhivko froze. A quick glance over his shoulder to assess the situation was followed by a rush of determination to escape, regardless of the consequences.

No way.

He grabbed the door handle. Pavel squeezed down on the trigger.

"No!" the desperate yell came from Simeon, who had a clear view of the situation. He thrust his arm forward and pushed Pavel's rifle.

Iliev felt as if a sledgehammer had just slammed into his abdomen. The blow threw him back like a rag doll, sending him flying into the corner of the elevator. His arms, back, and head hit the walls of the cabin, causing it to rattle from side to side. He collapsed in a heap on the floor.

The bullet had not pierced his bulletproof vest, but he was sure it had broken two, possibly three, ribs and left a hell of a mark. The wind was knocked out of him, and he was gasping for breath, attempts to raise himself on all fours proving futile. Ganchev was kneeling down next to him, asking if he was all right. Iliev moved his mouth, but no words came out. He tried a few more times. Shock overwhelmed all sense of time and space, but he did remember leaning to one side and spitting out a colorful mixture of saliva and blood.

The lieutenant then got up and started running, hollering for someone to call a medic.

The wall next to Zhivko's head exploded with an earsplitting bang, sending a cloud of debris flying in all directions and onto his head and face. He lurched to one side, shaken and temporarily deaf but aware enough to open the door and stumble through.

He made it into the hallway and headed toward the guest rooms. The ringing in his ear was intense, causing him a great amount of pain as he nearly tripped over his feet and grabbed the wall for support. For a second, the images around him were spinning and flashing. Zhivko cupped his hand over his ear and brought it before his eyes. His palm was bloody, and he could sense a trickle of blood sliding down his neck.

He groaned and cupped a hand over his abused eardrum.

He was hearing a hitherto unknown whistling sound, while simultaneously feeling as if someone was poking his brain with a needle. The pain was spreading, now coming from within his head and disrupting his thoughts. If they were chasing him, he could not hear.

I can't stay here long!

Zhivko retrieved his gun and fired three shots into the door of the room directly in front of him. All three bullets landed on or near the doorknob, damaging the locking mechanism. He charged forward and landed a heavy frontal kick on the door, cracking and bending it inward. Pieces of wood and paint flew in all directions. He stepped back, fired another shot, and gave it another kick.

The battered door swung open. Zhivko went in and pushed it behind him. There was no one in the room, which was neatly prepared for its next occupant. The ringing in his ear was getting worse as the blood continued to drip. He felt as if someone had put a knife in his ear and was slowly twisting its handle.

Furniture of all sorts flew against the door as he grabbed everything in sight and crashed it at the entrance to create an obstruction and buy some time. The fury lasted no more than ten seconds and completely rearranged the room. Zhivko made for the window and looked outside.

He was looking at the sleepy small street behind the hotel, on the side opposite the main boulevard. Two floors below was a sloping wooden roof that descended down toward the sidewalk. Zhivko had first made note of it yesterday when he approached the hotel. He grabbed the window and opened it, the frame swinging inward with ease.

"What are you doing?" Simeon yelled at his squad leader, his face showing fear and anger. "What are you doing?" The voice boomed rage. He had pushed Pavel into the wall by his neck with one hand while maintaining a grip on his rifle in the other. The door to the fourth floor was open, but the commandos were not chasing their suspect.

"Let go!" Pavel demanded, his voice raspy due to the pressure applied to his neck. He jabbed his elbow into Simeon's abdomen in an attempt to gain some wiggle room.

"Damn it!" he tried again, but his windpipe could only produce a whimper. "He's getting away!"

Simeon gritted his teeth and pushed harder into Pavel, crushing him against the wall. The eight other men filled the stairwell behind them but could not advance.

"Fuck you!" Simeon howled into the squad leader's ear, his warm breath uncomfortably close and his teeth gnashing.

Zhivko was on the other side of the window, standing precariously on the ledge and facing outward. His hands were behind his back, tenuously holding on. He looked down at the roof five meters below him. There was no breeze, and the area was relatively shaded, the sun hidden by the large building. The grass on the sidewalk was neatly trimmed and lusciously green.

His head was spinning, and he felt dizzy. He sensed difficulty keeping his balance and nearly slipped off the ledge.

There was no time. Zhivko let go with his right hand and quickly crossed himself, appealing for divine intervention. He then let go with the other hand and leaned forward. The onrush of air was at first negligible but quickly became much stronger. He tried to keep his legs even as he fell. The roof twisted and moved below him. Events transpired slowly, as if he were in a drug-induced trance. He felt disoriented.

The violent impact jolted him into coherence. He landed awkwardly, one leg hitting the roof before the other. The fibula of his left leg broke immediately and with a wrenching, snapping sound.

"Aghhh!" Zhivko screamed at the top of his lungs as he rolled down the roof. He reached the edge in two cartwheels and bumped against the top of a street lamppost. He grabbed at his shin with both arms and simultaneously forced his mouth closed, muffling the cries of agony. His cheeks flushed.

He reached down to feel the injury through his jeans and smothered a scream by burying his mouth in the windbreaker. The agony was profound.

Zhivko pushed his lower leg back into position, causing another blast of pain. He wanted to scream again. He reached for the lamppost and carefully slid down, mindful not to hit his left leg. The soft grass had cushioned his right leg when he landed.

He looked up at the open window. No one.

Thank God.

A look up and down revealed the street was empty. His injured leg was beginning to numb. Panting and desperate, Zhivko began hopping his way across the street and toward the opposite sidewalk. He reached it and fell into a tree for support, his good leg tired. The collar of his shirt was stained with blood and sweat.

He held on to the tree for a few seconds and then pushed off, making his way down the sidewalk toward the tram stop nestled under the trees beyond the end of the hotel. No one was chasing him—at least not yet. He could not hop anymore so he walked, taking quick, small steps and dragging his injured leg behind him. He stood a good chance of getting away if he could turn the corner without being noticed.

The sound of approaching footsteps was unmistakable. Zhivko stopped in his tracks.

So close.

He swallowed and tried to catch his breath with big gulps of air. *It's over.*

He turned around.

Chapter Forty-Nine

General Secretary Mitov was standing in the middle of the street, his gun pointed at him. He looked tired, with deep, dark pockets under his eyes. Zhivko was stunned to see him.

The men just stared at each other, neither saying a word.

"What are you doing here?" Zhivko asked, his breathing now nearly normal.

"I am arresting you," Mitov said, not relaxing his grip on the gun. "It's time to end this."

Zhivko looked around. A stray dog lazily crossed the street with the tram line, the animal's ears flapping as it arched its back underneath a fence and disappeared. The softened noise of traffic could be heard in the distance. It was a sunny, beautiful day. It wasn't even particularly hot.

"I was framed," Zhivko began, fixing his eyes on Mitov. "I didn't do what they said I did."

"I know, son," Mitov replied and let his gun hand drop. "I believe you."

Zhivko felt a tremendous sense of relief even though he could not understand the full meaning of the words. He hopped to the side to avoid getting a cramp in his only standing leg and spoke.

"I was set up," he said. "I've got proof."

"So do I," Mitov replied. He had moved closer and was now no more than five or six meters way. "Like I said, it's all over."

Zhivko decided to trust him.

"What happens now?"

Police sirens began wailing, the sounds getting ever closer. A blue-and-white police car turned off the main boulevard and headed his way.

Two officers were running down the other street, coming up behind Mitov.

"Let me bring you in, and we'll sort this out," the general secretary advised.

Zhivko fell to his knees and raised both hands to his head.

Chapter Fifty

Tuesday, September 9, 1997

The air in the packed room was heavy. Journalists were elbowing their way forward, attempting to secure a better position ahead of the anticipated question time. The camera crews were testing their powerful lights.

The prime minister and Mitov walked down the stairs and came into view. A cacophony of voices and flashes ensued, forcing Mitov to raise his hand for protection to make sure he did not lose his footing and fall over embarrassingly. The speaker's stand was so burdened with microphones the pile threatened to fall over. Numerous cameras flanked both sides, and cables snaked across the dark-red carpet. The prime minister put his hands on both sides and cleared his throat.

His hair was combed over, and an old gray tie was securely fastened around his neck. His bony fingers and continued weight loss made him look sickly, but for the first time in weeks, there was energy and optimism in his eyes.

"Thank you for coming," he said clearly, looking at the crowd at the foot of the stairs. "I will try to keep this short."

Mitov stood next to him, hands clasped in front for authority.

"As I am sure you all know, a lot happened during the last week," the prime minister began. "The efforts of this government have been successful, and we disrupted a major criminal network involved in international drug smuggling. We are very proud of this and commend all who made it happen."

He looked over at Mitov and nodded his head.

"At the same time, I am aware members of my administration were involved in criminal activity." The level of tension increased a notch. This was a historic admission, and the reporters stood on edge.

"I am here to announce a reshuffle of key positions and the launching of criminal investigations against all guilty parties. I'm sure you're all aware of the arrests we made in the past few days."

If there was a TV or radio station that had not been broadcasting the press conference live, it surely was now.

"Specifically, police in the Plovdiv area handcuffed four individuals, all part of a transnational criminal group. Among them is their leader, Kiril Dimitrov. The police have also arrested a truck driver involved in smuggling. I have talked with the general prosecutor, who has already raised criminal charges. I expect him to make a public statement shortly."

Some of the photographers were already putting in a second roll of film. In his haste, one even dropped the canister and was forced to dive to the ground before it rolled away in a forest of feet.

"Details!" someone yelled. "Tell us details!"

"Please don't interrupt," the prime minister admonished and continued. A microphone fell from the stand to the rug below.

"The leader of this criminal group resides in Sofia, and we have sent a team to his house. I've been told that someone there has been detained, but their involvement has not yet been determined and no charges have been raised for now."

"Which of your people are implicated?" a reporter shouted. "You mentioned members of your government are suspected."

"Indeed," the prime minister replied, not letting it show that he was annoyed by the interruption. "Over the weekend, we arrested Veselin Iliev, the former head of the special forces unit. There is specific evidence linking him to the drug smugglers, so criminal charges are pending. It appears his role was to tip off the smugglers before raids by the special forces, so they could move the drugs. It has also been revealed that he helped the smugglers gain access to the commando who helped frame Mladenov. Finally, Iliev is behind the fatal shooting last Friday. My condolences go out to the man's family; hopefully the ministry will give them some sort of compensation."

"Who will replace Iliev?"

"That will be discussed at the next cabinet meeting," the prime minister answered. "I can't say anything right now."

"What about the commandos?" another reporter asked. "Are they also guilty?"

"No," the premier responded. "They are innocent and were not aware of Iliev's collusion with drug smugglers. I am told that some want to leave the force but most would prefer to stay."

"And Mladenov?"

The prime minister looked at Mitov before answering.

"That's up to the courts to decide," he said slowly. "Our investigation is incomplete and ongoing, but Mladenov has been cleared of wrongdoing. He was framed by Iliev and the commando who was subsequently killed. As for the things he did to clear his name, I will leave it to the prosecution and the courts to decide, what, if anything, should be his punishment."

"What about the reporter who was kidnapped?"

"She claims she was not kidnapped and not forced to do anything against her will," the prime minister replied. "She is not pressing any charges."

He looked to Mitov, who nodded in confirmation.

"There is one more thing," the prime minister began. "Earlier today, I asked Mr. Stoyanov to resign. I received his resignation a few minutes ago, and he is no longer head of the Interior Ministry."

The journalists once more pushed against each other for a better position. A woman ran out of space on her recorder and hurried to turn over the tape but was inadvertently shoved by someone else and dropped it. Pens squeaked furiously against notepads as the crowd tried to transcribe every word.

"Is he also with the criminals?" someone shouted. "Has he been charged with anything?"

"No, no," the premier replied and waved his hand. Cameras flashed once more. "At this point, we do not believe he has been involved. However, I am not satisfied with his performance and do not agree with some of the things he did at the ministry. That's why I asked him to step down."

"Who is the replacement?"

"Have you decided already?"

"Who?" someone implored impatiently. The reporter who had lost her recorder had retrieved it and was elbowing her way forward. "Who?"

The prime minister did not answer immediately, taking time to choose his words carefully.

"The people of Bulgaria owe a lot to Mr. Mitov because his hard work made these arrests possible. His qualifications are impeccable, and I have decided to offer the position to him."

With that, the prime minister stepped back and invited Mitov to take the podium.

"Thank you," Mitov began and took his place, slowly clearing his throat and looking into the lights. "I have seen a lot of things over the years, but the recent events were arguably the most dramatic. I am glad all ended well."

He allowed himself a poised half smile. He was thinking of his wife, who lately was seeing more of her husband in the media than in person. He was supposed to take her to the beach this summer, a nice, quiet resort somewhere away from most tourists. Watching the sunrise over the Black Sea together would be nice.

Promises made, promises not kept.

"I thank the premier," Mitov continued, gratitude creeping into his formal tone. "It would be an honor to serve as minister, really." He looked over the heads of the reporters and into the distance, his thoughts carrying him away and over the mountains to a placid lake, his toes swinging freely through the water. He hugged his wife and tucked strands of hair behind her ear.

Mitov paused to exhale and steadied himself. "But I feel tired, and there are other things I need to focus on."

Epilogue

The morning came with the crowing of a rooster. It was shortly after sunrise yet the bedroom was already awash in bright sunlight, while the crisp mountain air was gently swaying the drapes dragged halfway across the windows.

Mira raised her head above the pillow and rubbed her eyes. Still half asleep, she turned around to lie on her back. The rooster sounded for a second time, blocking out the constant chirping of the spring birds.

Mira leaned over and saw Zhivko was sound asleep. She gently touched his jaw and let her hand slip down onto his chest, sliding over his scar and triceps with her fingers. She then swung her feet off the double bed and into the soft white slippers. She quietly walked over to the chair and picked up her silk robe, putting it on with two quick movements. The fashionable red-and-white cloth fell to just above her knees. She decided not to use the belt and let it hang loosely.

Mira made for the bathroom but stopped when she passed in front of the closet mirror. She parted the robe slightly and studied her body, admiring its shapes. There had been some inevitable sagging and weight gain over the years, but not much. Her breasts were still shapely and firm enough to excite any man. In subtle—and sometimes not-too-subtle—forms, the praise came almost daily. But she had long ago stopped paying attention to the reactions of random men, for she had found the one she needed.

Behind her, Zhivko moved. He straightened his posture and stretched one arm, no doubt trying to hug her as he usually did when sleeping. The sun's rays fell directly on his body, giving the skin a soft glow. The man was at rest, yet he looked so muscular, so powerful. He had eased into middle age with only isolated traces of gray in his thick, full hair.

Mira bit her lip and smiled. Her memories from the previous night were very pleasant.

She went into the kitchen and put coffee on the stove. She then splashed her face with water from the sink, and by the time she began drying it with a towel, a pleasant aroma had filled the little room. Mira grabbed two cups from the shelf and filled both, tossing in a cube of sugar in each. She picked up her cup and walked over to the bedroom, leaning casually against the doorframe as she watched the man sleep. The coffee steamed in her hands.

Behind the nearby trees, the golden domes of the Shipka Memorial Church loomed against the mountain. The tall building's striking pink facade was breathtaking, particularly for those walking up the memorial's steps for the first time.

It was Sunday, and the couple would be attending the service. Afterward, Mira wanted to do some gardening, maybe even prune the roses, if she had the time. She took a sip of coffee. Her husband could help her.